1-21-20

Henry

Henry

Sydney Paige McCutcheon

To Jesus Christ, Who gave it all.

CHAPTER ONE

"Three perfectly fertilized embryos!"

Dr. Hayward cheered, grabbing the yellow folder from her desk and lifting it high in the air as if it were a trophy. Perhaps it was.

I looked to my sister, Hannah. Tears ran down her cheeks as she smiled at me. We sat in plush gray chairs, arms and hands linked together, as Dr. Hayward, or *Juliet,* as Hannah called her, sat opposite us.

I gave Hannah a long hug, a smile to my own lips, and whispered in her ear, "Congratulations. It's going to work this time."

"I can't believe it!" she said, squeezing me tight. "Jacob will be so happy!"

"Now," Dr. Hayward said, garnering our attention once again. "Though there are three embryos, that doesn't mean you will be having triplets!" She laughed, and Hannah let out a chuckled sob. I passed her a balled up tissue from my purse, and though normally she would gag at the thought, she took the wad at once.

"I have full confidence that one of the three will mature

and fully develop, unlike past attempts." Dr. Hayward looked to Hannah sympathetically, but nothing could break my sister's happiness now. "Any questions?"

"How long before we know if . . . ?"

"Give it at least two weeks, then come back to the clinic and a nurse will draw blood for an accurate pregnancy test."

"How long until the results come in?" I asked.

"You can come back the next day, or I can call you over the phone."

"Ooh," Hannah gasped. "We can announce the news at the baby shower! Everyone will be so surprised!"

"You already have a baby shower?" Dr. Hayward said, the doubtful tone grating on my heart.

"It was Prue's idea," Hannah explained, then faltered. "Or do you think that's too hopeful?"

I looked to Dr. Hayward and raised my brows, my heart pounding more rapidly.

She then smiled. "That sounds like a fantastic idea. I am very confident that a pregnancy will occur, almost a hundred percent."

I let out a sigh of relief.

"You hear that sis?" I nudged Hannah with my elbow. "No doubts this time. It has to work—even your doctor says so."

Hannah smiled, her eyes shining. "You're right."

"As always." I laughed.

"Well, we can at least put everyone at ease that there is a great chance this time for a baby," she added.

"Good idea," Dr. Hayward said, and she stood from her desk, our cue to follow, and led us out of her office down the hallway. Emily, the receptionist, saw our enthusiastic faces as we came around the corner, and she gave Hannah a tight hug as I stood at a distance.

"Congratulations!" Emily squealed.

"Thank you," Hannah said, pulling back. She wiped the tears from her eyes, still smiling, and I grabbed her hand to lead us out.

We waved goodbye to Dr. Hayward as she called to us from down the hall.

"See you in two weeks!"

CHAPTER TWO

Two weeks later

"We both went to the blood test yesterday, but I haven't seen or heard from her since," I told my mother as I drove us to Hannah's house. We were picking her up to go look at cake ideas for the baby shower.

"That isn't like Hannah not to call," Mom murmured from the passenger seat.

I shrugged, my eyes to the road. "She is probably just busy planning the party next week. You know Hannah and her lists."

I rolled down my window and reached a hand to the keypad near the front gates of Hannah's neighborhood. She lived the wealthy life with a mansion, and a successful businessman-husband who could give her everything except the one thing in the world she wanted. A child. But that was over now, and finally—*finally*—her chance was here.

"I can't tell if the lights are on," Mom said when I parked in the driveway and turned off the car.

"That's because it's daylight," I said, grinning.

Mom rolled her eyes at me and opened her door. I followed, but got to the front steps before her. My hand reached to turn the doorknob, then paused.

"I forgot my spare key, do you have yours?" I asked just as the door slid back smoothly.

Odd, I thought. *The door wasn't even closed all the way.*

"Never mind," I mumbled, stepping inside the house.

Only sunlight lit the living room to our left and the shadows seemed wrong in the quiet setting. I headed toward the kitchen, the hairs on the back of my neck rising from the silence.

"I'll go see if she's upstairs," Mom said. "Maybe she and Jacob went out to the store or something."

I didn't answer, only listened to her hurried footsteps against the carpeted stairs, as I surveyed the kitchen.

The coffee pot was half-full, and a crème-colored mug sat on the kitchen table. I walked to it, taking note of the empty chair and an unfolded newspaper. Steam rose from the cup and the paper was barely opened. Hannah never drank coffee, which meant that Jacob was still home, but I didn't see her usual cup of tea.

The scent of eggs cooking had taken on a burn. I rushed to the stove and switched the knob to OFF, grabbed a towel, and lifted the blackened pan onto a cool center. My heartbeat was loud in my eardrums, and I didn't know why. Then I heard Mom scream.

"Hannah!"

"Mom!" I shouted, my voice shaking, and my legs moved without thought. I came to the stair landing and shouted again, but no response came. I ran to master bedroom, through the opened double doors, and slowed down.

Mom stood next to the bed, her hand covering her mouth

in horror, and I rushed to her side, almost stepping on Jacob's leg.

"No!" I gasped, bile burning the back of my throat as I looked down.

Jacob was on the ground, his blue eyes staring up at nothing. A growing circle of blood stained his abdomen, and another one spreading just above his chest, his hands covered with the dark liquid.

Mom and I stared at him for a second, frozen in place and in silence, but then his lips moved and we jumped back in sync.

"The nursery," he whispered, letting out his last breath.

I gave no second thought.

I ran from the bedroom and down the hall, not sure about anything, but barged into the nursery, my fist knocking the door open. I came to a stop at my sister's bare feet, a large figure hovering at her head.

"Hannah," I said, and my voice cracked.

The intruder's head snapped to me like a viper ready to strike, a bloodied knife in his hand. His entire face covered by black cloth, I could only make out his small eyes where he had cut out holes to see. I didn't know what to do, my mind was blank; I was a deer in headlights waiting for the truck to ram me over.

"Prue," her delicate voice sounded my name. "Run!"

All at once, Hannah came alive. She sat up, her hands grabbing at the man's face, tearing at his ears until finally ripping off his mask. He yelled as her nails dug into his skin, leaving red lines down his cheeks.

He shoved her hands away and then leaned back suddenly, only to plunge forward with the knife. Hannah let out a small breath as her back hit the floor, and she didn't move again.

Now it was my turn to die.

When he faced me again, I took in his every feature. His head was shaved, leaving only black roots. A brutish face with dark eyes and bushy brows and a sneer that made my skin crawl. He was large and tan. He then stood, taking a step toward me, the blade ready in his hand.

Sirens screamed in the distance.

"Prue!" Mom called frantically from the hallway. "I called the police! Where are you? Where's Hannah?"

I wanted to yell for her to stay away but my mouth wouldn't move, locked and frozen by fear. I felt the blood drain from my body before the knife could even come and make a wound.

The man hesitated, surprising me, and he stepped toward the window. He stared at me, his eyes cold, and slicing the blade before his neck in mime, he then pointed the tip toward me.

"Next time," he said. And without any justice, he broke the glass of the window and jumped out to freedom.

I hurried to Hannah, her face pale and her eyes closed. I caressed her brow, spoke her name, praying for her to wake up, to come back.

"No! Hannah! No!" Mom shouted at the doorway, sobs choking her. Hannah didn't respond to either of us.

I crept away from her body until my back hit the wall, needing something to keep me steady. I couldn't feel my hands. They must have been shaking. Tears fixed in my eyes, unable to release, and my mouth was still numb. Mom wailed, but the sound couldn't touch me, couldn't make it real.

Paramedics rushed in, cops rushed in, the world rushed in.

And they drowned me whole.

CHAPTER THREE

Three hours later

I sat in a cold room with a long steel table, two chairs, a security camera, and a two-way mirror.

The chair was hard, but nothing compared to the stares of the two cops facing me. One female, the other male, both wore dark-colored suits. My tired eyes could barely take them in, but my ears did, very much so.

"We believe that your sister and brother-in-law were killed for money," the woman, Officer Lee, stated firmly, resting her palm on the table. Her dark purple lip-gloss complimented her ebony skin and brown eyes.

I cleared my throat, blinking a few times before allowing myself to speak.

"Money?" I paused to let the question linger. "They didn't keep money in the house," I said, my gaze unfocused. "I mean, they put it in banks. To keep it safe." I almost broke right then, but something kept the strings of me together. "Are you sure?"

Officer Virgil spoke up, "Did you know the man Jacob started his company with?"

I shook my head. "All I know is that they were best friends in college, but had a falling out when the company started to grow, and they parted ways. Jacob was entitled to the whole business because the friend laundered money or something." My mouth was sticky with thirst. I needed a glass of water.

Virgil pulled a yellow folder from his armpit and dropped it in front of me onto the table. He flipped open the cover, revealing a profile with a photo inside.

"His name is Mark Brooks."

I stared at the square picture of a man a few years older than Jacob, with plain brown hair and a round face.

Lee cut in. "You see, if you get down to the final print of past contracts, even though the company was given to Jacob, Brooks is still named to inherit the company and all fortunes in case of Jacob's death."

"What about my sister?" I asked. Though I suddenly realized, it didn't matter now.

The two looked at each other, hesitating. Finally, Lee confessed, "According to the business contract, your sister would have never gotten a cent of the money."

"So they killed her for nothing?" I said. Fire burned inside my chest, giving life to my body.

They killed her for nothing! I watched her die for nothing!

"There was one exception," Virgil added. "If an heir was produced, then the company would be taken care of by the board until the child reached legal age."

His words silenced my rage. *A child?*

"Unless we can prove that Brooks was behind this, he gets everything."

"Prue," Lee called, and I didn't even realize they had asked me a question in the first place. "What is it?"

My eyes slowly roamed to her face as my finger slid to the photograph. "This wasn't the man I saw."

The room went electric.

"What do you mean? Who did you see?"

I thought of the man hovering above Hannah, stabbing her in front of me and wanting to spill my blood as well. Panic began to freeze my limbs.

"The man who killed them . . . I saw his face," I said.

"Then what happened?"

I spoke in a trance, ignoring the heavy smell of black coffee on Virgil's breath as he leaned close to me, his expression serious, and I replied, "He told me I was next."

They called the Chief.

Less than two minutes after my confession, an older man in uniform with graying blonde hair and a matching mustache walked into the fluorescent room, his nametag reading 'Chief Brandon'.

"Ms. Collins," the Chief said kindly, taking a seat opposite me. "We have a problem."

He waited for me to respond, but my silence gave him full reign.

"Since there is no way for you to inherit money from Jacob's business, we thought your safety was set. But now that we know you have seen the murderer's face . . . things have changed."

Again he waited, and again, I gave only silence.

He sighed, the compassion in his eyes making me think twice about him. "This man has made it clear you are his next target. With your testimony, once we catch him, he can be sent to jail for a long time, and we can get closer to getting Mr. Brooks. But we must protect you."

I scoffed. "What can you do?"

My sister was dead. She was my protection. She protected

me my whole life since she was eight years old and I was born. My shield against the world was gone and I vulnerable to it. *Who could protect me now?*

"We will send you to a safe house and you will be cut off from all connection to your friends and your family. There, you will go under a new name and a new way of life. Under no circumstances must anyone have knowledge of your whereabouts."

"How long?" I asked, my throat burning, and I wondered why they didn't have a glass of water for me like in the movies.

"Until the man you saw, and hopefully Mr. Brooks, are both in jail."

Chief Brandon stood up, the chair legs scraping the cemented floor. "I will have a uniform take you home so you can pack some of your things, and he will bring you here tomorrow morning where we should have a placement for you. Any questions?"

I stared up to him, and licked my dry lips. "Can I have a glass of water?"

CHAPTER FOUR

They had me see a sketch artist before I could leave.

I didn't want to see the completed work, but they insisted to make sure the photograph was accurate. It was.

The officer who drove me home had the name *'Brandon'*, and I wondered if the young blonde thing was the Chief's son. He had the whiskers.

I lived with my parents even though I was twenty-two years old and should have been in college—but college life was not for me. Thankfully, Jacob had found odd jobs at the company for me to fulfill and I loved every minute of it. *That was gone too, I guess.*

Mom and Dad weren't home, but I had already said my goodbyes at the station. They were going to stay with my grandparents in Ohio, though they asked if they could come with me. The Chief said I was safer alone.

The house was quiet without them. It caused my chest to tighten and I wanted to scream of my hurt and let the water rush from my eyes like a rogue river, but I swallowed it all back inside of me.

Brandon said he would check out the place in case of any suspicious signs as I made my way to the kitchen, never having gotten that glass of water.

The red light on the answering machine blinked, but I got a cup of juice before hitting the play button. It was Dr. Hayward asking me to come to her office as soon as I could, and saying nothing further.

I stopped the recorder. She probably had already heard the news and wanted to speak with me about it in person to give her apologies. I didn't want to see her, and even decided to start packing my clothes when something pricked my brain, and soon enough I asked Officer Brandon to drive me to her office.

Once there, he took a seat in the waiting room next to a few toddlers playing with blocks, and I went through the door leading to the receptionist desk.

"Prue!" Emily said too loudly as she came around to give me a hug. "I am so sorry! We all heard what happened—no one could believe it!"

Anger rose inside me, burning my skin, and I rebuffed her embrace.

"Neither could I," I muttered, "and I saw the whole thing."

I left her wide eyes and headed to the familiar office near the back. I didn't knock but walked right in.

"Prue," Dr. Hayward gasped. She came to me with open arms that I took like a cat to water. It only lasted ten more seconds before I pulled away and took a seat in my usual chair. My eyes scanned the chair beside me, a pang hitting my chest.

Juliet wiped tears from the corners of her eyes. A tinge of guilt tried to squeeze me, but I brushed it off as best I could, and Juliet became Dr. Hayward again.

"I wanted to show you something, Prue," she said, a hint of

hesitation to her voice. She took a folder from her desk, and opening it to me, I saw at once the blood test results.

"She was going to be a mother," I said, losing all breath.

Dr. Hayward nodded, and my heart squeezed as my fingers dug into the chair to keep control.

She had it! She had the very thing she dreamed of! And it was all taken away by a man with a knife! Why? Because of money? Because of a long ago feud! It wasn't fair! How could this happen to her?

I used the arms of the chair to help me rise, fighting the overload of thoughts, and went to the door.

"I have to go," I told Dr. Hayward, and her eyes looked up to me with red rims. "I have to go to a safe house for a while, and can't have contact with anyone."

"I will miss you," she said. "But Prue there are things—"

I didn't hear the rest. I had already walked out the door and was in the hallway, shock still fresh in my veins.

I kept silent my whole journey from the office to the waiting room, to Brandon, to the police car, to the stoplight, to the house, to my room.

Not a word left my lips. Not one.

CHAPTER FIVE

The next morning was hard for me.

When I woke up, my body did not rise in tune, only my eyes opened. They pondered the room, the ceiling, the very paint. As if my eyes had been dipped in bleach to make them clean, giving the world an overexposed tint.

It made me want to scoff at how different things looked now. How they would always look different from now on.

Eventually I sat up and pushed away the comforts of the covers for the cold outside world. Last night I had packed one suitcase of clothes and a few personal items, but this morning I had some difficulty choosing what to wear.

What do you wear to a place you've never been?

I decided on a simple shirt with old jeans and sneakers.

Officer Brandon took my suitcase to the car as I busied myself with breakfast. I put two slices of bread in the toaster, cracked a few eggs, and splashed milk into a pan on the heating stove, and started up the coffeepot. I grabbed a few tea bags from the pantry and heated a cup of water in the microwave. After about ten minutes, I walked with a plate in hand around the kitchen, scooping on the scrambled eggs, quickly throwing down the hot toast next, and grabbing another mug from the cabinet; setting it all on the table. I poured the coffee first, but added no sugar or cream, and then dropped three cubes of sugar into the tea and many splashes of milk until the liquid started to turn cold.

"Ms. Collins," Brandon called just as I had picked up a fork to eat. I stopped midway to my mouth but didn't look at him. "It is time to go, Ms. Collins. They are waiting for us at the station."

In the twenty minutes it took to make the breakfast, it took only one minute to throw it all away. Funny, how preparation took so much longer than destruction, and that the latter was never prepared for.

Instead of the cold room from before, I was taken to Chief Brandon's office where I sat in a more comfortable brown chair. Lee and Virgil were back, and all eyes were once again on me.

"Good morning, Ms. Collins," the Chief said to me. I spotted a sesame bagel beside his phone and my stomach growled.

"Good morning," I repeated the term for the day, my throat just waking. I noticed the many backs of silver picture frames on his desk and wondered what faces they held.

Were they the faces of life that kept this man sane from seeing so many images of death?

"We spent all night trying to find a suitable place for you to stay during the course of our investigation," the Chief began, taking a sip of his steaming coffee. He liked it black, too. "You will be taken to a small town just outside Astoria, Oregon. There you will have a new name, a new identity."

I held my reaction but felt the jolt of reality tinge my

cheeks.

"Only the four of us know of your whereabouts." Chief Brandon's sensitive eyes stared into mine. "If you try to contact anyone, we will be forced to lock you up Ms. Collins, and in a place you would think to be prison. I do not want that to happen, do you understand?"

I nodded with a thick gulp. "Yes, I understand."

But did he understand that I had just lost my only sister? Did he understand that my whole world was being turned upside down, and I could have no one to confide in about my pain?

I didn't believe so.

"Ms. Collins, are you ready for your new life?" he asked me, when I had yet to bury the old one.

CHAPTER SIX

The younger Officer Brandon and I left the police station at about seven in the morning, taking an unmarked car for safety—*my safety*. I sat in the passenger seat keeping my focus out the window, the bright sun coming up for the day. Though summer was over and August now here, Arizona overlapped this particular season, and I wished I had brought sunglasses.

I leaned the back of my head against the window and looked to the young cop.

"How long before we get there?" I asked.

Brandon's eyes darted to mine, then quickly back to the road, surprised I had spoken. I wondered if this was his first case.

"The drive should be about twenty hours, maybe less." He looked to the clock on the dashboard. "We'll probably get to the lake house around two or three in the morning."

"Lake house?"

He cleared his throat. "Yeah, it's a house in the backwoods, secluded from everything except a small town about fifteen miles away, and there is a lake nearby. Didn't they show you the picture before we left?"

I shook my head that I didn't, and he reached into the glove compartment and pulled out a beige folder. This was my life, it seemed, my world, composed into many different yellow folders.

I took it from his offered hand and flipped it open, my eyes catching the first picture I came across. A mixture of thin and thick trees cluttered a two-story cabin-like home. The colors of the house and the forest were dark and dramatic, the exact opposite of here. But it looked quaint. And cold. I hadn't packed for winter.

"My dad thought it the best place because it's isolated and the house isn't listed." Brandon shined when he mentioned his dad.

"Am I to be there alone?"

He laughed, then caught himself. "No, someone will be there with you."

"You?" Another foolish question and my cheeks burned. I kept my eyes to the picture, studying it, and trying to dismiss the embarrassing tension.

"No, I have to come back to Arizona, but I'm sure you will be fine," he said.

I nodded in response, and put the folder back into the compartment. I adjusted my seatbelt, trying to find the right spot between the seat and the window, my right temple pressed against the glass.

My eyes kept closing, and soon I was out. But this time when I fell asleep, I didn't have nightmares as I did the night before.

Instead, I dreamed of the lake house.

Chapter Seven

"Wake up, Ms. Collins."

I heard Brandon speak, but his voice seemed to be muffled out by a loud pattering noise. He shook my arm and my eyes opened, slowly adjusting to the darkness.

Had I slept the entire drive?

"Ms. Collins?" Brandon prodded again with an anxious tone.

My mouth was dry as if I had swallowed three large cotton balls, my brain foggy. I tried to figure out what the loud noise was, and finally looked out the car window.

"It's raining," I said, a yawn escaping me, as I had yet to move.

"A storm," Brandon clarified, pushing papers around in the car, trying to organize, it seemed. "Actually," he added. "Ms. Collins, we need to get inside before the car starts to get stuck in the mud. Do you have all your things?"

After a quick scan, I nodded, and he grabbed his papers, opening his door. I followed suit and stepped out into the cold rain, surveying the area. Trees lined the entire place and it was hard to make out the road from the bushes in the dark, but it didn't look to be paved. As I turned my head to the left, my breath caught.

The lake house was beautiful—even when drenched in pouring rain. Two hundred foot trees with long branches covered the sides of the house like a shield, their leaves dripping with rain; my nose itched with the smell of fresh earth.

I took a step forward and slipped.

"Ms. Collins!" Brandon rushed to my side, taking my elbow in a firm grip and helped me up, my suitcase underneath his other arm. An embarrassed laugh escaped me as mud coated my jeans and hands.

Together, we walked up the porch steps and stopped at the front door. I was drenched from head to toe and shivered as a strong wind blew. Brandon banged the screen door, hitting the hard wood behind it.

"Officer Clay!" he shouted against the rain, his mouth close to the door. "Officer Clay! It's Chief Brandon's son! Open up!"

"Are storms common?" I asked, my arms hugging my body to keep in warmth.

"From time to time," he said.

He banged on the door again but it seemed useless. Minutes passed and no one was coming.

"Officer Clay!"

I was about to suggest going back to the car when the door suddenly swung open, startling us both. Officer Brandon drew back and my eyes caught with a stranger's, the light from inside the house illuminating through the screen door.

I couldn't move, couldn't shiver.

"Officer Henry Clay?" Brandon questioned, water dripping down his face.

The stranger kept our eye contact for one more second before darting his attention to Brandon.

"You're early," he said, but backed up nevertheless, and Brandon twisted the knob of the screen door and entered, taking me with him.

I came face to face with the stranger, and felt shame for my response. It was not something I was prepared for.

"This is Prue Collins," Brandon introduced me, setting down my suitcase. The stranger waved his words away, ignoring him.

"I know the drill," he said with a rude tone, and gave me a look that said, *'No, we will never get along, and yes, you will be miserable here'*.

His dark eyes stared me down. "You must be freezing."

No, I wasn't prepared. I wasn't prepared at all.

CHAPTER EIGHT

I hadn't slept at all last night, my mind too awake with thoughts and flashes of images that I wished would disappear forever. Hannah's face mostly, and Jacob's from time to time, but the main mental picture was the burned eggs and uneaten toast—that the laid down spatula just waiting to be picked up again a short time later, but never was. Jacob didn't know he should have turned off the stove. No one would know about silly things like that. He thought he'd be right back.

A cascade of creaks came from downstairs and a chill swept through me like a passing storm.

Should I go down? I wondered, nervous at the thought. *Would if I just stayed up here all day? Or even until I was taken back home? Would he bring me food?*

Something told me he wouldn't.

I sighed, pushing myself up from the bed, and another series of cracking stirred up in the house like an old man waking.

The room was small, but open with minimal furniture: a

twin-sized bed, beige wallpaper, and a draped window overlooking a cluster of trees. Everything seemed to fit in its place.

Last night I had changed out of my mud-covered clothes and into pajamas of a white shirt and old cotton shorts, but wasn't sure if it appropriate to wear downstairs in front of the two officers. After a moment of wavering, I decided it should be fine—I also being too lazy to change. I tiptoed to the door and it creaked as it opened, like everything else.

My nose stuck out of the gap and my eyes criss-crossed about the hallway, seeing if anyone was there. With the coast clear, I walked out, trying my best to walk lightly, and rested a hand on the railing of the stairs. The living room was just below next to the front door. I held my breath as I continued to tiptoe down, not wanting to make a sound or bring attention to myself. However, the stairs groaned with each step.

Just hours ago, I had been down here freezing and dirty while the stranger gave me directions to my new room. I hadn't dared ask about dinner, and my stomach growled in retaliation.

I hurried toward an open entryway that I assumed lead to the kitchen, and was right. I caught sight of a head of dark untamed hair, and my eyes scaled down.

"Are you going to come in, or not?" His sharp voice startled me and I stubbed my foot into the wall.

Muffling my cry of pain, I left my hiding place and quickly sat in one of the empty chairs at the table, saying nothing.

He had his eyes to a newspaper, the movement of his reading so quick and deft, and yet, he continued to speak to me without even glancing my way.

"Your officer friend left you," he said with a hint of amusement, and flipped the black and white page, licking his finger first.

I suddenly wanted to run. I didn't like the fact of being alone here, with him. *Who was this stranger?*

"You must be hungry," he said, and took a sip of orange juice from a half-filled glass near his plate of toast.

"Do you assume everything?" I asked without thinking, and blood rushed to my face. His eyes looked up from the newspaper to mine, taking my outspoken thought as a challenge.

He then returned his gaze back to the paper, and I let out a deep breath of relief. But not knowing what else to do, I said, "I am . . . thirsty, though." I could practically hear his eyes roll. "Never mind."

He dropped his newspaper on the table, and the next part I couldn't help but keep my eyes trained on.

The locks clicked as he released the brakes of his wheelchair, and I watched as he backed up from the table and swiveled toward the cabinets. I then returned my eyes to my lap.

Some racket was made, and I even regretted to hear his groan as he must have had to stretch up high. The fridge was opened, liquid poured, and the fridge closed, and he returned to the table. Though I had kept my eyes straightforward the entire interval, the idiot inside of me forced my eyes to look at him. *All of him.*

"It's a wheelchair," he snapped, and I flinched, feeling the blow of his words.

"Sorry," I whispered, and moved my gaze back to his face, but even that was hard to bear. His brown eyes were stern, the thick brows the same, and the line of his mouth kept downward in a continuous frown.

He reached out past me—another stretch for him—and set the glass of orange juice down, the foam sitting deliciously at the top.

"Thank you," I said quietly, but still at a loss as of what to do as he returned to his spot.

The munching noise as he ate toast made my stomach churn, and I tried to hide my discomfort. Taking a few sips of juice, I gagged.

"Is something wrong?" he asked, turning his focus a second time from the newspaper and toward me, the jut of his jaw saying it all.

Yes, I thought, *he hated me.*

"Nothing," I said, a mouse not wanting to disturb the sleeping cat.

"What is it?"

I jumped at his sharp tone, unnerved and irritated all at once with his rudeness. *Is this how he treated all his guests?*

"I don't like pulp," I said, trying not to sound ungrateful, though I assumed that was how he'd take it.

He did.

Another groan. Another roll of eyes—and of his chair—as he unlocked the brakes, and went to the fridge. He returned with a new glass full of milk this time, and set it beside the orange juice. He picked up his paper again, exhaling loudly through his nostrils as I kept still, my arms slack against my lap.

Not even a minute went by before he spoke unkindly, his newspaper covering his face. "What is it now?"

I dared not speak, but he dropped the paper for the third time, complete irritation written across his face.

"It's nothing," I lied, giving a small smile.

"Then drink it."

My heartbeat skipped with every edged tone of his voice. I opened my mouth to speak, but it took some time before the words finally came out.

"I can't drink milk before ten o'clock . . . it makes me sick."

His brows rose. I wondered if he thought I was kidding. It seemed like that at first, as if he were waiting for a punch line, and instead got punched.

Keep waiting, I thought. Because the fact was true. Every time I drank milk before ten o'clock, it made my stomach hurt.

The brakes were once again unlocked; the tiring sigh expressed; and even more noise this time with his added aggravation. The third glass set next to the other two held clear liquid. He exhaled again, locking the brakes, and he scanned back to his place in the paper, only to fold it minutes later as his eyes locked with mine.

"Are you allergic to water?" he demanded, his piercing stare threat enough.

I gulped the sucker down, leaving only a quarter of it left.

A slight ripple crossed his mouth, as if he enjoyed that last bit of mine, yet was quickly concealed with the firm line again.

Now I had to burp because I drank too fast and too much at once. But the silent room wouldn't allow for such a noise, and I tried to think of something else.

"I didn't mean to stare," I tried to apologize.

"Thought you'd never seen a wheelchair before," he said and nothing more.

I sighed, trying again. "It wasn't that. They said—"

"*They said* I was an officer, or rather, you heard Officer Brandon call me that, and so it was a grand surprise for you to see me—*a supposed officer*—in a wheelchair?" The paper fell for the last time, and I knew it wouldn't be picked up again.

"So, you are an officer?" I asked, not wanting to lose our chance at conversation.

He let out a deep sigh, clasping his hands together and resting the joined fists onto his lap.

"I'm an ex-cop," he said, and I tried to keep my focus on his nose rather than his eyes. "Chief Brandon knew me when I used to live in Arizona, and somehow found out where I live now." This seemed to depress him immensely, but he continued on. "Because I used to be a cop, and I live in an unlisted home in the middle of the woods, he assumed this to be the best hiding place for you. I mean, why would anyone think to look here?"

"Why is it unlisted?"

"Because."

After a pause, I said, "That makes sense, I guess."

He feigned a smile. "It does, doesn't it?"

I gazed about the room, a break from his hard stare. It had a cozy feel but dark, and it matched well with the man. "So, Officer Clay—"

"Henry."

"Henry," I said. "Do you live here alone?"

"I do."

Well that was informative. I rubbed my shoulders, looking back at his nose again. "Sounds lonely."

"Hence the term," he said, taking another bite of toast.

I couldn't help myself.

"Do you have any ice?" I asked, a pushed grin through my cheeks.

Yes, I thought, *we are going to get along just fine.*

CHAPTER NINE

The faucet ran as he rinsed the dishes, his elbows holding his stretched body as he leaned against the sink. Only when I held out the first glass, did he look my way.

He took the cup without a word, and as the water continued to run, my legs shook.

I passed him the other glass.

His gray sleeves were soaked at the ends, and it amazed me he wasn't tired after holding himself up for so long, but I guessed he had to do this every day. He then spoke with heavy annoyance,

"Is something wrong with your legs?"

"What's wrong with yours?" I felt the blood drain from my face; my brain had no time to stop the retort.

His head turned and he kind of stared at me, maybe in shock, maybe just bewildered at the brash question, I didn't know for sure, only that I wished I could take it back.

"I'm sorry," I whispered.

His jaw clenched, as if he were holding back his first reply, and he took a silent breath before speaking again.

"What is it?" he asked, his less rude and more tired tone, surprising me.

"I have to go to the bathroom."

"Follow me."

I did as told, studying the back of his head and shoulders as we went to the wall of the stairs and I realized there was a door. He pulled the handle, opening it for me, and I hurried inside.

Once the locked clicked, I dropped my bottoms and sat. I didn't have to put the toilet seat down, and the thought burned my cheeks.

He is in a wheelchair, I remembered.

I pushed further thought away and relaxed enough to pee. I wouldn't be surprised if the town fifteen miles away heard the waterfall.

After I finished and opened the door, the man was sitting in the living room with the only furniture being a green couch and a red chair. I sensed a theme, recalling the same colors on the blanket in my new room.

"There is no TV," I said, and took a seat on the couch.

"I don't watch TV," he said with little emotion except the ever present bothered one. He kept his hands in his lap with his elbows resting on the arms of the chair as he faced nothing in particular.

"What do you do all day?" I asked. The place had no personal touches—no photos, no art, no true decoration other than mainstream furniture and lighting. Like my room though, it was open and quaint.

"I sit," he said, then added with a hint of eccentric edge, "stare at walls."

My tongue jabbed my inner cheek as I realized something obvious. "So basically, you think all day, and nothing else. Just sit, thinking."

"That's right."

"What do you think about?"

No response. His eyes rested at the bare fireplace while I stared at him, the nervousness from before fading.

I sighed, feeling my bladder fill up again during the awkward silence.

"Can we go to town?" I asked, hoping for something, anything. A spark in his pitch-black world.

"Why?" he said carelessly.

I thought fast. "It's a girl thing."

And that made him uncomfortable.

"You understand?" I beamed with laughter as I rose from the couch. "Good."

His car had five seats but only two doors, and I wondered how we'd go about the whole 'wheel-chair-thing'.

"You can drive?" I asked, wondering if it was another stupid question.

"No," he replied coolly. "Whenever I need to go somewhere, I have someone who comes by and takes me."

"Who is she?" I made a guess at information.

He threw me the keys and swiveled to the passenger's side. "She likes to call herself my physical therapist."

My lip curled and I gave him a 'too-much-information' face.

He rolled his eyes and opened the car door. "But I don't need physical therapy," he clarified, then looked to me with impatience. "Get in."

"You want me to drive?"

"Get in," he said, and that time I obeyed.

I pushed the key into the ignition, twisting it, and the car roared to life as he locked his brakes. I watched from the corner of my eye as he picked one of his knees. The leg hung numbly in the air before he set it on the ground, and then did the same to the other, both lifeless.

Grabbing the coat hook with one hand, he pressed his other palm against the leather seat. Lifting himself inside, he made a *huff* noise as beads of sweat coated his upper lip. I didn't dare help.

Once in the seat, he adjusted himself and slumped back, letting out a short breath.

"Are you just going to leave it outside?" I indicated toward the wheelchair. "I can get it for you."

"I don't plan on getting out of the car," he said, shutting his door.

"Then why come at all?" I was done with his constant attitude. *Did they expect me to stay with him all day? Couldn't I have some time to myself?*

His next words answered my silent questions.

"Because I have too," he said, looking at me as if I were an idiot. "I have to stay with you twenty-four-seven, and no matter how much of a sick joke it seems, I have to protect you. Now drive."

CHAPTER TEN

Driving through the woods wasn't as hard as I thought it would be. A path remained in the drying mud from where Officer Brandon came through, and I followed it easily enough. After about fifteen minutes, we passed a sign reading, "Welcome to the Town of Fay".

"It means faith," he scoffed. "Or is a short term of the word."

I held my tongue and watched as children played in front lawns, ran through sprinklers, and rode on bikes, laughing and screaming with joy, until finally I had to look away, mist in my eyes, and a pang of guilt in my chest.

We reached a circle of shops shaped like a horseshoe enclosing a big parking lot, and a convenience store was first to the left. I parked and turned off the car.

"You're just going to stay in here?" I asked, trying to take in his features, but the harsh eyes were all I could focus on.

"How would you expect me to get out?" he said, keeping his attention out his fogging window. It looked like it was going to rain, gray clouds covering the sky, and it was weird for me to see rain in August.

"Okay." I held back my sigh and got out of the car. I could feel his stare the entire time as I walked away, and I hurried inside the store.

"Good morning," a man in his fifties greeted me from the register counter.

"Morning," I answered him back, the first smile to my lips in a long time. I walked closer, noticing the small display of rocks. "Are you collecting those?"

"Just the most unique," he said, taking me in. After a moment of quick inspection, he handed me a purple rock with specks of black. The surface was smooth and warm. I set it down and took an orange one.

"It is not just the color, or appearance of a rock or pebble, that matters," he explained, his pale blue eyes meeting mine as he spoke. "It is the touch, the feel, and shape, that is also important."

"What do you think of that one?" he asked about the purple.

"Hmmm," I thought a moment, trying to think of what to say. "Well, the purple and black was cold, but this orange is neutral."

He took the orange from my hand, his soft skin the first contact I had in what felt like forever.

"Then what I do, if the pebble is as you say, I take it back to the lake and let it mature, grow some more." He laughed lightly, as if knowing the silliness of his hobby but didn't care.

"If only you could do that with people," I said, thinking of the man in the car.

"Ah," he countered, "We are more like rocks and pebbles than you think. At least, that's what my wife always said. Collecting rocks was her hobby." His face grew soft at the mention of her.

"I'm Prue," I said, offering my free hand.

He took it kindly. "James Wilson. You must have just moved here."

"How'd you know?"

"Small town." He grinned. "Where are you staying?"

"Uh . . . ." I paused, not really knowing what to say. "The lake house in the woods." *Should I be saying this?*

The color left his face. "Did something happen to Henry?"

"Henry . . . ?" *Oh yeah,* I remembered, *that was his name.* "Oh, Henry, yes—um no, nothing happened to him."

"So, he moved?" Mr. Wilson prodded, eyebrows still quarters high above his eyes.

"No." I swallowed something thick. "He still lives there."

Crap, I thought. *I should have kept my mouth shut. Was anyone allowed to know about us?*

The store suddenly felt stuffy and hot, and I needed some air.

"Um, actually, I was wondering if you had any, uh . . . candy?" I said, not so quick on my feet that time.

Mr. Wilson looked at me as if to say something more, but didn't. He pointed behind me. "In the back there is a nice selection."

"Thank you." I smiled and turned around. I passed shelves of canned goods and boxes of food, not even giving a second glance to the small displays of pads and tampons.

I tried to catch my breath as I scanned the candy bags, hoping I hadn't just ruined my entire cover. I grabbed licorice, chocolate covered peanuts, and gummy worms, then headed more cautiously back to the counter. Without a single word, Mr. Wilson rung up the items and placed them in a bag for me. Then I realized something.

"I didn't bring my purse." I frowned, then looked up to the kind man. "I'm sorry, I can't pay for it."

He waved his hand, smiling. "On the house."

"Oh, no, I don't want to impose—and I can always come back."

He chuckled. "Well, if it troubles you that much I can just put it on Henry's tab."

"Okay." I grinned ear to ear, taking the bag. "Thanks."

I reached the door and waved goodbye, one foot outside.

"Come again," Mr. Wilson hollered, and I nodded that I would.

Once the shop door closed behind me, it was instinct to head toward the car where the gloomed man sat waving for me to come on, but something else drove my intrigue harder.

I turned on my left heel and walked down to the window display of a boutique. A tiny pink dress with white lace and black shiny shoes stared back at me through the glass. I couldn't help but think of my sister as a heavy ache pulled my heart.

Hannah couldn't wait to shop for baby clothes, and strollers, and cribs. She was most excited about the decorating. She would have bought the dress at first sight, even if the baby were to be a boy, then would say, *'for next time'*, as if there truly was going to be a next time.

A car horn honked. Loudly.

I turned around and sure enough, it was him pressing the steering wheel. He did it three more times until finally realizing that since I was near the car, I was coming.

"Did anyone ever tell you about patience?" I said as I slid into the driver seat and passed him the grocery bag.

"Well, she was a lovely girl, but I was too short for her," he said without smiling and rifled through the bag as I started the car. His head jutted up to me. "You only got candy?"

Oh. Right.

"I must have gotten distracted, I was talking to the man

who runs the store."

"Do you need to go back?" he asked as I put the car in reverse, and I could have sworn that I detected a tinge of concern in his tone.

"No," I said, veering the steering wheel back to where we came from, and changed the subject. "Did you know Mr. Wilson collected rocks?"

"Yes, I did. Wait." He paused. "He introduced himself to you?"

I shrugged a nod but kept my eyes to the road, entering the woods.

Technically, it was I who started introductions, but I didn't want to go into any more detail than needed. I should have guessed he wanted to do the exact opposite.

"Did you introduce yourself to him?"

"Well, it's what you do," I said, cringing from an oncoming shout.

"You told him your name!" And there it was.

"Hey," I snapped, moving my eyes off the road and to him. "You're the one who forgot to give me my new identity, remember? So don't blame me for telling someone my real name—it is habit after all."

He let out a loud, angry groan, running his hand through his hair.

"Wow." I mocked. "Such vocabulary."

"Watch it," he said. "Because of you, I have to fix this."

At his first order, I returned my gaze to the road, nearly missing a squirrel, and my hands froze on the wheel. I was glad he didn't notice.

"Fix what?" I asked. "So he knows my first name, we can always tell them a last."

"Them?"

"Whoever he tells," I clarified. "No big deal.

"Oh, so your life is no big deal?" he countered. "So your sister and brother-in-law's life, were no big deal? Do you not understand the kind of people we are dealing with here?"

My foot stomped on the brake and we plunged forward. His head almost hit the windshield, but I didn't care. My chest heaved up and down rapidly as my hands began to shake with anger. I faced him.

"Hey!" I growled through clenched teeth. I wanted to slap him, shake him, make him hurt as he hurt me. But I forced my feelings to remain at bay.

After I took a deep breath, I released the brake, and said, "Put your seatbelt on."

CHAPTER ELEVEN

I ran up the stairs first thing after I opened the front door of the lake house. My sneakers squeaked as the floorboards groaned beneath my weight, and I rushed into the first room I came to and plopped onto the bed.

But this wasn't the room I originally slept in the night before. It was his.

My eyes, blurry with tears, looked at my fingers grazing the red comforter. I turned on my back, facing the ceiling, the lighting of the room a low glow against the dark cherry wood walls.

There were no decorations, no pictures or painted frames, just like the other rooms in the house, yet it still contained a cozy atmosphere somehow. Slowly, I got up from the bed, wiping the corners of my eyes, and walked to the adjoining bathroom, investigating the place.

I took the opportunity to pee, and the toilet seat was already down, I noticed once again. I flushed and went to wash my hands, seeing the claw-foot tub adjacent to a glass shower, with nothing much else besides towels hanging on the walls, and a mirror. The sink was high and I wondered how he managed to get ready in the mornings since he was wheel-chair-bound, but then again, I guessed everyday things were a challenge for him.

When I could find nothing more of interest, I stepped back into the bedroom and that was when I noticed his closet cracked open. I didn't think there would be much to a closet except for clothes, but my curiosity needed its spark and there was the match. I tiptoed—thankful that the floors did not creak in here—and pulled the knob.

A string dangled out in front of me and I tugged until a light clicked on, illuminating a rack of clothes with no bright colors or short-sleeves. I pushed between the hangers, biting my lip with fear of being caught. Shoes were in the back, only three pairs lined up, one of which being worn slippers, and nothing else of intrigue, until I looked up.

"Prue!"

I jumped back, my face burning, and looked behind me, ready to be chastised. I was relieved when no one was there—he had called me from downstairs.

"Prue, come down!" he shouted louder, but there wasn't anger in his voice like times before.

I wavered, wanting desperately to stay, to find out more about this mysterious man, but knew I should answer him. The box would have to wait for another day.

He was waiting for me at the bottom of the stairs, his face solemn as usual, but with a more sympathetic tint to it. I waited at the landing.

"I'm sorry, Prue," he said. "I sh—" he paused, clenching his jaw; I could hear the grind even from here. "I shouldn't have said that about your family. It was out of line."

I took the first step down.

"It's just, you could have jeopardized your safety—and

now I have to change your identity again."

I went on alert. "I don't have to leave, do I?"

"No, you don't have to leave," he said, and I thought he almost chuckled.

"Okay." I had nothing else to say, I just wanted to rest. When he started to speak again my voice won over. "Actually, I just want to get some rest. I don't really feel well."

"Oh, okay," he said with some understanding, taking me back a little. He must have felt pretty bad for what he said. "You have been through ... it ... it takes a lot out of you."

I had to wonder if he actually did know how much it took out of someone. *He was in a wheelchair.*

"It's perfectly normal," he added.

"Good to know," I muttered, and went to my original bedroom. Though I had wanted to go back to the closet, I decided against it, my head and stomach hurting all at once.

I swam under the covers, relaxing my limbs, and stared up at a different ceiling as awaiting thoughts plunged through.

Could Hannah really be gone? No longer by my side in this life? I saw her just two days ago . . . . I shook my head, and my heart plummeted. *She would have loved to be a mother. I would have given anything . . . but at least she believed she was going to have a child before she was . . . before she died.*

I have been told to leave revenge to God, but . . . what am I supposed to do now? I feel so helpless . . . especially here, right now. Left to the protection of former Officer Henry Clay, a.k.a. the man who hates my guts because I stared at his wheelchair? My apologies, then.

But what do they expect me to do here? My eyes rolled. *Sit all day and think like him? Maybe we'll even get matching chairs.*

Hours later, I woke to a loud crash resounding from downstairs. I jolted up from the bed and ran to the banister. When I looked down, he was on the ground next to the bottom step, his wheelchair tipped on its side feet away.

The wood cracked as my foot moved forward.

"Go back upstairs!" he yelled, red veins pulsing at his temples and throat. His stomach lay against the ground, his hand straining for the railing as his face looked up toward mine.

I pushed past my fear and continued down.

"You need help," I tried to say with sympathy, but it was full of rebellion.

"Go back upstairs!" he ordered again, his dark eyes aglow, and I could tell that such a proud man would never take my help, or my sympathy.

So I did his bidding and walked away, the feeling not so good. I slammed the bedroom door shut, and did not come out for two days.

CHAPTER TWELVE

He knocked both days.

Knocked when he first got up; knocked for breakfast; knocked for lunch; knocked to go to town; knocked for dinner; even knocked for bed. He never said a word, except my name after his knuckles hit the wood three times.

Knock. Knock. Knock.

"Prue."

Silence.

Knock. Knock. Knock.

I had to survive on my bag of candy, but that quickly ran out, and I felt so sick. I only took bathroom breaks at midnight.

Then, I could take it no longer.

He had just knocked for the third morning less than two minutes ago when my hand flew to my mouth, and I broke free from the room and out into the hallway. To my left, there he was, going to his room. I dashed to his side, taking a quick turn before running into him, and headed straight for his bathroom, knowing there was no time to ask if another one was on the second floor.

Thankfully, the toilet was separated from the bath by a door and I could confine myself inside, turning the lock.

Too bad that the toilet seat wasn't lifted. I wasn't sure about my aim, but didn't care either way. I purged the life out of me.

"Prue!" A loud pounding hit the door, shaking the tiny room. "What's wrong? Are you sick?" His tone was not so much of panic, but of inexperience—as if he didn't know how to show compassion for another human being. "Prue!"

I vomited a second time. My shoulders shook with tears, my heart convulsed as my nose clogged with stinging bile, and sobs were evident.

"Prue," he called again, "open this door."

I flushed the toilet.

"Open. This. Door!"

I wiped my mouth with shaking fingers, using toilet paper to soak up the residue. I reached a hand toward the knob and unlocked the door, the click a lingering sound. Tears continued to flow as hiccups threatened, and I tried to focus on my breathing.

The door swung back and he sat before me a foot away, his gray robe disheveled as was his dark hair, but I could not take in his face, the water in my eyes blurring everything.

"Prue."

"She's dead," I said.

I rested the back of my head against the wall and blinked the water away. I could finally take in his features, his eyes not so harsh now.

Uncombed, dark brown hair that was almost black, short matching brows over darker eyes, a long but contained nose reaching to his full mouth that was kept in a forever firm line and surrounded by a week's worth of five o'clock shadow. Maybe two weeks.

Henry. I tested the name, thinking of him as such, and less of the isolated and wounded officer I deemed him to be.

"She's dead," I said again, as my stomach lurched. "And she's not coming back. It should have been me."

His mouth opened, but no words came. *Could* come, it seemed. Until he swallowed, only then did he speak.

"Prue, I—"

He tried, oh yes, he did try. Like the boy who chased the firefly yet could not catch its flame.

But those words were not the words I wanted. Longed for. From anyone.

"Just leave," I said, facing the inside of the toilet once more. "Leave me alone."

And I kicked the door shut.

Another hour later, with smudged eyes, clogged nose, messy hair, and a red mark on the side of my face from resting on the toilet seat, I came downstairs.

Henry, as I now called him, sat opposite the green couch. He watched as I descended the steps, and I took the seat facing him.

He cleared his throat, obviously not sure whether to have his left hand on his right arm, or right hand on his left leg. I waited, my eyes beginning to swell from so many tears, something that always happened after I cried.

"Are you all right?"

"No," I said, my throat raw.

Henry sighed, his eyes actually looking to me now, for once. Or twice, rather. The first time was in the bathroom.

"I know this is difficult for you, losing your sister and

brother-in-law, but . . . ." He paused, and took another deep breath. "I don't know what to tell you, I mean we just met days ago—two of which you kept yourself locked up—and we know practically nothing about the other. How could I ever relate to you, right?"

My eye twitched.

"We have to at least try to get along," he said, but I wasn't sure if he knew all what that statement entailed. He then shrugged, forcing a smile. "Or we could just keep out of each other's way and not speak at all."

I didn't move a muscle. Only my eyes. They continued to look at him, inspect him, because once again, the harsh stare was gone, and I was given free reign.

He was older than me, a little more than ten years past my twenty-two, and had modest gray about him; in his hair at the temples; the salt in the pepper of his shave.

It was his face that gave him away, though. The *aged-by-years-in-a-matter-of-seconds*-look. And the constant frown did not help. But I bet if he smiled . . . he would lose those years between us. If only he would smile.

At first, I thought he gave up, but then he surprised me by unlocking his wheels and coming closer, holding out his hand to help me up from the couch.

"Look, I don't want you to be sick. Let's go to town and we'll see the doctor to find out what's wrong. You shouldn't be throwing up like that for an hour."

I didn't give him my hand, only looked at him, a challenge in my eyes, a tremble in my chin.

"I'm not sick," I said, my lips chapped, and my heart pounding loudly in my tired chest. "I'm pregnant."

CHAPTER THIRTEEN

Henry's eyelids fluttered and he shook his head. "What?"

I exhaled, and said, "I'm pregnant."

"Excuse me?"

My next sigh was of irritation. "I'm *pregnant.*"

"I heard that part," he growled. "I only asked again because—*I don't know*—I thought you'd be less vague!"

I flinched, my habitual reaction, and this, he noted. He rubbed his face and groaned, his eyes closed between the slits of his fingers.

"Get in the car," he said.

"What?"

He shouted. "Get in the car!"

I jumped from the couch, almost knocking into him, and ran out—*in my pajamas*—to the outside world.

A few minutes later he rolled out, his gray robe replaced with a gray shirt, and I watched wide-eyed as he skidded down the steps of the porch.

Coming to the car, he threw me the keys but I didn't react in time and the sharp ends scratched my arm. They fell to the ground in a short jingle, but he said nothing.

"*Ouch,*" I said, staring at him in bewilderment. He gave me a dirty look in return, waiting for me to unlock the doors.

After a short-lived staring contest, I gave up and grabbed the keys. I unlocked the car and slid inside as he grunted and groaned his way into his seat. I didn't speak until his door shut.

"Where are we going?" I asked.

"To town," he said.

"Why?"

"I need to make a call."

My senses revved. "W-why?"

"Because," he said. "Chief Brandon—*and whoever else is supposed to be working on your case*—needs to know, and while we are on our way you are going to tell me everything."

"Everything?" I asked with more curiosity than timidity, wishing I could ask him the same.

"Everything."

My foot hit the gas, and I knew that this would be the longest drive of my life.

CHAPTER FOURTEEN

My palms perspired against the steering wheel as I drove, my knuckles cracking every other minute from the tight grip. I tried to keep my focus on the road ahead but the dark glare in my corner vision made it difficult.

"Go on," Henry said. He leaned against the window, his gaze still on me, and I felt the intensity of it.

"Hannah couldn't have children," I said before I could lose nerve. "She and Jacob got married when she was twenty-three, and though they tried to have a child, seven years passed without success. Numerous tests were done and drugs given, but the one time she did get pregnant, she lost the baby."

I gripped the wheel tighter, trying to release the nerves inside of me, my knuckles white. Silence enveloped the car like a hot blanket and I was suffocating.

I looked his way, too much silence on his part, and his wide-eyed expression said it all. "Are you telling me that—"

"After the last attempt failed, I did research on different methods and came across In-Vitro Fertilization. At first,

Hannah and Jacob were against it, but I convinced them."

"Ah huh."

"Everyone thought I was too young, that it would be asking too much." I paused again, remembering it as if it were yesterday. When I made a decision, I stuck to it.

"Two weeks ago, Hannah and I found out that the three embryos they put in me, survived. She was so excited because all my chances were good. She was finally going to be a mother. Before I left to come here, her doctor called. She had the blood test results that said I was pregnant."

"How old are you?"

"Twenty-two," I said.

"What does your boyfriend think about this?"

I laughed, a relief to my heart, and I couldn't believe he just asked me that.

"Is that you coming on to me?" I grinned, but didn't give him time to respond. "I don't have a boyfriend," I said, wishing we could turn back around. I wanted to see the actual lake part of the woods, but then something else caught my eye. "Is that a church?"

His eyes scanned past the square building, then back to me. "Yes, it is."

"Can we go?"

"What?"

I shifted my gaze to him and narrowed the lids. "Is that you wanting me to be less vague again?"

"No," he said, relaxing back. "I shouldn't even be letting you into town, let alone drive me here."

His controlling issues prickled my skin. "Look, you can't keep me locked in the house—I will go nuts like you," I said, a surge of emotion running through me. I moved my attention back to our destination. "Where are we headed to anyway?"

"The payphone."

50

I slammed the brakes of the car, both of us plunging forward again. I waved my hands around, motioning to nowhere as I fought nausea. "And where is that?"

"By the convenience store."

I held the impulse to roll my eyes and hurried to find a parking space, which wasn't hard. I cut the engine when realization occurred. "How are you going to get out?"

He began to speak, a smarty-pants remark no doubt, then stopped, realizing the same thing I had. He growled just as a fresh set of rain began to pour.

"I don't know."

Something came over me, compassion perhaps, or pity; I hoped the latter; and I tried to be helpful, knowing that such a thing could slap me back in the face one day.

"Don't you have a phone at the house?"

"No," he said, not meeting my eyes.

"What?"

He growled again. "Get Mr. Wilson."

"Do you want me to ask him if he has a cellphone?"

"Just go get him!"

"Fine," I said, opening the door, then slamming it shut after me. Cold drops of heavy rain pelted my hair and shoulders, a storm no doubt coming. I looked around, wondering where all the town people were.

The window then rolled down. "I don't have an umbrella," he said. I assumed he was sorry about the fact. After all, I was doing this for him, though I doubted he would see it that way.

"Don't worry," I said as I began to slip away. "The rain never bothered me."

"Mr. Wilson!" I called for the older man once I entered the store. Seconds later, he was shuffling down a back aisle and towards me, concern on his face.

"Prue, so good to see you again. Are you all right?"

"It is Officer Clay who needs your help, actually."

Crap! Does he know he's an officer? I tried not to let the thought stop me, and with my big mouth, I led Mr. Wilson to the car.

I waited by the bumper as Mr. Wilson went to the passenger's side. The window rolled down again, revealing the tired looking ex-cop.

"I need to use the payphone," he said carefully, as if someone could be listening even though there was only the three of us around. "And I forgot my chair back at the house."

"Ah," Mr. Wilson concluded with a slight nod. "Ms. Prue," he called to me as he opened the passenger door. "Would you mind getting a few umbrellas from my store and bringing them to Ms. Martha down the street in the bakery? I was just about to bring her some."

I nodded slowly, wanting to stay, but did as asked and went back into the store. "They are by the counter, first thing you see," he hollered as the shop door closed behind me.

I saw the three umbrellas right away as they sat in a tall holder and grabbed them all before leaving again.

I watched as Mr. Wilson helped Henry out of the car. He had both of Henry's arms slung around his neck as he held onto his waist. Turning toward the payphone, Mr. Wilson held him with care as Henry's feet dragged like deadweights against the ground.

The sight tugged at my heart, but I knew this errand was supposed to be my distraction, and with devotion, I turned away and went about my business.

The bakery wasn't far, just a few shops down like Mr. Wilson had said, and soon I was face to face with a window displaying rows of pastries, small cakes, and other sweet treats that caused my mouth to water and bile to rise, all at the same time.

The grammatically incorrect pink-lettered sign read, "Marthas' Bakery". I opened the white framed door with ease, and walked inside.

"Well, hello there my dear," a woman a little older than me with black curls and ivory skin cheered from behind a flour-covered counter. She wore red lipstick and mascara, her dress white with black polka dots covered by a white lace apron, and a hint of pink for her nametag, *Martha*.

"What brings you here?" she asked. "What's your name?"

"Oh, uh Pr—" My throat caught on the words. *Should I tell her my name? Was I allowed now that Mr. Wilson knew?* My mouth moved soundlessly like the village idiot.

"What?" She laughed kindly. "Cat got your tongue?"

"Um . . . Mr. Wilson sent me . . . with umbrellas." And the idiocy continued as I held them up before me. I shook my head and laughed a little, handing the umbrellas to her, which she happily took.

"How thoughtful of James," she said as if they were a bouquet of flowers, and I felt as if I were invading on a personal moment or something. She then returned to my attention. "So, you're the new girl in town. Prue, right?"

I nodded slowly. "Yeah, I live at the lake house."

Ugh. Could I ever stop blowing my cover?

"Really?" Her eyes widened. "How's that Henry Clay doing?"

"You know him?" I asked, amazed he ever came out enough to be seen.

She chuckled. "Well, I used to. He's mostly an urban legend now."

"An urban legend?" I parroted.

Her head bobbed in a positive reply as she took the umbrellas behind the counter, and I followed from the opposite side to where more cakes were displayed. She motioned for me to take a seat at one of the stools. I sat down as she turned her back to me, pulling out a metal cooking sheet, and then placed it on the counter.

"Try one." She smiled down at the rows of small squares covered in white icing. I popped one into my mouth and glowed with the first bite. "I take what is left from cutting cakes and make them up into squares, then freeze them overnight and dip them in icing. I sit them out in the morning and right around this time they are perfect."

I took another.

"So, urban legend?" I nudged the subject, and she grabbed a short stool from the other side, taking a cake for herself.

She then hollered behind her at the kitchen door, "Hey, Martha!"

I was instantly confused.

"Bring some fresh coffee, will ya, dear?" She looked back to me, taking in my stumped expression, and laughed.

Another woman came through the swinging door, holding three mugs in her left hand and a pot of coffee in the other. She wore her blonde hair in a loose bun, a pen sticking at the top, and she had a firm smile that somehow oozed warmth.

"Both of our names are Martha," Martha #1 explained as Martha #2 poured each of us a cup of steaming coffee.

"Oh." I formed a grin. "So, the sign isn't wrong outside?"

They both smiled. "No, it's right," Martha #1 giggled. "Call me Evie." She extended her hand formally, and I took it.

"Just call me Martha," the other replied. She took a seat of her own and leaned an elbow against the counter. "What are we discussing, ladies?"

Evie smiled. "The Urban Legend of Officer Henry Clay."

"Ah, that's a juicy one."

"What exactly is it?" I said. I took a sip of the coffee and jerked my head back in surprise.

54

"Chocolate." Evie laughed again. "We never liked the taste of real coffee, so we decided to make our own, and chocolate was the only option. What do you think?"

"It's good." I took another sip. "You were saying?" I leaned forward, wanting desperately to know what they were talking about.

Did Henry have a scandal about him? A dark past? Who was this man I am forced to live with—be protected by? And do I even really want to know the truth? Or should I do the right thing and ignore silly rumors, giving him the benefit of the doubt? But the image of a certain box in a specific closet pestered me, and I needed something, if anything.

Martha spoke first. "Well, to start with—"

"Mr. Wilson, how good to see you!" Evie gave her cheer again, and I looked behind me. "Care for some coffee?"

"Oh, no thank you," he said, looking at me. "I have only come here to fetch Ms. Prue."

"We were just telling her about the Urban Legend of Officer Henry Clay," she chimed in tune with Martha.

My cheeks burned at once. *Great.*

"Oh, really," Mr. Wilson said quietly. "I am afraid it will have to wait for another time, then." He smiled at us, but not like before.

I stood, thanked the girls for the coffee and cakes, and followed Mr. Wilson out the door. Once outside, and away from the Marthas', he spoke close to my ear. "I would like to offer you some advice, Ms. Collins."

Chills went up my spine. "How did you—"

"Henry told me," he said. I could only wonder how much Henry had told him. Mr. Wilson continued. "I hope that you will not let your thoughts about Mr. Clay be poisoned by idle gossip." His blues eyes stared into mine. "For instance, this urban legend folly."

I felt like a child being punished. "I didn't—I didn't mean to pry like that," I said, not wanting him to think of me as a person who thirsted on gossip. "I just wanted to know . . . something."

He patted my hand gently and gave me a smile that calmed my fears. "If you wish to know something, simply ask him."

If only it were that easy, I thought to myself. "He won't tell me anything."

We reached the car, the rain a little less vigorous than before, but Mr. Wilson still held my hand. Henry watched us from inside, his face always seeming to be hardened at normal state.

"Give him a chance," Mr. Wilson said. "This is new for him too."

I only nodded, and got in the car.

CHAPTER FIFTEEN

"You should probably take a hot shower," Henry suggested as he wheeled himself into the kitchen. I followed behind him rebelliously and watched as he stretched high into cabinets, grabbing a saucepan and two wooden bowls. I was homesick and wished to call my parents, but had seen plenty of mystery movies to know where that conversation led.

"You need a hot shower yourself," I said and he looked back to me as if he had forgotten I was even there.

He looked back to the heating stove. "There is only one working shower. I figured you would want to go first."

"Oh," I said, then stopped midway my exit. "Which shower?"

"Mine."

"Oh," I repeated, my voice rising an octave, and I quickly fled the room, cheeks aflame.

The floor creaked as I walked up the stairs and to Henry's room. I glanced toward the closet, wondering if this would be a good time. Then I remembered Mr. Wilson's advice and kept my feet to the bathroom.

I took a quick shower and hurried to my room to change, a delicious smell from downstairs hitting my nose as I crossed the hallway.

I followed the trail into the kitchen where Henry had his head stretched over a saucepan, stirring with a long wooden spoon.

"Almost ready," he announced, speaking into the pan and startling me. "Take a seat and I'll bring the soup."

I sat in my original spot from my first breakfast here, and waited patiently, looking around the room. The wooden table was bare with no cloth and only dark curtains dressed the sides of the window that out-looked the beautiful woods. Not a feminine touch in sight.

"I had to use your shampoo," I told him, my cheeks burning again. He rolled to his spot at the table and set a bowl of red soup and a slice of bread before me.

"That's fine," he said.

When he settled in his seat, he reached for his spoon.

"Aren't you going to pray?" I asked.

A muscle jerked in his cheek and he looked at me. "You can. I'm eating."

I sighed, closing my eyes, and clasped my hands. "Dear God, I thank You for today and ask You to bless this food we are about to receive, nourishment to our bodies in Jesus' Name I pray, Amen." I paused a moment, my cheeks warming again, then added, "And thank You for Henry."

I opened my eyes, not daring to look his way, and dunked the corner of my bread into the hot soup.

"It's good." I smiled after taking a bite, and dunked a second time.

"I need to tell you," he said slowly, and paused to slurp a spoonful of soup. "What Chief Brandon and I discussed over the phone."

"Okay," I agreed, my heart pounding a million miles a minute. *What had they planned for me this time?*

He dropped his spoon into his bowl and pushed it away, not even half-empty. His focused gaze held mine.

"I told him about the pregnancy," he said. "You're in more danger now than you were before. I assume you know the conditions of your brother-in-law's contract? About the heir?"

"Yes," I said quietly, remembering the cold room at the police station.

Henry hesitated then, eyeing me more strangely, and said, "Is that why you said it should have been you?"

My hands fidgeted in my lap, my own soup forgotten. I looked down. "The only reason they killed Hannah was because they saw the nursery. I'm sure of it. But they killed the wrong person. I'm carrying the heir, not Hannah. She would still be alive if—" I stopped, my throat tightening.

"You can't blame yourself, Prue," Henry said, surprising me. "Which do you think Hannah would want more? Her life? Or your life, and that of her child's?"

Guilt was clay in my mouth, and anger burning coal in my chest, giving me fuel. I wasn't sure how to let go of them both. "But that was the only reason they killed her."

"Blaming yourself is a pit that you can only get out of yourself," he said, then continued the other subject. "Sooner or later, this Brooks guy is going to find out your pregnant. Since you saw the man who . . . was in the nursery, he is going to find out everything about you. It's only a matter of time."

"How could he find me? I mean . . . ."

What did I mean? Did I truly think that the bad man couldn't find the long lost princess? That perhaps, her supposed knight-in-shining-armor was truly a crippled, no offense to the man, and that just perhaps, she could be stolen and killed? I cringed. *But what of the prince she carried inside of her? The very last thing that was left of the king and queen? How could she fail them?*

She couldn't.

"What am I to do?" I said.

Henry's expression changed into something I could not quite name. *Anxiety? Trepidation? Thinking the same as me and that there was too much pepper in the soup?*

"The thing is . . . ." He cleared his throat. "Your parents couldn't come because a group stuck out. Now that you're pregnant, and single, you stick out again, so . . . ."

"So?"

He shifted uncomfortably in his chair, then let out a groan. "The Chief thought it best that we . . . ." His jaw clenched, hard, and a stirring of nausea overcame me. "That we get married."

I had no response. Couldn't even try.

"Prue?"

I felt my eyelids droop and saliva rush into my mouth. *Why was I so hot all the sudden?*

"Prue, are you okay?"

"I think . . . I am going to be . . . sick."

He backed up instinctively. "Go to the bathroom."

I stifled a burp. "I can't really move right now." My head throbbed, the light in the room so bright it made me squint, and I began to sway.

Henry didn't seem to know how to react to a pregnant girl about to pass out. At least that's what I gathered from the blank look on his face. If I could have laughed right then, I would have, and loudly.

He handed me his glass of water after mine emptied and rolled back and forth across the kitchen in a pace, then finally stopped when I said he was making me dizzy.

"We should probably take you to the doctor. You shouldn't have been in the rain like that."

"You mean drive?" I moaned.

"Go lay on the couch," he said. "Unless you can make it upstairs?"

"I think I will just sit here."

Silenced reigned, and then:

"What do you think, Prue?" Henry asked quietly, his breathing deep. I suddenly noticed the unique line of his mouth, the way it curved down at the tip. "I mean, you could go somewhere else. You've only been here a few days, and it wouldn't be hard to find another safe house for you. I'm not making you do this, marry me, I mean."

Marry him?

What had I gotten into? Marriage? Marriage! Would this be real? Would I legally be married to this stranger? Pregnant with another couple's child? When had my life become a soap opera?

But then I thought of Mr. Wilson and his rock collection, how I could not wait to find a special one for him. I thought of the Marthas' and their small iced cakes with chocolate coffee and their urban legends, how I wished to be able to share a recipe of my own. I thought of the lake house, how I had yet to see the lake and the woods surrounding. I thought of the town, who I would miss meeting and never get to know. I thought of Henry, and how somewhere deep inside of my heart, I did not want to leave this stranger in exchange for a world who would never truly understand loss.

Henry understood it. He enveloped it. Surrounded himself with it. I might not ever know the story, but I did know that there was something, and that only he could understand me. Tragedy connected us.

"I want to stay," I said, determination rising in my voice. *I could do this. I could do this for Hannah, for her child. I could choose a different path than I originally thought for my life. I could be strong, no matter the cost.*

I heard Henry's deep inhale, the cold air rushing into his mouth and filling his lungs, his chest expanding until the next release. I listened to his voice, soft and low, as he spoke.

"Chief Brandon thought that if you and I were . . . *married*, then that would make your pregnancy less suspicious."

I thought of the child inside of me. All my life, Hannah had protected me. Now it was my turn to protect something of hers.

"Okay, Henry."

His brows lifted. "Are you sure? If people ask about us—" He didn't finish, and I wanted to ask if he was so sure.

"I'm sure," I said.

"Tomorrow we'll make it official with the judge. I have your new identity papers, and the only way any one will be able to find you is by my name."

I closed my eyes as he continued to speak, listing details. I wasn't sure if he ever realized I had fallen asleep.

Prudence Clay.

The name quietly sang in my mind. I didn't think the two names went together very well, but then again, neither did we. So perhaps it fit just as it should.

By not fitting at all.

CHAPTER SIXTEEN

"I was wondering," I told Henry as we sat in the car outside a doctor's office.

"What?"

"Since we are changing my last name, and since *I am supposed to be undercover*, you could say, do you think...."

He faced me, annoyed it seemed, that I broke his thoughts. He had been staring out the window the entire drive here.

"Yeah?" he said, the rude tone never changing.

I bit my lip. "Can I change my first name, too?"

"Why do you want to change your name?"

"Because I was thinking about it, and my name doesn't really go well with your last name. I mean, *Prudence Clay*?" I gagged. "*Prue Clay*? It doesn't sound right."

He scoffed outright, but I did catch the laugh there, even if it didn't read across his lips.

"You're not changing your first name. It sounds fine." He then added with a more forget-it-tone, "Besides, it doesn't really matter, does it." It wasn't a question.

"If it's to be my new last name, then yes, it matters."

He threw his hands in the air dramatically, hitting the roof of the car and I laughed. He almost did too. A very quick and overly stifled chuckle escaped like a light within a light; outshined before it could truly be remarked upon.

He softened. "What would you liked to be called, then?"

"Sheridan."

"No."

It wasn't even up for discussion?

"Why not?" I whined unbecomingly.

"I am not going to call you Sheridan, when that's not your name." The corners of his mouth twitched, but only a little.

"Well," I said, determined. "That is what I want."

"*Well*," Henry repeated with my fervor, "I'm not going to change your name to Sheridan just because you don't think Prue Clay goes together. It sounds fine."

"Sheridan Clay," I pressed. "It sounds so much better."

"You are right," he agreed, and I smiled with triumph. "It does sound better, but the answer is still no."

I frowned. "Why?"

"*Because* Mr. Wilson and the Marthas' both know your real name—and most likely the whole town does, too."

I got out of the car with a groan. We brought his wheelchair this time and I reached into the back to pull it out.

"I'm going to guess that everything here is in this circle of shops?" I said as I tried my best to figure out the strange contraption. He watched from the passenger seat.

"Yep," he said, obviously annoyed with that fact, then mumbled, "nothing can hide here."

My brows knitted together as I instantly thought of the urban legend I never did get to hear, and my heart accelerated in speed from the fact that I truly knew nothing of this man.

"Is that why you live in the woods?"

"I like my privacy."

I am sure you do, I thought, rolling my eyes and dropping the subject.

We entered the small building and garnered looks from everyone in the waiting room.

"Henry," I whispered out of the corner of my mouth, but he ignored me and went straight to the front desk, signing a brown clipboard. I quickly fell behind him, the hot stares burning my back, and I looked down to the name he wrote. *Prudence Clay.*

I slapped his arm, causing looks from the other patients, and a very shocked and dark look from Henry himself, but I simply didn't care.

"Hey," I snapped. "It's not official yet."

CHAPTER SEVENTEEN

Twenty minutes later and I was in an oh-so-sexy backless gown with my legs spread on stirrups. *Thank you, Henry!*

Dr. Seymour was an older fellow in his sixties with the color brown still in his gray hair. He had a kind, big-toothed smile, and a warm voice that calmed my nerves.

He gave me a physical exam per the request of a certain handicapped officer, and various other tests to figure out why I was so sick. Now I sat with my legs completely crossed on the exam table, waiting for the doctor to return.

Soon a nurse, Sarah, came in. "Well Mrs. Clay, Dr. Seymour is just having a chat with your husband—"

"Oh, no." I laughed nervously. "We're not married."

She looked at me in confusion, then peered down to her chart in hand, her brow furrowed.

"I'm sorry, the name said . . . ."

Oops. I wasn't cut out for this *'secret-keeping'* thing.

"I mean," I said quickly with a smile, though it waned. *What did I mean?* "I mean, we're not married yet."

"Oh, well I guess he just thought to put it like that since . . .

you guys are having a baby after all." She spoke cautiously, not quite sure of herself again.

"Uh." My mouth opened, but no further sound could come out. *What now?* "Actually we are married . . . but then we found out . . . it wasn't official?" I lied, badly, and one of my eyes squinted. The nurse looked at me as if I were insane. "I mean, uh, well you see, we met a couple—almost a year ago, you know, and fell in love." I squirmed girlishly for effect. "And, uh, we wanted to get married, and we did, but later we found out that our ceremony pastor-person was not certified, legally."

Sarah's eyes widened and she clutched the clipboard close to her chest, listening with intent.

"Because we weren't in the U.S. at the time." My heart raced with the spewing lies that I knew would come with much guilt, and I had no idea where this ridiculous tale was going, only hoped for the best on the ride there. "We were in, um . . . Bagheera."

"Oh, I've never heard of that country," she replied, still intrigued, and waited for more.

"Yeah." My eyes got big. "It's uh, it's a, uh, a hidden . . . country."

Hidden country? What? Now I couldn't stop.

"Next to Bulgaria. And so we met there in a market place and just clicked."

"Oh really, what did—"

"In fact, you know," I cut her off, getting into the scheme of things. "He actually saved my life."

"Really?" she said with even more bewilderment. "How?"

I swallowed nothing. "Funny story, um—"

The door swung open and another nurse walked in. "Sarah, Dr. Seymour said Mrs. Clay can come out to the waiting room now. Her husband and the doctor are waiting for her there."

Sarah didn't even glance at the other nurse's way, only kept her sight on me, her eyes filled with wonder. "Okay, Pam, we'll be out in a sec."

I hopped down from the table, all out of ideas for the present time, and quickly changed beneath the gown.

"I will have to tell you the rest later," I hollered behind me as I ran to the waiting room. I almost hit Dr. Seymour, and stopped just in time in front of him and Henry. I gasped for air from the run.

"What . . . are you . . . guys . . . ." Deep Inhale. "Talking about?"

Dr. Seymour had a dour expression on his face while Henry looked at me, ballistic, and then shouted,

"You're a virgin!"

I blanched, an entire room of strangers staring at me. The pin needles spreading through my limbs kept me alert.

"Just tell the whole room, why don't you!" I growled.

"Mrs. Clay, I—"

"Ms. Collins," I hissed.

"Prue!" Henry yelled, then grabbed my arm to pull me away. I jerked from grip, narrowing my eyes even more.

"What is it?" I asked the doctor, ignoring the crowd and Henry.

"Mrs. . . . . Prue," Dr. Seymour began slowly, trying to keep professionalism. "You know that you are more than three months pregnant, correct? Though your chart said otherwise?"

"What?" Henry shouted again.

My heartbeat pounded in my ears as the room began to sway. "Yes, I know that," I said.

"Then—"

"How are you more than three months pregnant?" Henry

68

asked, now every eye officially on us—the strange new couple from the lake house who met in a fake country named after a panther who didn't like water. "You said two weeks."

"No, I said—" I paused, looking around the room, my cheeks flushing. *What would all these people think now?*

I turned to Dr. Seymour. "Will you excuse us?"

I didn't wait for permission. I roved around Henry, grabbed the handles of his chair, and pushed him with angered force out the door, letting his feet kick it open themselves.

"What is the matter with you!" I yelled once outside. I didn't wait for his answer either, letting go of the handles and crossing the street, leaving him on his own.

"What's the matter with me?" he said, spinning his wheels ferociously behind me. "What's the matter with you!"

I turned just in time for his legs to crash into my shins.

"Ow!" I groaned through my teeth.

Henry met me head on, and said loudly, "You told him—*and everyone else in that room*—your last name! Do you realize what you've done? You just blew your only cover!"

"You told everyone that I'm a virgin!"

His cheeks reddened, and he stumbled over his next words. "Dr. Seymour said—you said, or rather, *never* said—"

I bent down to his level, face to face, not having it anymore. "I'm pregnant! Don't you think telling them that I am a virgin already blew the cover!" I screamed, and the echoes frightened me into silence.

What was happening? What was he doing to me! No one's ever made me feel so out of sorts before! Was this even me anymore? Or just this crazy pregnant girl with a now messed up life—and all because of her?

"Where are you going, Prue?" he called as I walked away.

"I'm getting away from you!"

"Oh yeah?" he challenged. "And just where would that be?"

"Somewhere that actually cares! Understands!"

I continued to storm off, my fists jammed into my jacket pockets. And the first few drops of coming rain fell against my face in knowing tears.

CHAPTER EIGHTEEN

"Give me three—no, *four*—crème-filled ones with the chocolate glaze on top."

My nose pressed against the display glass. Dozens of donuts stared back at me with promises and I was feeling gullible. "Then the chocolate ones with the glaze—*no*, actually, just give me two plain chocolates."

"Six more, my dear." Evie peered down with me at the collection, a white box resting on the palm of her hand. "I would recommend the powdered ones. Sometimes the originals do the job."

"Give me three."

"Three left."

Something poked my brain, and I grudgingly looked up to Evie, rolling my eyes. "Do you know which kind Henry likes? I guess I could get him the last few."

"I would get him the one with sprinkles." Martha grinned. "He is a cop after all."

But it didn't seem to fit the gloomy man.

"Nah." I pondered the selections thoughtfully, sizing each

one up. "I'll get him two plain ones." Evie reached inside and grabbed the two, then waited for the last one. "Hmmm. Which is Mr. Wilson's favorite?" I asked.

At this, she smiled ear to ear. "The crumb cake ones."

My mouth watered. "Yum. Okay—put back one plain donut and grab two crumb cake ones instead," I said, and squirmed as she rang up my order.

"Okay," Evie said kindly. "Anything else today?"

I thought a moment, and even felt a little soft. "Three cups of your chocolate coffee."

Martha grabbed three to-go cups and filled them to the brim with the steaming, dark liquid, and placed them into a carrier. She handed the trio to me as I held the box of donuts on my other hand.

"That comes to thirteen dollars and twenty-two cents," Evie concluded, then winked. "You get the family discount."

"Oh, thank you." My heart melted and I thought I would cry right then. I didn't have any cash, not thinking of taking any on my rush here, but was not the least bit worried. "You can just put it on Henry's tab."

"Of course."

The door to the bakery opened, and a disheveled and damp Mr. Clay rolled in.

"There you are," he replied monotonously to our surprised looks.

The Marthas' coughed.

"Ready?" he asked carefully then, obviously realizing he was treading dangerous waters with me.

I feigned a yawn. "I guess. Goodbye Martha, Evie." I smiled to them, but gave a stone cold face to Henry as I swept passed him and out the door.

I walked toward Mr. Wilson's shop. Opening the lid of the donut box, I grabbed a crumb cake donut and quickly replaced the lid once more.

"Where are you going now?" Henry asked.

I took a bite of the crumb cake, warmth spreading through my mouth as I held the box with the coffees on top of the lid, and muffled an answer. "Mr. Wilson's."

Henry rolled to my side and groaned with impatience. "Give me that," he said, but it did not come out sounding helpful. "Or else you're going to drop everything."

I handed him the carrier, keeping the box close to my heart, and finished off the crumb cake. "I can taste why he loves those," I chimed, happier now than I was before.

"How did you pay for this?" Henry asked more innocently, keeping the cup carrier on his lap as he kept pace with me in his wheelchair.

"I didn't." I reached inside the box a second time and pulled out a plain chocolate that had no glaze.

"You put it on my tab?"

"Thanks," I said with a soft chuckle. I strolled into Mr. Wilson's shop and pushed the door hard enough so the swing would give Henry time to roll inside.

"That's stealing," Henry said.

I smiled and spoke in a sing-song tone, "We're married."

"Not yet," he retorted.

"Ah, Henry, Prue, what brings you here today?" Mr. Wilson greeted us from his usual spot.

"I brought you a donut," I said, walking toward the counter. I reached inside the box and grabbed the last crumb cake, handing it to him. "Evie said you liked these best. I got one too. They're delicious." I gave a side-glance to my fellow man. "Henry bought them."

"That was kind of you, Henry," Mr. Wilson said, but his tone said more, and he took a bite of the crumb cake as I watched with intent. "Always the best." He smiled after chewing with dramatic critique. But then his tone became more serious as he looked beside me. "I saw your car, Henry, parked by the doctor's office. Is everything all right?" He glanced quickly my way with anticipation.

Henry only shrugged. "Just a check-up, James. Nothing to worry about."

Silence followed, and I turned my focus back to Mr. Wilson. A thought then popped into my head. "Do you go to church, Mr. Wilson?"

The man smiled. "I do."

"Would you mind saving a seat for Henry and me next Sunday?" I could practically hear Henry's jaw drop.

Mr. Wilson looked at Henry for a moment but then smiled to me. "I will be happy to, Ms. Prue."

I winked. "Mrs. Clay, right?"

"What?" By the expression on his face, I suddenly felt like I had done something wrong.

My head hung back. Crap! *Again? Seriously—again! He knew my real last name—but doesn't know this? Ridiculous!*

Henry muttered behind me, pulling my arm, "I think it is time for us to go now, *Mrs. Clay.*"

I rolled my eyes at him, then smiled to Mr. Wilson as we headed toward the exit. "See you soon."

I dropped Henry off at the town hall and waited in the car with my box of donuts. I had to run back inside the shop because I forgot to give Mr. Wilson his coffee, and though he thanked me kindly, he seemed indifferent. I decided to seal my lips until speaking with Henry and telling him all of the other things I had spilled to strangers since I had been here—things true and not-so-much.

Twenty minutes and two donuts later, Henry came back

to the car and I pulled down the window. "Everything good?"

He squinted in the brightening sun as it fought for space between the clouds. "You need to come inside."

"Why?" I asked through a powdered donut, positive I looked a sight right now.

"You need to sign the marriage license."

"Oh." I got out of the car, reluctantly leaving the donut box behind, and followed Henry inside as I wiped donut residue off my mouth.

"Why can't we just tell the judge our story, and get a fake license or something? That way it doesn't have to be official." I laughed, mostly to myself. "I only planned on getting married once."

"As you should know, things don't work out the way they are planned," he said under his breath. "This is still a small town and even judges are human. If we told him the truth, someone else could find out and you would be in danger. Besides, we aren't using your real last name."

"Oh," I said, nothing else much coming to mind. An officer escorted us the judge's office and we met a large man with thin, square glasses sitting behind a mahogany desk. I liked him instantly. He had character.

"Hello, Ms. Jones," the judge said with a hearty smile, and I tried not to pause on my new last name.

"Hello," I murmured, still chewing on something.

"I gave the judge all of our papers, now we just need to sign the certificate," Henry explained.

"Goody." I grinned dramatically and walked over to the desk as the judge handed me a porcelain black pen. But actually holding the pen and looking to the printed line where I was to sign my name, my heart quivered.

We would really be married, wouldn't we? Legally. But then again, it wasn't my real name I was using . . . so I guess it won't be that legal at all. I held my breath and signed.

"Okay," the judge said. "Henry, your turn."

My head snapped to him. "You didn't sign it yet?" I asked. *Did he think I was going to back out?*

A ripple of something washed over his face. I heard his thick swallow, and with a brief pause, he pushed his palms against his wheels and rolled forward. I held out the pen to him and he took it gingerly. He inhaled a short breath as I had, then signed, backing up again before the ink could even dry.

The judge collected the papers, rising.

"All right," he said loudly as he signed something himself, and I waited in the back, the door my new friend. I didn't notice at first how Henry had done the same, us closer now than when we signed our lives together, and the judge's next words rang out against the world:

"I now pronounce you, Mr. and Mrs. Henry Clay."

CHAPTER NINETEEN

"I want you . . . to tell me everything," Henry said when I parked the car outside the lake house.

I grabbed a crème-filled donut from the box and took an inspected bite.

"Do not be so vague, Henry," I replied nonchalantly though anxiety gripped me. "It doesn't suit your façade."

He exhaled through his nostrils. "How are you more than three months pregnant, when from what I have been told, you should be only weeks into the first month?"

My next bite caused a squirt of crème and it slipped down my chin so elegantly. I used my fingers to wipe up the mess and licked them clean, taking another quick bite before the entire thing squished out. I focused on my task, not answering, or looking at him.

"Prue!" he said loudly, awaking my attention, and I took my last bite, snipping my tongue.

I sighed. "Hannah wanted to try one last procedure on herself before letting me go through with the In-Vitro. But Juliet—*Dr. Hayward*—told me it wouldn't work, so I went ahead with In-Vitro. Hannah never knew, and I wasn't going to tell her until I was absolutely positive I was pregnant."

I lifted the donut lid cautiously, eyeing Henry, and took out another crème-filled, not hungry anymore, just stressed.

"But at our last office visit, Dr. Hayward told us that three fertilized eggs survived. What Hannah didn't know, was that they were already inside of me." The blood from my cut tongue filled my mouth with a metallic taste, numbing the sweet of the crème. "I waited to do the pregnancy test with Hannah, though I had my suspicions."

Henry watched me as I ate like an animal, his eyes concrete.

"So, what?" he said, his dark eyes clear. "You thought she wouldn't be confused by the birth date? That you would go into labor two months earlier than planned? Three months?"

I licked my sticky lips and put the half-eaten donut back. "I was going to tell her—after we got the blood results. I wanted it to work so bad that I had to try it first without Hannah. I didn't want us to get excited and then it fail. I knew she would never let me try again if that happened, and then she would never get the child she wanted."

"But," he said, still stunned. "You're a virgin."

"Haven't you ever heard of Mary?" I chuckled, willing my flamed cheeks to cool.

"That was different," he replied without any humor.

"There have been virgin surrogates before," I reassured, taking the bitten-into donut again. "It isn't a true rarity."

"You obviously are not getting my point," he muttered, looking away, and yet I heard every vowel.

"Then say your point."

He looked back at me. "Did you think about how this would affect you? How it would affect your entire life?"

For a moment, I thought he cared, but I knew I could not

let that feeling last or else it would hurt me in the future. If only I had stopped it in time. If only I had wanted to. Then maybe the strings of my heart would have never been pulled to his.

"I thought about it every day," I said. "I thought of the happiness I would be giving my sister and Jacob." I paused, then added, "But I know what you really meant, when you asked if I had thought."

Henry's eyes flickered with a shadow and a spark, all too quickly. He could not seem to tear his gaze from me. I held his attention in my grasp like honey to a bear. It takes a while for it to calculate its advantage, its plan, but all the while, it stares agape in memorization. Not even bees can hinder its devotion.

"I knew people would automatically assume something about me. That guys wouldn't glance my way. I knew that I would be giving birth to a child I had held for nine months, only to let it go."

I couldn't blink the mist from my eyes, but took a deep breath, forcing my voice to remain steady. "Let me be the first to tell you, I have never had a boyfriend. Not by choice, really. No one ever asked me out except maybe one or two guys who I only saw as a friend. But I'm waiting for the right one to come along, and as you can guess, I am saving myself for marriage."

I broke our staring contest, my cheeks still hot, and grabbed the box, returning to a third crème. "Having a baby for my sister did not faze me. At most, I felt guilty that she couldn't experience everything I would go through, though Hannah told me she was so happy nonetheless."

I finished off my donut and wondered if we were going to get out of the car now, but something seemed to be pressing Henry's thoughts.

"You were sure you could give up the child in the end?"

"It *is* Hannah's egg, and it *is* Jacob's sperm—not to be crude—but this baby in all rights is theirs. Not mine."

"Yet, you are the one who is connected to it," Henry said, and my chest squeezed. With Hannah gone, her child and I were connected even more now that we no longer had her. "How can you be so casual about this?"

"Because he was never mine."

Henry turned toward the window again, staring out and away from me. My eyes gazed at the back of his head.

And what is your story? I wished to ask, wished to be bold enough. *What made you the way you are?*

I unlocked the doors, grabbing his attention.

"I thought a lot, Henry. Just like you." His eyes shadowed, blocking me out once more. "But soon comes the time to speak."

My words sunk into the air, but I knew our vulnerable atmosphere was dispersing, and such was confirmed with the rebuffed change in his demeanor.

"Fine," he replied, stretching his shoulder blades back and cracking the stiffness out. "Stop putting things on my tab."

I shook my head a little, scoffing, but not hindered, and I reached into the emptying box, only to hold out my hand in front of him a moment later, as if I held the world.

"I got you a plain one."

CHAPTER TWENTY

As Henry cooked dinner in the kitchen, I was upstairs changing. My eyes wandered to his room again, wanting to get the box from the closet, but I knew it wasn't right, nor the right time. I needed to stay patient until the moment would come—until the guilt of looking wouldn't be too much to bear.

I headed back downstairs, smelling the familiar soup, and took a seat at the table as he set a steaming bowl in front of me. I prayed over the food, and ate in silence, not quite sure what to say.

"I was thinking," Henry said into his soup. "About taking you to the lake tomorrow." He took a thicker slurp and a tickle of surprise spread through my cheeks. "I mean, we keep calling this a lake house, you should at least see why."

I looked to him, but he didn't meet my gaze. "Why do they call this the lake house when it is in the middle of the woods?"

His eyes hesitated, then finally roamed up to mine. "It's the attic. From the window up there, you can see almost the entirety of the lake."

"Can we go up there?"

"No," he said. "It's a deathtrap. I wouldn't want you getting hurt." He gave me one more glance before returning to the captivity of his soup. But something in my curious mind— *suspicious mind*—told me there was something more.

"So," I toned slowly. "In the doctor's office, while Dr. Seymour was talking to you . . . a nurse and I were talking."

It was confession time.

"About?" he asked, the soup suddenly solid in his mouth.

"Well . . . you and me." I felt like a young child telling her parents what really happened to the neighbor's cat.

Henry dropped his spoon and it clinked like chainmail against the bowl, almost chipping the ceramic.

"What did you tell her?" he said, his voice sharp. I highly doubted he'd have a problem with me going into the *'deathtrap'* attic now.

I sucked in a deep breath, biting the insides of my cheeks. "Uh," I chuckled nervously, trying to remember what all I told the woman, but Henry found no humor. "I said that we met in the hidden country Bagheera where we got married but found out the ceremony guy wasn't legit and so we aren't 'officially' married, but that we still . . . are?"

"*Hidden . . . country?*" His glare was unyielding as he spoke through clenched teeth. "Is that all?"

It was funny how hopeful he sounded, and I almost chuckled again. "Hmmm . . . yeah."

"Are you sure?"

"I also mentioned that you, uh, saved my life."

"What?"

The words flooded out of me like a bubbling brook.

"I didn't tell her *how* you saved me—we got interrupted— but what was I supposed to say? I accidently said you weren't really my husband—then it was weird because I am pregnant with *your* last name on the clipboard—so I had to cover that up and said that we did get married, but that it isn't really real yet. And then I was getting into how we met in a little market place in Bagheera, but thought it sounded more interesting if you saved my life. Before I could say anything else, they told me to come to see you in the waiting room." I didn't stop to breathe, only tried to make him see that I meant no harm—that I was just not good at keeping secrets, or making up lies.

"A market place?"

"Hey!" I said defensively. "The Marthas' believed me!"

Oops.

A red wave washed over Henry's face, veins throbbing at his neck. "*The Marthas'*! You told the *Marthas'*!"

"Only as much as I told the nurse," I reassured, and gave a small, pathetic smile to win him over.

It didn't.

"What is wrong with you!" he shouted, his hands balled into fists. "First you tell Mr. Wilson your real name—then you're pregnant—then you tell an entire waiting room your last name—and then you make up some random story about us and you tell it to three people—two of which are the biggest *gossips* in town!" The anger rose in his voice even more with the finale. "And lastly, you tell Mr. Wilson we're married!"

Tears swelled my eyes. "I thought he knew!"

"*Why*," he mocked, "Would he know?"

"Because he knew my real last name—and I never told him that!" I said, glaring now. "Now it's your turn to explain!"

Henry quieted instantly, his jaw clenched shut, his eyes focused on the table. His palms rested on their sides, no longer fists, and it seemed he was thinking over the past few days, where he could have taken a wrong turn.

"*Oh*," I said, callous, and his eyes shot to mine. "So the great and majestic Officer Henry Clay made a mistake?" My voice then dropped suddenly into a dry tone. "Alert the media."

That did it.

Something in my words made him leave.

Made him softly unlock his brakes, push the wheels back from the table. His face was slack, void of recognizable emotion, and he did not meet my gaze once as he rolled out of the room in complete silence.

It was the worst sound I had ever heard.

CHAPTER TWENTY-ONE

"Henry!"

It had not even been thirty seconds before I called out his name. I got up from the chair and ran into the living room.

What was it that I had said? I wondered anxiously. *Or was everything I told him too much to handle? Perhaps . . . perhaps that was what drove the others away. My words.*

I came to an empty living room. "Henry!"

Relief washed over me as I spotted the front door ajar. I rushed out onto the porch where he sat facing the trees.

"I'm sorry," I said.

The wind played through his hair as I waited for him to speak, to yell, or something, but he didn't.

"It's obvious, Henry," I said quietly. "You and me . . . we can't get along, and we can't pull off being married. People will see right through it. Right through us. We both have issues, too many issues, and I can't see how this will work. I think it's best if we call Chief Brandon tomorrow—or tonight even—and tell him I need to be relocated somewhere else."

No response. No movement or acknowledgement of my

words.

With a pull in my chest, I went to the door and twisted the knob as it gave a loud click.

"Wait," Henry said in the background, but it wasn't enough. The door squeaked as it continued to open, and I was about to step inside, readying to pack my bags and leave. He then let out a growl of frustration.

"Sylvia, wait!"

I turned on my heel, eyes wide as I faced Henry. But he wasn't looking at me, his head still toward the forest.

"What did you say?" I asked. He didn't answer and I stepped up behind him. "Who's Sylvia?"

Again, nothing.

"Fine," I said, boring my eyes into the back of his skull. "Does she have something to do with that box in your closet?" *Why was I such a snoop? Why did this man cause me to want to know so much more than his façade?*

Henry's head snapped at me so fast, I tripped backward, almost falling on my butt. But something forced my left foot toward the house.

"Don't you dare," he said. Fire was in his eyes and a hard line to his mouth.

But I had too.

I ran into the house, scraping my arm against the door as I rushed to reach the stairs. I made it to the top landing when I heard his yell behind me.

"Prue!"

I couldn't stop. Not even as my ears caught the sound of his struggle in his wheelchair as he bound for the same stairs with anger. A small crash and a loud groan was heard quickly after.

My head turned to the steps as my body remained posed toward his room. After one last moment of weakness, and another furious shout as he fumbled against the floor, I turned to him.

Henry lay at the bottom of the steps, his arms straining to pull himself up the stairs after me.

"Give me one good reason why I shouldn't look what's inside that box," I barked, staring down at him. My chest rose and fell heavily. Terrified of my next threat, I took a quick breath, forcing the words out. "Why I shouldn't believe the Urban Legend of Henry Clay to be true?"

Rage drifted across his face like a gust of wind.

"Yeah," I said with a defiant nod. "They told me. Right before you came into the bakery, they told me everything."

"What did they tell you?" he said with venom, his arms shaking with the weight of his body.

"Who is Sylvia?" I pressed.

"What did they say!" Spittle flew from his mouth. "What did they tell you, huh?" He pulled himself up two steps, the veins in his neck throbbing with the strain. "Did they tell you I killed her!"

Chills ran up my spine as my eyes widened in fear and I stayed frozen.

"Did they tell you . . . I drove her to suicide! That I was left crippled when I tried the same!" he shouted again. "Huh? Answer me!"

"No," I finally gasped, afraid of my own speech. "You did."

His face fell.

"I lied," I said, and my whisper echoed the air. "They tried to tell me at the bakery, but I told them no, I didn't want to hear it. Then you came in, and we left."

Henry stared at me in bewilderment, his eyes and mind registering my trickery.

I had tricked him, and it felt so wrong but I couldn't let myself pull back now.

"Give me a good reason not to look in the box," I said.

His body went limp against the hard steps. The side of his face pressed against the wood, and I could see his lips move as he spoke the one word. "Please."

I looked to Henry, to his face and splayed body, and closed my eyes, knowing he wouldn't take my help. "I'm going to bed."

I turned away, hating myself for it. And I decided I wouldn't leave him like that again. No matter what.

CHAPTER TWENTY-TWO

A few days had passed since the fight, and Henry and I had kept our distance. Good thing I brought plenty of books and crossword puzzles to keep me entertained.

I still wasn't sure about this stranger, or what secrets he held, but I didn't feel the threat of panic like I had when I saw the man in the nursery. Instead, Henry's secrets drew me closer to him, causing my curiosity to grow, and I wasn't going to give up so easily.

I took my usual seat at breakfast and waited as Henry set the food. Toast, scrambled eggs, and coffee. Orange juice for me.

I sipped through the fizzy top of the glass and was instantly taken aback. "There's no pulp."

Henry chewed on a bite of plain toast. "I had James—Mr. Wilson—drop off a few groceries for me this morning." He continued to take another bite and spent a great deal of silence chewing.

"Thank you," I said quietly as I stirred my fork into my eggs, then thought of something. "But you don't have a phone? How could you—?"

"We have a schedule." He eyed me from his plate, holding his newspaper at a level that gave him the ability to read, watch me, and eat, all at the same time. "Aren't you hungry?"

The very thought made me gag. "No, I was sick this morning, and I don't think I can eat anything right now."

"All those donuts." The corner of his mouth rose, and a tickle in my stomach erupted. Before I could retort, he asked, "Did you want to go to the lake today?"

"Yes!"

He chuckled under his breath, and I wished I could have heard it out loud.

"We'll go after breakfast," he said and reached under the pile of papers, pulling out a white square envelope, and handed it to me. "The Marthas' gave this to Wilson to give to you."

I grabbed the envelope timidly, only to have my fingers rip open the letter with zeal and pull out a card. I read aloud:

"Dear Mrs. Henry Clay, you are cordially invited to the community center on October 17th in honor of your welcoming party."

I grinned ear to ear at the news, and then paused as I calculated the days inside my head. "October 17th . . . what day is that?"

Henry dropped his newspaper, looking up at nothing as he thought. "Well, today is Sunday . . . so that's about a month away . . . which should be on a Friday . . . and oh yeah, we're not going." He picked up the newspaper, and swallowed a spoonful of eggs, pretending nothing had occurred.

I rolled my eyes. "We have to go." I then added, "It's rude not to." Only to have something entirely different pop into my brain.

"I don't think that would be—"

"Wait," I cut him off. "What did you say today was?"

He took another sip of black coffee. "Sunday."

"Crap!" I jumped up from the table, hitting my knee against the wood and could feel the bruise forming. "We're late for church!"

I scrambled out of the kitchen and ran up the stairs and to my room to change clothes, seriously doubting Henry moved a muscle.

"You better change or I'll make you go in your bathrobe!" I hollered, positive the thin walls carried my voice.

"I'm not going!" he said just as effectively, then yelled louder. "And I don't care if you made me go in my underwear!"

I hurried to the dresser, pulling out different shirts to wear. I grabbed a purple long sleeve and pulled it over—only to quickly rip it off. It didn't fit.

Crap! I groaned. *I hadn't even noticed I was gaining weight!* I rushed over to the mirror in my bra and pajama pants, and stuck out my plump tummy to examine the evidence.

Almost four months.

All the stress made me forget.

My stomach popped out in a sloped bump, enough so that you could see I was pregnant. *Is this what people saw when they first met me?*

Henry didn't know. But then again, I did try to hide it from Hannah with the bigger clothes and always having a jacket on in the closing summer heat. But this seemed to grow almost overnight.

I switched sides, pondering the very child inside of me.

I must have started growing the day I first got here, not too long ago. I guess you hit a certain stage and bam! There it is.

I took one last glance, then searched through the dresser

91

until I found a stretchy top and inhaled as I slid up some PMS jeans. I quickly redid my ponytail, my strawberry-blonde bangs hanging along at the sides, and headed back to the kitchen.

"You didn't change," I said in surprise at Henry who remained in his breakfast attire.

"Did you really expect me to?"

I rolled my eyes, and ran up to his bedroom, coming back with a gray shirt and jeans.

"Change in the bathroom," I said as I threw the clothes to him. Then added off-handedly, "How did you not know I was pregnant when I first got here? I mean, I must have grown overnight or something." I stuck out my stomach to show him and he looked at me strangely.

"Maybe I thought you were just chunky."

My eyes narrowed. "Thanks."

He gave a fake grin that quickly fell away, and rolled into the downstairs bathroom as I waited another fifteen minutes by the stairs, tapping my foot with each passing second. Finally he came out, and a little winded too.

"Tell me again, why are we doing this?"

"Because," I said firmly, taking his car keys from the coffee table and not waiting for him to follow. *Let him figure that out!*

Life Church was a short, square building with welcoming ushers, and lively music coming out the doors. I actually knew a song playing inside and was surprised the church in a small town like this wasn't an old timer.

"*Life Church*," Henry scoffed as we came toward the building.

"We need a little life around here," I said.

He only rolled his eyes, and into the church.

We weren't too late, only by a few minutes or so, and the worship music was still going. People stood out of their seats, clapping, rejoicing with smiles on their faces, and only a few peeked our way as I pushed Henry down the aisle. He tried to escape into the back, but I stayed firm with my grip, and steered to find Mr. Wilson.

"What are you doing?" he growled, squirming in his seat. I only smiled as if nothing was wrong, and continued on our way.

Thankfully, Mr. Wilson reached us first and led us to his spot near the front. I could barely hear him over the music, and he had to speak closer to my ear. "I was not sure if you two were coming or not," he said, and I smiled back at him with relief.

"Henry couldn't say no." I grinned.

I clapped along with a song, singing familiar words, and suddenly thought of Hannah. We had all went to the same church together. She had met Jacob for the first time at the church our grandfather spoke at, and it was all love after that. They married in my home church and moved closer to that area, our families always going together, then eating out for lunch.

I continued to clap, but hadn't the heart anymore to sing, suddenly very tired. After praise and worship, the pastor walked up to the platform.

He spoke of King David, the hardships and battles he went through—the ones with the sword, and the ones with the heart. He taught how whenever David did something wrong, made a mistake, he would always cry out to God of his sin, and ask forgiveness. And God always forgave him, He loved him, after all. David would always be honest and outright with God—even if it took a little while to do so, and God was there for him every step of the way—even after the adultery, murder, and glory. God took a man no one looked twice at and made him someone great.

The service ended, and I wished to stay longer and get to know the friends of Mr. Wilson, but the uncomfortable Henry seemed to be worn out.

"Thank you, Mr. Wilson, for saving us a seat," I said.

He smiled, grabbing his bible and notebook. "You are very welcome, Miss Prue."

I looked to Henry, questioning him with my eyes, and after a brief moment, he nodded. I returned my gaze to Mr. Wilson slowly.

"Actually," I said, laughing nervously. "It's *Mrs. Clay.*"

His eyes widened to the man behind me. "You never mentioned this, Henry."

Henry inhaled through his nostrils, his cheek sucked in. "Well James, I guess things moved a little faster than my mouth could reveal."

"Ah," Mr. Wilson said, giving Henry a peculiar expression, then quickly fading into a gentler one. "Congratulations are in order, then." He smiled warmly to me, but I saw a strange shine in his eyes.

"Thank you," I said. I was glad I told him the truth, but wasn't this marriage just another lie?

"Could I speak with Henry for a moment, Prue?"

I nodded, and watched them both move toward the exit in heavy talk. Only a quick tap to my shoulder was able to pull me away.

"Evie!" I almost squealed at the sight of her bubbly face. I reached over the chair to hug her and she returned it warmly.

"Did you get the invitation?" she asked.

"Yes, but why is it so far away?"

She giggled. "The community center is booked till October. I figured we needed to give people notice ahead of time—let them find great gifts to buy!"

"No!" I laughed, shaking my head with embarrassment. "We don't need any gifts!"

Did I just say we?

"Oh, don't worry my dear, everyone is so excited to have a reason for a party—they won't mind! The scandal alone of the mysterious Henry coming out of his lake house did the trick!" She led me out the exit doors as I thought about her words, and the angry words of Henry from before. *What parts of his speech rang true?*

Church-goers stood in small groups, chatting away, some even saying 'hi' to Evie as we passed by, arms linked, and I had to pull away at the sudden thought of my sister. Evie didn't seem to notice.

"Where are we going?" I asked as she ping-ponged through the horde of people.

How will Henry find me now? I wondered. *Hope he doesn't get too mad.*

"A friend of mine wants to meet you!" Evie chirped, retrieving my wrist once again, her black curls bobbing in the air. "I told her all about you and how you and Henry met—and she just couldn't believe it!"

My heart raced as the blood slowly drained from my face. *So this is why Henry didn't like me to talk to people. It led to this.* I could only hope it wasn't a jealous ex-girlfriend—though I doubted he had any of those here . . . right?

When my foot stepped onto the road, I pulled back from Evie.

"Isn't she at the church?" I asked, knowing that if I went any further, Henry would indeed be mad at me for making him wait alone, with people, no doubt.

"No, she's across the street. She works at Dr. Seymour's office. After church on Sundays she gets things ready for Monday."

"Couldn't I just meet her another time?" I asked, suddenly nervous at meeting a stranger. "I mean, Henry is probably wondering where I am."

Could she be connected to Hannah and Jacob's murder? Did she want to meet me now and then kill me later? Or is Evie part of this too? Sweat beaded across my upper lip as my alert senses heightened.

"We're right here," Evie said lightly, yet with underlying determination. This caused me to be more suspicious, but then again, this was Evie—socialite of the town . . . right?

We crossed the street to the doctor's office, a churning in my stomach at the thought of my last visit and the new one to come. Evie hurried through the chillingly dark and empty waiting room, and past the office doors before I could even read a sign as to where we were headed.

Was there a back alley they were going to jump me in?

"Natalie!" Evie said after opening a side door, and a woman filing through an old cabinet shot her head up to us. I gulped in fear, wondering if this was it.

"Evie." The woman smiled her pearly whites against pale pink lips, and her clear eyes took me in, as I did the same. Her light blonde hair was up in a bun with sharp bangs at her temples that hung against her thin black-framed glasses, making her look even more sophisticated.

"Natalie, I would like to introduce you to Prue," Evie said with a smile, and the woman, garbed in a white lab coat, reached out to shake my hand.

I took it uneasily, and felt her firm grip as a threat.

"Hello, Prue." We released hands. "Evie tells me you are Henry's new wife."

A lump formed in the back of my throat, but I managed to speak lightly. "And who are you?" I don't think the question came out as innocently as I wanted it to appear.

"Oh." She adjusted her glasses on the bridge of her nose. "I am Henry's physical therapist."

"Hmmm." My mouth formed a firm line, but I realized this woman wasn't going to kill me, and that I should at least try, for Evie's sake, to be friendly. "He did mention you, actually," I said more enthusiastically.

I noted how her smile widened at that tidbit of info. "Well, now that he is married, maybe you can make him come to his sessions." She laughed, and I hated how cute it sounded. *Why?* I don't know.

"Yeah," I replied, not knowing what else to say to this woman, and feeling very out of place. I guess I sensed something from her. She knew Henry in a way I didn't, that much I could see, and it caused a knot to form in the middle of my stomach, or my chest, I wasn't quite sure, couldn't tell just yet. "W-what do you do in his sessions?"

Natalie closed the file cabinet and shuffled through papers on her desk as she spoke. I noticed a few picture frames of friends, but no true outstanding man in any of them, and she wore no ring on her left hand.

But neither did I. I pushed the thought aside, and listened intently to the beautiful woman.

"Stretch the muscles, work on balance, and so on," she listed casually. "But the best thing for Henry would be swimming."

"Swimming?"

Her eyes looked up to me with a spark. "Oh yes. I tried to get him in the pool a few times, but . . . you know," she trailed off. "And so I gave that up. But it really is the best thing if he ever wants to regain mobility back in his legs."

"So . . . it isn't permanent?"

To that, she did not seem to want to answer, but after a second pause, she sighed. "I don't know. But the body can only do so much without the mind's willingness."

"Right," I said, and left it at that.

"How far along are you?" Natalie motioned to my stomach, and I looked down to the forming bump. My hand rested tenderly against the valley, something I hadn't even realized I was doing.

"Four months," I said.

She eyed me. "I never did hear the story of how the two of you met."

I kept a straight face. "Come to the welcoming party and Henry will give you every last detail."

"I will," she said, and I could feel the challenge and suspicion in the air. I knew she smelled something fishy with our tale, and I couldn't blame her. Henry had to of been living here a good deal, and wouldn't they notice if he left the country? Maybe. Hopefully not. But I knew this woman was going to want proof, I could see it in her sparkling eyes.

And I was going to give it to her.

Chapter Twenty-Three

Henry was not too annoyed that I had disappeared, and even seemed more docile after speaking with Mr. Wilson.

"I need to use the payphone," he said as we met outside the church, people passing us and saying hello. Henry ignored them.

"You should be polite."

"Why? You're the one who wanted to come here, not me. I stopped coming a long time ago."

"Stopped?" I said.

He groaned but didn't answer, and kept his eyes on the pastor who was making his way to us now.

"Hello," he said and held out his hand, which I took. "I'm Pastor Eli, and what is your name?"

"Prue Col—"

"Clay," Henry interjected.

The pastor looked to him, surprised. "I haven't seen you here in a long time, Henry."

"Yeah." His lack of speech surprised me. *Where was his usual retort?*

"Is this your relative?" the Pastor asked.

"No," Henry snapped. "Why? Because she's pregnant and that goes against your views of an unwed mother?"

"No," the Pastor said, his soft eyes scanning my face. "She has your last name, but I hadn't heard you were married, and I didn't want to jump to conclusions. Forgive me if I offended you, Mrs. Clay."

Henry rolled his eyes.

I tried to smile. "Henry and I got married a few months ago, and I just moved here with him after I got things settled back home. Mr. Wilson was kind enough to save us a seat at church, and here we are."

"Many folks will be surprised to hear that, I am sure." His eyes looked to Henry, then back at me. "It was very nice to meet you, Mrs. Clay, and I hope to see you again at church."

"Thank you," I said. He walked away, and my mind flooded with questions.

Did this have to do with the mysterious Sylvia—with the urban legend? Was that why it was a surprise to everyone that Henry got married—because he had an urban legend to scare all women off?

"What did he mean?"

"Nothing," Henry said, wheeling ahead of me. "I've got to go make a phone call."

It angered me how he did not even wait for me to follow, only left without another word. I almost marched right to the Marthas' Bakery to find out the truth about Henry, once and for all.

But . . . *how much 'truth' could be in an urban legend? And why did Mr. Wilson warn me not to listen to such a thing? How did he know? Why did he care?*

Maybe he saw Henry in a different light than the other people in this town. Or perhaps, maybe he saw what caused his shadow to appear in the first place, saw what had crept into his life to cast such darkness. But who was to be the one to show him that it didn't have to last? That such a way of life, did not have to be.

Not a girl like me. The doubt shouted in my mind. *You are far too damaged yourself to fix another—just look at your life—your situation! Who could you help when you are the one needing saving?*

The thoughts pulled me down, weakening my resolve to even try, but then gently, like the way a puddle forms on the pavement during rain, another voice spoke through the doubts.

A girl like you.

My heart pinched at the notion. I realized I really wanted to help this man. He needed someone to help him, to reach out. Still . . . .

I watched from inside the car as Henry struggled into the passenger seat after making his phone call, his face haggard and worn, his spirit broken. A stirring soared into my heart, a hope of some kind, a confidence.

And it was enough.

CHAPTER TWENTY-FOUR

The lake was nothing like I had ever seen before.

About ten minutes from the house with no trail in the overgrown paths of the woods, Henry managed through it easily. The trees thinned out around the shore, the ground a mixture of sand and dark pebbles. Peaceful. Beautiful. The blue water seemed to go on forever, no horizon to separate earth to air. I didn't realize I was holding my breath until I let out a cough, and I drew closer to the water, Henry beside me.

"Does it ever end?" I said.

"At some point," he replied dryly.

I ran my fingers against the earth, fiddling with the textures, knowing what I had to do, what I had to say.

"What happened, Henry?" I asked, keeping my eyes toward the sky. "Who's Sylvia?"

He let out a long breath and said, "She was my wife."

A tingle spread through my limbs like beginning fire. *Wife?*

I looked at him. "What happened to her?"

"We lived in Arizona, but grew up here. That is why the

townspeople have known me since I was a kid. We got married sixteen years ago, but were only together for five."

I thought back on his words from the other night, about the rumors that he drove her to suicide, killed her even, and shivered.

It couldn't be true. He's an officer.

Was an officer. The doubt crept loudly into my thoughts.

But how could being an officer exempt you from murder— from killing your own wife? It couldn't—could it? Who was I really sitting next to? Had I only run from one murderer, just to meet another?

"One night . . . we got into a fight," Henry explained as he stared at his hands. He scoffed. "I can't even remember what it was about."

I couldn't remove my gaze from his unshaven face; the hot water stuck in his eyes, not allowed to come out.

Henry took a deep breath, forcing down a rolling sound in the back of his throat. "She got in her car and drove off. Later that night, I got in my car, figuring she went to her friend's house, and started toward that way when a call came in on the radio. They needed more men at this crash site. A drunk driver. Reporters were flooding in like ants, and the area was hard to keep clear with so little backup. I didn't even think twice about it. I only thought of it as another job. So I went, it was only a few miles away, and I couldn't believe the hype." He paused, his gaze shifting back and forth at nothing particular, then said, "There were reporters everywhere— people everywhere—and only one paramedic van. The other cops couldn't get through the traffic. I got out of my car and hurried to the scene, but there was only one car on the edge of the road. The front end was crushed, the driver pulled out quickly, and I didn't understand what all the commotion was about.

"I walked over to the edge and looked down to the canal below . . . . Five cars were in the water being sucked down to the bottom. Officers and paramedics were at the edge next to me, trying to get down to the people, but it was almost impossible. And then I looked to the last car to be reached, saw the familiar license plate . . . Sylvia's car."

A cold wind blew against us suddenly and I tucked my bangs behind my ears, shivering. I couldn't believe what he was telling me; it was so terrible.

"I went insane," Henry said. "I screamed out to her, then went to kill the driver who caused the crash. I pulled out my gun and aimed for his head, but just before my finger hit the trigger, officers tackled me down. After a struggle, I pushed past them and dove into the canal.

"I couldn't save her. She was too far gone," he protested. "While I was in the water, the current kept spinning me around when I felt something stab into my back . . . and then I felt nothing at all."

Henry looked at me suddenly, then moved his gaze to where my hand touched his.

"I wanted to kill him," he said.

I pulled my hand away, and the brief flicker of his eyes showed betrayal. But I was to surprise him. My hand reached out palm open, waiting for him to make the choice, to take my hand.

His eyes held mine and I didn't know how much longer I would have to wait, but I've heard that some of the best things in life take time.

CHAPTER TWENTY-FIVE

It was starting to get cold and my hand was tired of waiting for his that never came, never would come, though my heart pressed for me to keeping waiting. The sky started to mix into a deeper gray as the lake waters turned a seductive sapphire blue.

"I think we should make a pact, Henry," I said. "We need to help each other."

"You're acting as if we know each other," he said. He held his scruffy chin in his hand, his dark eyes blatant before me, and his expression, ludicrous. "The only thing the two of us know about the other, is tragedy. And only one tragedy, I might add."

What did that mean?

I stood up from the ground, keeping my eyes with his. "I know that you get up every morning at seven o'clock. You make scrambled eggs, and toast with the occasional bacon— always depending on whether Mr. Wilson brought some or not. And I know you like your coffee black, and your newspaper to your right side so you can hold it as you read and eat. I know you never read the front page—only the articles in the middle—and that when you finish reading, you fold the paper back like it was, and read a different page at night after dinner."

He stared at me. Shocked at my observations, my revelations, of him. Of the dark gloomy man bound in a chair, who might not be so gloomy.

"I know that you treat Mr. Wilson in a close manner, even though you ostracize yourself from every other person here, when it seems that despite your isolation these people know you. More than you think. And I know that you once believed in God. That you once had faith. And that for some reason, most likely related to your late wife, you have given up such belief—or frankly, you just don't care anymore."

His gaze turned into a glare, irritation on his face, but it had no effect on me.

"I know that you still have your police uniform—that it hangs dry-cleaned in your closet, along with a mysterious box." I licked my lips. "I know that you are stuck in this wheelchair, angry at everyone. That you have to struggle everyday up those stairs on your elbows just to get to your room; that you would refuse any help offered. I know that you love your wife, and that it wasn't your fault that she died."

"Then who's was it?" he hissed.

I knew he wanted my answer, but I had to ignore his question for the sake of our current atmosphere. I needed to preserve what was left of it. "And I know that by refusing the help of Natalie, it is your way of punishing yourself for what happened to Sylvia." The first name was like pepper on my tongue.

Henry's face was pure distrust. "How do you know Natalie?"

"Evie introduced us," I confessed lightly. "She told me that you rebuff her attempts at helping you, and the best thing for you is swimming, but you won't even try."

"Don't talk to Natalie."

"I also know your ever present mood swings. Aren't I supposed to be the pregnant one here?"

"So, what?" he said, mocking me. "Now is it my turn to tell all the things I know about you—that way we can have our in-depth, emotional moment that connects us somehow? Let me make this clear, we are not connected."

His curt words hurt, but I was determined to hold my ground. "I am not an idiot, Henry. I know you watch me as I watch you. What else are we to do all this time in such silence? We have to work together, or else *this* cannot work. People won't believe us."

He said nothing.

I sighed, almost giving up, but an idea popped into the back of my mind. It was bold, and it was outrageous—but it was all we had left to make this *'relationship'* work.

"Do you trust me?" I said.

"As much as I can walk a mile," he replied.

There is hope then, I grinned. "Will you?"

His brow furrowed, thinking, wondering perhaps what was up my sleeve, and what he had to lose.

"Maybe," Henry said.

"Good."

"Why?"

The corner of my mouth rose, pulling up the smile, and I felt the glint in my eyes.

"Because *we*," I said triumphantly, "Are going swimming."

CHAPTER TWENTY-SIX

I shoved Henry's wheelchair against rock and sand, not listening to a word that broke out of his enraged mouth. The idea was already formed in my mind, and could not be killed.

"Prue!" he yelled. "Don't you even dare!"

The rubber wheels crashed against the first wave, cold water splashing against us. I slid in front of him, a smile not able to leave my lips.

"Come on, Henry."

But he crossed his arms like a child. "No."

"Hey, you said you trusted me."

"I said maybe."

"Do it anyways."

My choice of words worked. I could see it clear across his face—the belief, the trust, and even the taste of suspense of what was to come.

Now was the hard part—getting him into the water. My hands were timid when I reached to touch him; memories of earlier rejection washing over me anew; but I pushed aside my lip-biting indifference, and held out my cold hands.

"You know it has to be freezing, right?"

"It's still summer," I muttered, forgetting the date today.

"It's September," he reminded me ever so readily.

Was it really? Soon was October. Just yesterday August was creeping in. Just yesterday, Hannah was alive. The lurch in my heart caused me to wince with pain, and I took a sharp inhale, causing a strange and almost worried look from Henry. I shook it off.

"We will be fine," I reassured, waiting with less patience than before.

"How do you expect me to swim?"

"Let's just first get you *in* the water before we worry about what happens after," I said through clenched teeth, taking initiative and quickly diving my arms under his pits. I locked a tight grip across his back and felt the shockwave course through him, and me. This was probably the closest thing to a hug he had in a long time. I, on the other hand, had never been this close to a guy before.

Henry's arms enclosed around my back cautiously as his hands held my shoulders. The sides of our heads touched, and it was too good to be this close. I could smell the scent of his hair and it smelled of the woods, the cabin, the lake, and something else. My breath caught in my throat, my heart racing, and for a moment, I forgot that I needed to move.

"Ready?" I finally chirped, my voice barely able to keep from breaking.

"I guess," he said.

I leaned back slowly, the heels of my shoes sinking into the sand, and tightened my grip on him as my feet shuffled backward on the slippery slope. A groan escaped him as we leveled up, my heels still digging into the earth as we balanced back and forth, his legs completely underneath him now.

His weight caught up to us. I almost fell on my butt when he leaned closer, his chin hard against my shoulder, the scruff scraping my skin. I was sure we looked a sight.

"Whoa," I gasped, my left foot planted farther behind me than I remembered, and my back arched as Henry could do nothing to help. It was up to me now to move us, and just as the realization occurred, I prayed,

God, please help me get this man in the water before we both fall and break something. And please don't let this be a waste—please make this count for something.

"Told you," Henry said, exhaustion full in his ragged voice. His fingers dug into my skin as he held on helplessly, one hand reaching for his chair. But I wouldn't give up. My mouth set in a firm line. I readjusted my grip on his back and we began the strenuous trudge into the lake.

The water wasn't that cold as it soaked into my jeans, waves crashing against my calves. I tried my best not to make much noise of my struggle as I pulled Henry along, but he was no fool.

"This is pointless," he said, "And not good for the baby. Let me go crawl back into my chair."

"I wouldn't even let you crawl into this lake, Henry," I said, my knees reaching into the water, my shoes filling with wet sand. "Not so bad," I said under my breath, but spoke too soon. My next step backward was in a sand hole, and I tripped into the water full-fledged, Henry atop of me.

Water filled my mouth and nostrils as I was submerged, my elbows scraping into the sand. Henry at once propped himself on his elbows, lifting his body up from mine, though his legs kept me anchored from washing away. I broke to the surface, laughing.

"Are you okay?" he asked, cupping the side of my face as I coughed out water, my throat, lungs and nostrils burning.

Occupied with the thought of how he could hold himself up with one hand, and touch my cheek at the same time, I suddenly realized he was touching my face.

"That was fun." I grinned, my vision suddenly so clear, and I noted for the first time ever how handsome Henry was. My cheeks burned and I hoped it didn't notice.

He pulled his hand back, steadying himself. I shook my head of flooding thoughts, forcing my heart to be light, and proposed a new idea.

"How about I just pull you in the water instead of trying to carry you?"

Less than a minute later, we were up to our necks in the water, our bodies huddled close. Henry's grip lessened now that the water helped keep us afloat, and I tried not to think too much about how this was the most we had ever touched.

"Ready to float?" I asked.

His brown eyes stared at me, not into my own eyes, but near that point. A close call. He almost tripped from his hard exterior; almost fell into compassion.

He scoffed, per his usual response to everything. "How do you expect me to float?"

I grinned, the plan already formed in my mind at the shore. "I am going to help you."

The plan was to hold him up as I swam beneath him. So far, it was working.

At first, Henry had a fit about me being underneath him in the water, afraid he could drown me or harm the baby somehow, but I only pushed his 'worries' away and went ahead with my plan. After a few moments of flailing around, he settled, and even now, I could hear his calm, deep breaths so close to mine.

My palms rose and fell against his chest as he breathed, the side of my face close to his, our cheeks almost touching. Water swam through my hair, untangling it and pulling it toward separate currents.

"Not too bad, huh?"

He didn't respond, but I wasn't bothered. My eyes closed as I took a deep breath, inhaling it all, and I squeezed my eyelids tighter together, not wanting to lose this moment. This brief relief of the world's pain.

"What's wrong, Prue?" he said and I heard the crisp tone. I was a girl after all, and we know that tone, that inclination, that withdrawal, that heartbreak, that slight rebuff that is more of a shove.

My emotions were getting the best of me; my hormones taking over; and I had to shake them away for good. If only it weren't too late.

"Just cold," I mumbled.

"We should get out then," he said. "You don't want to get sick."

A beat skipped in my heart, whether at the thought of leaving, or his presumed concern, I didn't quite know—only that I shouldn't be so starved for both.

"A few more minutes," I whispered, opening my eyes.

In the bottom lids of my vision, I saw his arm lift from the water with little noise and so much grace as his warm palm clasp against my intertwined fingers. Then he ripped my grasp apart, and swam toward the shore, using his arms and the current to carry him.

I had to suck in my lower lip and bar it against my teeth to keep the sobs inside; like bats in a cave, the darkness their blanket. I knew it was only pregnant hormones making me feel everything with heightened emotion, but still, it hurt that he wouldn't just give a little, wouldn't just try.

My hands swept to my stomach, cradling the stretched skin and growing child inside me.

All alone, I thought sadly, *yet connected just the same.*

And I wasn't so sure if I spoke of me and the one inside, or me and the one so very far away.

CHAPTER TWENTY-SEVEN

Henry swam back to the shore with surprising speed, his legs deadweight dragging behind him as he climbed against the sand. My knees gave way as soon as I stepped onto the beach, my breath ragged.

"You did a good job," I encouraged as convulsions started to take over. The wind blew stronger and chilled me to the bone from my damp clothes and skin.

His brown eyes scanned mine, then he brushed me off, rummaging to his chair and grabbing the armrests as he pulled himself up.

Boldly, I reached out a hand and caressed one of his legs, feeling the soaked jeans against the muscle, and my heart raced with each new second of contact. He tensed, not by feeling but by seeing, and my child-like eyes roamed up to his face. I saw the lines around his mouth where laughter once graced him, where someone in the world, Sylvia maybe, made him laugh. Something I could not seem to do. No, I only knew how to anger him. And this wasn't helping either.

But I didn't care. I wasn't going to let his hurtful looks and comments stop me all the time. I guess that was the problem.

"Do you feel that?" I said. "Can you—"

"No," he said, and I knew that if he could, he would have kicked my hand away. I retrieved my fingers in silence.

"It's getting late," he said, and that was that.

Chapter Twenty-Eight

I woke up the next morning to the sound of nothing. No creaking floors, no pots and pans clanking against the other, no sound of Henry. At first, I had the slight fear that the murderer was back for me, somehow found me and hurt Henry, or worse, killed him in his sleep. I took a deep breath, let it out, pulled the covers back, and prayed to God for courage.

The hallway was clear and no noise came from downstairs—very strange for a morning person such as him. My first instinct took me to Henry's door and I pressed my ear against the wood, listening carefully. The hairs on the back of my neck rose at the silence—and then someone sneezed. A cough quickly followed.

I turned the knob and pushed the door, poking my head inside.

"You!" Henry yelled, making me jump, but the word sounded funny, not like his usual voice.

I walked inside, relieved to see him alive.

"Me? What did I do?"

"You made me sick!" Then I heard it clearly. It sounded as if someone were holding his nose as he spoke, which made me smile. "It is not funny," he growled as I came to the bed. His eyes were watery and his nose very red, which made him so much less intimidating.

"You cannot honestly blame me for this—I told you to take a hot shower when we got home."

Henry only glared back in response.

I patted his arm gently. "Don't worry," I said. "I will take good care of you." I got up from the bed, grabbed his thick comforter and pulled it over his body, tucking the edge under his chin. "I'll make you some soup."

He shook his head in protest, but then a heavy sneeze took over and he finally gave up. "You'll have to go to the store," he said. "There are no more cans."

"Are you sure I should go all by myself?" I teased.

"I think you will be fine. You seem to get along well with the townsfolk."

"Is that jealously I hear, officer?"

"You don't have to be worried about me being jealous when it comes to you," he said.

I couldn't deny the tiny rebuff that hit my chest, and I got up from the bed, turning toward the door to hide any signs.

"I'll go get that soup, then," I murmured, wondering if had seen my widened eyes at his statement.

"Prue," he called after me, but I was already through the door.

"Henry's sick," I informed Mr. Wilson first thing upon entering his store. He was back to looking at his collection of rocks, and with a wounded heart, I joined him. "Find any new ones?"

He held up a pale stone. "Found it on one of my walks in the woods." He handed it to me. It was cool to the touch and fit nicely in my palm.

"What is the matter with our Mr. Henry?" Mr. Wilson said.

"I guess it's partially my fault."

His brows raised and my grin widened. "I took him swimming last evening and it was cold by the time we got out."

"Swimming?" he asked with a tone of surprise.

"I told him to take a hot shower, he didn't listen." I grabbed a fat brown stone with an odd bump to it and thought begrudgingly of myself. *Did I pull off this whole pregnant thing?*

"Henry has not been in the water since . . . ." Mr. Wilson faltered, and my eyes forgot the stones and went to him with hardened brows. He knew.

"Henry told me what happened," I said.

"He did?" This seemed to shock him even more than the swimming.

"Is he permanently disabled? Paralyzed?"

He gave a small sigh. "The doctors gave little hope. You see, a loose pipe embedded into Henry's lower back when he was in the water."

"He said he didn't feel a thing."

Mr. Wilson only eyed me with care and then he spoke gently, as if he were telling a young girl she was too old to play with dolls; that she needed to face the world.

"He lied to you Prue. Henry felt everything."

But in truth, the dolls were what prepared her to face the world, taught her to fight, to keep going, taught her to believe in things like love, happy endings, and most of all, courage to want those things. Even tea parties could be simple discussions of war.

118

"But he *is* paralyzed. How then—"

"When the paramedics got to him, they had to carry him out of the water with the pipe still intact. They took him to the hospital, a ten minute drive without traffic, and there wasn't enough time to administer drugs to put him to sleep or relieve much of the pain. The doctors went to surgery at once, Henry barely conscious by then, and their first priority was removing the pipe. The moment they pulled it out, an excruciatingly sharp pain ruptured throughout his entire body, and then he blacked out."

Mr. Wilson paused, his eyes full with memory of the horrid event, and I wondered how he knew so much about this man. "When Henry woke up, he had no feeling in his legs."

I didn't know what to say. No words could come to mind. Only images. Images of Henry, diving into the canal after his wife; Henry, trying to shoot the man who caused her death; Henry, in the hospital with a pipe ripped from him; Henry, waking up no longer able to walk; Henry, stuck in a wheelchair; Henry, all alone. But then another image came to mind, followed by another, and another.

Henry, eating breakfast as he read the newspaper; Henry, sitting in church by my side; Henry, angry and telling me his life story; Henry, not believing what I did for my sister; Henry, refusing my help up the stairs; Henry, getting me orange juice with no pulp; Henry, saving me in a hidden country named after a panther; Henry, floating in a cold lake as I held him close; Henry, sick in bed, needing me to get him soup. And then the last image, idea, quiet thought:

Henry . . . and Prue.

CHAPTER TWENTY-NINE

The tray was heavy in my hands, the bowl of chicken soup swishing back and forth with each new step up the stairs and the hot tea even more menacing with its rising smoke. *Good thing I brought towels.*

"Henry?" I asked the room as my back pushed open the door.

A light snore answered.

I walked to the sleeping man and set the tray carefully on the nightstand, then took a seat on the bed, trying my best not to wake him. Henry seemed more peaceful in sleep, though his eyes roamed back and forth hurriedly behind closed lids, and I heard the grinding of his teeth.

I couldn't help myself.

My hand reached out to his face, and my finger traced across his forehead, touching his brow, then boldly trailing down his temple, cheek, and stopping at the downward slope of his mouth. Ever so lightly, I brushed his lower lip.

"Prue?"

I reeled back, retrieving my hand as hot blood fled to my

cheeks and every hair on my body was on end. Thank goodness, his eyes were still closed.

"Hmmm?" I hummed through tight lips, my heart racing.

Henry started to move, rubbing his eyes awake as he cleared his throat and looked at me, a little surprised at my presence but nothing more. Meanwhile, I think I peed my pants.

"How long was I asleep?" he yawned, not seeming to notice my ragged breathing.

"I don't know, I just got here." I exhaled, and quickly grabbed the tray with his soup and tea.

Only, I miscalculated.

I was in such a rush, not to mention flustered, that when I took the tray, I didn't hold it securely enough and it flipped out of my hands, the steamy contents falling all over Henry.

"Prue!" He pushed the bowl and cup off the bed and they both broke into pieces on impact as I tried to help, grabbing towels and patting down his chest. "Just stop!"

"Sorry," I mumbled, embarrassed and hurt. My hand cradled my belly, and I sat there in pity, tears stinging my eyes.

He sighed, his shoulders sinking, and his eyes flickered from my stomach to the mess, and back again. "It's not your fault. You were only trying to help."

"Is that kindness I hear in your voice?" I said, even though I knew that could have pushed it. Pushed everything.

"Prue, at the lake—"

"It was a bad idea," I agreed. "It won't happen again." I got up and turned toward the door, but only made it a foot before his voice stopped me.

"You were right," he said.

The corner of my mouth rose in a crooked grin, and I faced him.

"About?" I inquired, joy clear in my tone.

He rolled his eyes for effect, but I knew it was farce. "We need to start acting . . . like we're married. Helping . . . each other." He choked on that last verb.

"Does this mean I get a ring?"

Henry blanched. "What?"

"Just kidding," I laughed, and sat beside him again. "So, what should we do now?"

His gaze held mine. "Consummate?"

My eyes widened as my entire body went hot with embarrassment. The only thing that brought me back from my stunned state was Henry's laughter. I had never heard it before, and now, I would do anything to keep it from ceasing.

It wasn't too loud, but anyone in a crowded room could hear it, and there was heart in it too. The skin around his eyes crinkled and his mouth opened wide as his teeth showed behind full pale pink lips. I had to smile, even laugh. It couldn't be stopped.

And that's when I felt it.

My palm clamped tight against my stomach, and Henry reached toward me. "What's wrong?"

A smile crept to my lips. "Like a flutter of bubbles." I leaned forward and pulled his hand to my stomach without another thought. "Can you feel it?"

"No, I—" He tried to retrieve his hand, but my grip was firm. He needed to get over his whole 'don't-touch-me' phase.

"Just wait," I said, feeling the warm pressure of his hand against my belly. But the bubbles wouldn't return, and reluctantly, I let Henry go.

"It was so strange," I confessed, lost in my own world of the baby and me.

When did my thinking change? When did this wonderful thing inside of me take first place?

And it dawned on me. "I am going to be a mother."

Henry cleared his throat twice, obviously uncomfortable by the small amount of space between us. He tried to speak matter-of-factly, "You know that you are sitting on soup, right?"

I quickly scrambled off the bed and looked at my backside. "Great, now I have it all over my butt."

This only cracked a slight grin from him. "We have to change the sheets, but take a shower first."

My smile instantly dropped. "You mean in there?" I pointed to his bathroom six feet away. "With you in here?"

Realization occurred for him and that brought out a very faded tinge of pink through his scruffy cheeks.

"Just go," he said, not meeting my eye. "And don't take an hour."

Once I closed the bathroom door, I discarded my soup-soaked clothes outside the shower, and pulled the glass door shut. It had a built-in shelf for a seat, and disconnected showerhead to hold.

It amazed me how Henry actually got about such things: up the stairs, in the bath, in the shower, in the bed, down the stairs. I never saw these things, except for almost one, but now I was going to change that. Now, I wanted to see everything. The lowest of the low.

No matter how much Henry screamed.

I guess I should have thought about this whole *'taking-a-shower-while-Henry-was-in-the-other-room'* idea. First off, the only clothes I had were the ones drenched in soup, and second, the only towel in sight was a washcloth.

"Henry?" I called, my voice cracking as my head stuck out the shower door, my body beginning to freeze. "Henry!" *He better had not of fallen asleep.*

"Yeah?" his sarcastic response finally came.

"Where are your towels?"

I didn't miss the short laugh before he spoke again. "Uh . . . I washed all the clothes and towels yesterday and haven't put them away yet."

"Great," I muttered as my eyes surveyed the room. *Did he plan this humiliation?*

Then my eyes spotted the only thing I could possibly use, and I had to force a chuckle to my lips—or else I would have felt completely embarrassed.

Five minutes later, and out the bathroom I walked.

CHAPTER THIRTY

"Is that my robe?"

My mouth ruptured into a smile, and I couldn't stop the giggle that escaped.

"Yep." I laughed, looking at him with feigned superiority as he sat holding the newspaper. "It is."

The thin gray robe was soft, as if worn for years. Now I knew why he always wore it.

I took a few steps closer, modeling my wardrobe casually.

"What's the matter?" I grinned. "Bothered by the fact that I am naked under *your* robe?"

His arms crossed, the newspaper discarded. "What makes you so sure I haven't been naked in that?"

I froze, wide-eyed. I almost ripped the thing off then and there—but some rational thinking told me that might not be such a good idea.

"Funny," I said weakly, trying very hard to keep my mind on something else.

"Bring me my chair so I can clean up, and while I am doing that, take the sheets downstairs to the laundry room."

I didn't argue, or mind, and rolled the wheelchair from the corner of his room and to his bed, my cheeks still warm. I waited while he struggled to get in, but as I watched, I saw it less as a struggle and more as a routine; there was strain in his muscle, yes, but also familiarity in how he positioned his body and turned to sit properly.

"Are you taking a shower or a bath?" I asked as I followed him into the bathroom, standing idly by the sink.

"Shower," he said, rolling toward the glass door and I didn't know if I should leave now or wait to see if he needed help.

So I asked.

He groaned. "I can do it myself, Prue."

At any other time, I would argue this fact since he did finally agree to let us work together, but this situation was not my forte, so I left, closing the bathroom door behind me and exhaled. I heard the shower turn on and my eyes scanned sideways to the closet. *I could look now in the box and he would never know.*

But I would, I told myself and forced my legs to the bed so I could pull the sheets free. Once I had the bundles in my arms, I found myself closer to the closet, my heart hammering with anxiety.

"Prue!"

I flipped around toward the bathroom, but didn't go inside.

"Y-yes?" I called nervously.

A slight pause.

"When you can . . . bring me a towel."

I laughed all the way downstairs and started up the laundry, the box and the closet out of my thoughts.

I gave him thirty minutes before heading up to his room, two fresh warm towels in my hands, and knocked quietly on the door, no longer hearing the rush of water.

"You finished?" I asked.

"Yeah."

Now I was at a loss as of what to do. *Should I go inside, my eyes closed, and my arms outstretched? Or leave the towels by the door for him to crawl naked against the floor in agony?*

Both scenarios made me shudder.

"Well, come on in," Henry said dryly after a minute of pure silence, startling me with his voice and his suggestion.

"You're still wearing my robe?" he asked when I stepped into the bathroom.

My eyes opened and I looked at him, a surge of emotion rushing through my veins at his sarcastic tone.

"I was a little busy doing the laundry!" I snapped. "Does it really bother you—you—you—" My gaze widened as it skimmed from his dark eyes down to his bare chest for a split second, and my head then shot up to the ceiling before I could see more, my face on fire.

My foot stepped on something soft against the floor and I fell hard on my butt, my left leg slamming into the bathtub's side. The stinging pain made me cry out.

But all I could hear was Henry's laughter again.

"Ow!" I said dramatically, keeping my eyes shut, and tried to gain some order with my body. My knee throbbed and my butt was still pulsing from the slap of the tile.

"I could have really gotten hurt, you know!" I growled childishly and his laughter suddenly stopped.

"Are you okay?" he asked, and I almost felt bad about my overdramatized words. *Almost.* "Should we go to the hospital?"

Air rushed out of my nostrils as I scrambled to keep the

robe tightly closed around my waist.

"I'm fine," I said, feeling completely embarrassed.

A last chuckled escaped him. "Relax, Prue, I have underwear on."

My eyes flipped open once again, but only to glare. I threw the towels at him as hard as I could, annoyed when he caught them effortlessly. With a roll of my eyes, I gripped the bathtub and pulled myself back to my feet, straightening out the robe as he dried off.

"It looks good on you," he said, and I looked him in the eyes to see if there was humor there. There wasn't. "You look comfy. Keep it."

I shook my head slowly. "It's fine, I can just wash it."

"No, it's yours."

I gave a small smile and took a careful seat on the edge of the tub, discreetly watching him as he continued to dry off.

He was strong, that was clear right off the bat. Even for a man in a wheelchair, he still kept in shape. Rolling that chair all those years gave him toned arms, and his chest had just as much contoured muscle. But his legs, though still full, were clearly unused; slack and awkward as they pressed against the floor. He needed physical therapy, no matter what he thought, or else he would lose his better chance of regaining mobility. Of course, that wasn't all that my eyes saw.

I walked closer to him, my hand already stretched out like a child seeing a star in the night sky for the first time. My fingers quickly made contact to his right shoulder where a marred scar laid worn. It was no bigger than my thumbnail.

"Is that from a bullet?" I asked. Only when his eyes scanned up to mine did I realize that I was touching his exposed chest. I quickly retrieved my hand as if had just touched fire, and I couldn't deny the tingle beneath my skin.

"Dove in front of my partner." He rubbed the towel

through his hair and over his face. "Do you mind bringing me some clothes?"

I didn't ask any more, sensing he wouldn't share if I had. A minute later I came back with a shirt and jeans in his favorite colors: gray with the exception of dark blue.

"Uh," he chuckled, his smile becoming a new habit.

"What?" I asked, feeling the shine in my eyes and the grin on my own lips.

"I'm going to need some dry underwear."

I pouted playfully. "Ah. Such a shame."

I started to walk away and he grabbed after me, but missed.

"Prue!"

I actually giggled as I ran out of the room, and I only made him wait ten minutes before bringing up the next load.

CHAPTER THIRTY-ONE

Henry was sick the rest of the week, but I was glad that my morning sickness had taken its course, and I could look at fish again without gagging. During the week, I somehow managed to convince Henry to start up physical therapy again—*Natalie said she would be here in fifteen minutes*—and Mr. Wilson, along with the Marthas', had something to show me and talk to me about. I guessed there was much to do since the welcoming party was only about two and half weeks away.

My belly was much bigger. Bigger than I thought it would be at this stage. My clothes didn't fit.

Still, I had not wanted to go back to the doctor's office again, and Henry didn't make me so long as I took the vitamins needed and didn't have any unusual symptoms. While he stayed sick in bed, I visited the bakery every day, even helped make new recipes with Evie, and Mr. Wilson always had time to chat or just sit on his porch swing outside his shop. Sometimes we would even look at the baby clothes next door.

"Have you and Henry set up the nursery yet?" he asked one day as we sat on the swing drinking icy cokes from the old-fashioned bottles. Martha had brought over some cookies and I scarfed them down as Mr. Wilson politely took one.

"No, we haven't yet." I stuffed another cookie in my mouth to keep the words—*the truth*—inside. I had to keep reminding myself that to everyone else, Henry and I were a happily married couple expecting their first child.

"A baby needs room. Needs a bed, clothes, toys." He then smiled to my anxious face, patting my hand that lay against my belly. "I'll have a talk with Henry about it."

"Oh, no, no, Mr. Wilson, H-Henry just wants to wait I guess . . . you know until the birth . . . um, because we don't know if it is a boy or girl yet."

Besides, Henry wouldn't be interested in any of that anyway. This was all an act.

Mr. Wilson's eyes looked to me, then back to the square. "I think it is okay to go by my first name now, don't you think?"

"James?" The name sounded strange on my tongue.

He seemed to have heard the oddity of it in my voice. His brows furrowed, then he shook his head, and said, "Jim."

"Jim?" I liked it. But not even Evie—*who was in love with the man*—called him that.

"My wife used to call me that."

"Oh." The gesture touched my heart. "What happened to her?"

"She got sick . . . a couple of years ago. Too many years ago."

"I'm sorry," I said, the very condolence spoken to me many times before. I took a deep breath and looked down to my fingers caressing my protruded belly.

"Have you picked a name, yet?"

"No, I haven't even thought about that."

That's because I wasn't supposed too. When Hannah and Jacob were alive . . . it was their baby, is still theirs, and theirs to name. But Hannah never told me a name; she wanted to see his or her face first before deciding for sure.

"What about Henry? Has he any ideas?"

"No." I shook my head and started to stand, grabbing my scarf and wrapping it around my neck. Fall was here and the crisp air too, but I loved it all the same, not missing the heat of Arizona.

"Goodbye Jim," I said softly as my boots crunched against the porch stairs. "I'll probably come by tomorrow."

He stood as well, following me down. "I'll be here. But you might want to see Evie first, or she'll have a conniption." He laughed and I joined, remembering how 'hurt' Evie was when she saw me with Jim when I supposed to be at the bakery with her.

"All right." I smiled and waved as I got into the car.

A couple weeks later, I had set up an appointment for Henry with Natalie.

A knock at the door could be coming any minute and I headed upstairs to Henry's room to see if he was ready. Sure enough, he was still in bed.

"Natalie is almost here."

Henry was still in his pajamas—long light blue pants and a gray long-sleeved shirt—but I wasn't about to push my luck by suggesting he change. Natalie would probably make herself at home, with him, though the very thought made me feel funny.

"Where are you going?" he asked.

"To see the Marthas' and Jim. I shouldn't be too long but I'll miss lunch."

"*Jim?*"

I shrugged innocently. "Mr. Wilson."

Henry quieted, and it seemed only I heard the front door bang shut. It sent a rush of nerves through me. Though my nightmares had lessened, I still caught myself jumping at shadows.

"Only Laura called him that," he said, his eyes holding the same memory fog Jim's had before. "It's been a long time . . . ."

"I guess you both know how that feels." The words were out of my mouth before I could even think, but Henry's features only showed sympathy, pity.

"So do you, Prue."

And with one last lingering look in his dark eyes, I headed down the stairs to find out who had just broke in the house.

"Goldilocks, I see."

Natalie's head snapped around and toward me the instant my words met air. A full smile formed her pink lips and her light eyes were unfair.

"Sorry," she sang out the two syllables like a canary and reached out a hand to me in greeting.

She better not dare call me mama bear, I thought.

I took her hand with rigid flare.

"I forgot you were here, that's why I walked in," she explained smoothly. "I figured Henry might be in his room or something."

Sure, I thought, but to Natalie I only gave a sweet smile.

"Of course. Well, you are right, he's in the bedroom." My cheeks lightly burned. I wasn't about to call it '*our*' room, even for safety's-sake.

I grabbed my coat and reached for the keys on the coffee table.

"You're not staying?" she asked.

Another forced grin. "No, I have to run some errands. Evie wants to discuss different desserts for the welcoming party."

"Oh, yes, the party," Natalie said with poorly masked skepticism. Her lips pursed. "I am surprised Henry is going through with that."

"Why?" I asked, the defense instantly in my veins, and I knew it wasn't baby hormones talking. This girl was on my territory.

But wait—she really wasn't, was she? This wasn't real, and Henry wasn't . . . mine. Who knows, before I came along, he could have been *hers*. I shook the unbelievable nightmare away.

"Oh, you know Henry, he isn't one for town affairs and such. But now with you at his side, I guess things have changed."

I shuffled the keys in my hand. "Yeah. So, are you coming?"

"Oh, no, no," she said. "Evie gave me an invitation, but I have plans that day. I hope you two have a great time though."

She sure said 'oh' a lot.

"Mhmmm," I hummed. "Well, I'm off. Tell Henry I said bye."

My fingers clamped against the doorknob and all things were right with the world, until she just had to call my name. Until I just had to answer that call.

Because curiosity didn't kill the cat.

"Prue," she said, and my neck craned toward her. "You are awfully young; impressionable. You may think that certain choices are for the better, like marriage. But come later you find out that sometimes foolish mistakes," her eyes scanned down to my belly, and my hand instantly cuddled the bump in protection, "cause people to make foolish decisions in contrast—even so for the pitying participant." Her eyes seemed so genuine I wanted to slap her. *Was this her philosophical way of saying I trapped Henry into marrying me because I was alone and pregnant?*

"I just hope you think about what I said the next time you are with Henry."

"Thanks for the input," I said, stifling my anger, and walked out the door.

No, curiosity didn't kill the cat.

Courage did.

CHAPTER THIRTY-TWO

"I want to know everything there is to know about Natalie."

I had just entered the white and pink bakery free of customers when the declaration popped out of my mouth like fireworks. Evie stood behind the counter balling up scraps of cake for her small iced squares, and Martha was starting up a fresh pot of her new caramel chocolate coffee that many women in town were raving about.

"Whatever happened, my dear?" Evie asked, her eyes full of concern.

My shoulders slumped at once and I trudged to my usual seat at the counter. Martha met me with a cup of original chocolate coffee.

"It's Natalie . . . ." I mumbled. ". . . . And Henry."

My eyes shot up to Evie as she grabbed a nearby bowl of dough and set it before me. I helped her roll them up into balls and stick chocolate kisses in their center.

"What's their history?" I asked.

"Oh Prue, you have nothing to worry about," she said, waving her hand at me in dismissal. A cough from the back told me otherwise, and my eyes flickered to Martha.

"What is it?" I said.

Evie glared at Martha, but didn't protest as the older woman spoke. "They do have . . . *history*."

"Are we talking President Lincoln history, or global warming?" I asked.

Martha smiled weakly, a wince coming. "More like . . . ." She looked to Evie for help.

Evie thought a moment, then chimed, "Acid rain."

Martha and I gave her matching confused looks and Evie explained, "It's kind of always been there."

Martha hit her arm with the doughy spoon. "That's her husband."

"What?" Evie shrugged innocently. "I could have said the pyramids."

My hands hit the table in defeat, and I let out a loud groan. "So, they have had something since the beginning of their lives?" I was so confused, but also new at wanting such gossip. I didn't let myself listen to their tales of the Urban Legend of Henry Clay, but now, I couldn't wait to get the truth about him and Natalie.

"Don't worry about it, Prue," Martha said. "There is nothing between Henry and Natalie anymore—he picked you."

A shiver ran through me at her choice of words, and they gave me no reprieve. Because he didn't pick me, he was just stuck with me. He didn't want me, he was forced to have me. *So, why did I let this bother me when I had no stance in this?*

I growled. "Tell me."

Evie was first to break.

My heart was next.

CHAPTER THIRTY-THREE

Jim was waiting for me on the porch swing with two opened coke bottles in his hands, and a smile that wished to lift my spirits.

"Good afternoon, Jim." I tried to smile back.

"Afternoon, Prue." He handed me a bottle. "Why so glum on such a day as this—your favorite?"

He was right. The clouds were just how I loved—gray with darker tints spread out, a cool wind with the smell of harvest, and the seductive threat of rain.

All the same, I sighed. "I was just over at the bakery. I asked the Marthas' what was between Henry and Natalie."

"Prue, I told you not to listen to idle gossip."

"It is not gossip," I mumbled, taking a seat.

"What did they tell you?" he asked a little harshly, and the foreign tone burned my eardrums.

"Why do you protect him so much? Why are you always quick to defend him?"

"Because if I do not defend him, Prue, who will?"

His eyes kept their train on me until I had to look away.

Not a moment later, I felt his hand cup over my frozen fingers.

"You must understand the way things are in this town. Henry . . . has made himself an outcast to everyone, but years ago, he belonged. In high school, Henry was the top of his class in sports and academics, and he had acceptance letters to many great colleges. But then he decided instead of going off to another state, that he wanted to become sheriff of this town." Jim paused, and only when I met his gaze did he continue. "Henry married a girl he grew up with, Sylvia, and after a quick marriage, he got a job offer in Arizona that he couldn't refuse. The two moved away within the following month without telling anyone."

"Why didn't they tell anybody?"

"Henry had a . . . falling out with someone very popular in town at the time, and he just wanted to get away from it all as soon as possible. Start a new job, new town, new life."

"What was the falling out about?"

"It is not my place to tell you, but you may ask Henry yourself if you wish. He and Sylvia were cut off from here for five years, and the town didn't forgive him for it."

"Why?" I asked. "Just because he moved away that means the town has to hold a grudge against him?"

Jim placed his hand on my shoulder, calming me down before saying anything more. My blood cooled as grief swept across Mr. Wilson's features.

"What is it?" I said, anxiety swelling my chest.

"Things would have been different . . . the town would have been more forgiving . . . if Henry hadn't come back alone. If Sylvia had come back alive."

My eyes widened, my breath taken. Because I understood.

"The town felt that Henry took her away from them, and they blamed him for her death. That is why Henry is so bitter.

Because once, long ago, he had their love—their accolade—until he realized that it could all be taken away with one simple act. Now though, he just blames himself."

"How does Natalie come into this?"

Jim's eyes closed as if in pain, and I didn't know what to expect. "I was the one who trained Henry to become a cop. I was the town sheriff." The news caused my jaw to drop. "We were close. I have been like a father to him since his own parents died when he was a little boy. I mean, to me, he *is* my son."

My eyes stung with water, and I knew something else was coming. Something that would hurt deep inside where the pain of Hannah was already throbbing.

"*Where does she come into this?*" I pressed.

"Natalie is my daughter."

The blow to my heart wasn't something I expected, and I jumped from the swing.

"No," I said. "She can't—s-she c-can't be your daughter. Y-you're—you are supposed to be on my—"

A car engine turning off just feet away cut the words.

"Hey Dad," I heard her call our way, my back to them now, and my body went rigid at how easily the words came to her.

In the corner of my eye, I watched as Henry allowed Natalie's help getting out of the car and into his wheelchair, and my eyes quickly found sympathy in Jim's gaze. I couldn't catch my breath.

"What brings you here?" Jim asked, his voice light as I wiped my face in case of escaped tears.

My ears pricked at the sound of Henry's voice. "Well, after I was tired of the pointless exercises—no offense, Nat—we came by to see if you both wanted to go out to dinner tonight. Plus, I need to make a quick phone call." I could feel his eyes at my back with his last sentence.

140

I turned around quickly, a forced smile to my lips. "That would be nice," I looked to the happy Henry, another crush to my heart, "but I have plans."

"Oh," he said, his face construed and eyes perplexed, but then added more easily, "What about you, James?"

"He's free!" I volunteered, looking to the older man. "Weren't you just telling me that?" I said, and could feel the hardness of my eyes pressing against the sockets.

"Yes," he lied for me, "I did, but Prue I—"

"Come on, Dad," Natalie urged. "It will be fun. Like old times."

I flinched, and did not know if I hid it or not. According to her father's face, I didn't.

"Is everything okay?" Henry asked.

"Everything is great," I chirped like a good little girl and faced the smiling couple with believable happiness. "He was just giving me a history lesson." My eyes chilled to Henry as my voice went just as cold. "And boy, did I learn something."

I hurried down the porch, passing Natalie's car.

"I'll see you all later," I called, then looked straight to the man on the porch. "Goodbye, Mr. Wilson."

CHAPTER THIRTY-FOUR

Where is a girl to go when there is no such place to be? Where can she find comfort, love and . . . love. Only one place came to mind but there was no way back to my family anytime soon. Instead, I picked another spot that offered hope for relief.

The waves were stronger this time at the lake but the sound was delicious to my ears, and I took a seat on one of three large black rocks near the shore.

I wrapped my arms around my stomach, trying to find that kick of warmth from before that didn't seem to want to return, and my eyes stared off past the trees in the distance and into the mesmerizing cool gray sky.

The wind caressed my body and loosed my hair, the strawberry waves seeming redder in the edgier atmosphere, my skin so white, and I closed my eyes. The next few hours were a comfort, but my mind still rambled with thoughts and questions. It was still hard to fathom Natalie being Jim's—Mr. Wilson's daughter.

No, I didn't see him as mine. I already had a father, but I did like the familiarity of one being close by. Plus, he was supposed to be on my side.

I guess that explains Evie's crush on him. She is best friends with Natalie and must have spent years at her house where he was. And that means the same for Henry. *Did she have something to do with the falling out, and why must I care so much?*

I was done with my thoughts. They needed to be cleared. And there was only one way I could think of accomplishing this. Henry would probably kill me for going in the lake at this sun-setting hour, but who cared about him? He didn't really care about me, I was just a job. Besides, he was one of the thoughts that needed to be gone.

I dove into the water hands first, air rushing out of my lungs as large bubbles floated to the surface of the lake. The water was chilly, but my body grew warm to it, and I kicked slowly as I floated on my back.

My clothes clung to me as my shoes and socks were heavy water, but I liked the feeling. I had kept my scarf on the beach, an image of it tugging around my neck and choking me under water full in my brain, and I chuckled at my silly thought.

The rocking motion lulled me into unconsciousness, and I let my eyes close, just for a second. My arms spread out, lightly bobbing with coming waves as my breathing slowed. It was so peaceful here, I could stay for hours. The pulling water eased my heartache and erased my thoughts as I just let myself float, relax.

I had just entered a sweet dream about a prince trying to rescue me but couldn't get his legs to work, when a shout broke through.

"Prue!"

I jolted up in the water, forgetting to swim for a moment. Rain hit my face and splashed the water violently around me, muffling the next shout that came from somewhere on the beach. I had not bobbed too far from the shore and I could just make out the black rocks.

I ducked under the water and kicked as hard as I could, my arms branching out, cupping the water to push me faster. Soon, my feet touched the shallow ground and I stumbled the rest of the way, exhaustion filling my limbs.

"Prue!" the same hoarse voice yelled again, and I could see the figure clearly now.

"Henry!" I called back, my legs regaining speed against the choppy waves and I felt heavier with each new step, but didn't care. "Henry!" I grinned, happy to see him, and hurried toward his way. His head snapped to me, rage in his bulging eyes, and I suddenly wished to retreat back into the cold waters.

"Are you insane!" he said.

"What?" I asked, dumbfounded, my hair sticking to the sides of my face as my clothes suctioned to my skin. "W-what are you doing out here?"

"Looking for you! What is wrong with you?"

My arms crossed tight against my chest, ignoring the shivering wind and pouring rain. "Typical," I scoffed. "You're all nice and buddy-buddy with *her*, but when I come into the scene you flip like a fish out of water."

"What are talking about?"

"Just forget it."

"Fine," he snapped.

I glared at him when he said nothing further. "What do you want?" I asked.

"I couldn't find you," he said, and apprehension prickled along my shoulders at his tone.

"Why were you looking?" I said, arms still crossed yet not wanting to be anywhere else but here, arguing with him, if

144

that was all God would give me.

"They found the murderer, Prue."

All fight left me. "W-what?"

"They want you to come back to Arizona to identify him."

"Go back to Arizona?"

"We leave next week." He was quiet as I soaked in his words, but soon his anger got control of him again. "This is so stupid of you! Why would you swim in this weather? Huh?"

I stilled my quivering chin and brushed past him roughly.

"I've got to go pack."

CHAPTER THIRTY-FIVE

"What is she doing here?" I growled at the sight of Natalie's car when we neared the lake house.

His shoulders dropped suddenly, and a cold fog left his mouth when he spoke. "They know."

"Know what?"

When he didn't answer, I pushed the front door open and let it slam against the wall, entering the house as despair started to take over. I was met by Natalie on the green couch, and Mr. Wilson coming out of the kitchen. He hurried past me with a fleeting glance, and went to help Henry up the porch steps and into the house.

So now, she knew.

Which meant I had nothing, no upper hand. She knew we were not really married. She knew I was just a case and nothing more. Though I suspected she knew something was off from the beginning, what with her telling me that just because I got Henry to marry me doesn't mean it accounted for my single-mother pregnancy thing. But she didn't know the whole story. *Or did Henry already reveal the sore subject as if it were nothing?* I felt so betrayed.

"Get out," I said, and the thunder aided my threat.

Natalie remained calm though, much to my regret. "Prue, you have a lot going on right now, a lot of stress coursing through your body, and it is not good for the pregnancy. Especially given your new situation."

"Well, Henry shouldn't have told you about that." I sauntered over to the stairs, but I wasn't about to leave.

"He was worried someone found you. You are an even bigger target now that there is a chance at a trial. The man who killed your sister—"

"Don't you dare talk about my sister like you knew her. You just found out about her existence five minutes ago."

"But that was not what I was referring to," she added.

"What were you referring to, then?" Henry asked once inside of the house, dripping to the bone. "Natalie?"

Her lips pursed. "Dr. Seymour wants you to come to the office so he can personally speak with you—and he only told me because you didn't set up another appointment."

"Is something wrong with the baby?" I asked, not believing I could lose my sister and her child too.

Henry rolled to my side, and even dared to grab my hand. "No, no, they are fine."

I froze. The only movement was a rush of butterflies as my stomach did a somersault, warmth igniting my body as my hand touched my abdomen. My other hand squeezed tightly to Henry's as my eyes scanned up to Natalie's face. "*They?*"

She nodded, and her smile was genuine with no malicious intent. Just one friend to another, sharing joyous news. "Prue, you're having twins!"

A returned squeeze caused my gaze to shift and move down to the intertwined hands of Henry and me, then to his face, to which, I finally realized he had shaved.

I reached out in a dream to his smoothen face, skeptically brushing my finger against his cheek, my ring finger barely grasping the edge of his lower lip.

His eyes stared into mine, searching, until I ripped both hands away.

"I need to pack," I excused, returning to the steps.

The last thing I heard was Henry calling my name.

Chapter Thirty-Six

I had just closed the zipper of my suitcase when Mr. Wilson knocked on the open door and took a step inside.

"Henry wanted me to tell you that you're not leaving for another week."

"Why wait," I said as I kept my eyes to the bed. The flannel color reminded me of him, and I had to look away, meeting Mr. Wilson's softened eyes.

"I know you are hurt, Prue, but—"

"No," I said quickly. "You don't know. You don't know how I feel, how it hurts to be here right now. And how it hurts to have to go away."

He sat down on the bed. "You have feelings for him."

The blush gave me away at once, and my watered eyes searched for escape.

"I have grown attached to this place, this town. I have no one back home except a family who couldn't possibly understand my situation, though they will try. All everyone, my family, my friends, will do is pity me and Hannah's children. But here . . . here things were different. I had friends who weren't burdened with my story, I had you . . . . I had Henry." My lips pressed together tightly as I inhaled a deep breath through my nose.

Mr. Wilson placed a hand on mine, and I heard his smile. "You still have me," he said, then added, "And Henry."

"She has you first," I protested quietly, and stood, grabbing my suitcase, ready to leave.

"What did Evie tell you about Henry and my daughter?"

"Just that Henry proposed to Natalie, but she refused him . . . less than a year later he got with Sylvia and soon they were married."

"Then why does this sadden you, when *she* refused him?"

My hand tightened on the handle of the suitcase as my gaze stayed heavy with tears.

"Because I know what happens when the one you care for, rejects you," I said. "You get stuck."

CHAPTER THIRTY-SEVEN

"Prue, we are not leaving," Henry said firmly when my hand grabbed the car keys, and I stepped out of the lake house.

"Prue!" He called after me from inside, but the car's engine quickly drowned out all other noise.

He skidded down the porch steps dangerously, his anger keeping him from caring, and I pulled down the driver's window.

"Where are you going?" he demanded, eyes aflame.

I wanted to caress his face as I had before. I wanted more time to memorize his new look. It made his eyes more prominent, and he looked younger. Still, it wasn't the Henry I knew.

"Home, Henry," I sang softly, not wanting to ruin this.

"I have to go with you."

I patted the passenger seat with a free hand, challenging him, daring him to make a move for me. To show something of himself, for me, like he did for her.

Alas, I had too much faith—in him. And I was suddenly reminded of a certain warning not to place faith in man, but in God alone. Here was why. People didn't know how not to hurt other people, even I was a practitioner of such cause.

"It's too early," Henry said, "Brandon was clear on when he wanted us to arrive." Part of me wondered if he was stalling because of his newfound friendship with Natalie. This caused me to put the car into drive, and wait no longer.

"I'm going Henry," I said, my tone serious.

His arms crossed. "And just where do you think you are going?"

"I already told you."

I pulled up the window, and drove away.

I had the car parked outside city limits when a loud bark jolted me awake. An engine revved in the air and my heartbeat skipped as I sat up in the driver seat, looking out the window. I let out a sigh of relief at the sight of Mr. Wilson's face, and rolled down the window, letting in the cold fall air.

"Someone here for you," he said, then backed away, letting Henry take full occupancy. He nodded toward the passenger seat where my purse was.

"Move your stuff. I'm coming with you." His words were sharp but brought a smile to my face all the same. I unlocked the car doors and dropped my bag in the back as Henry struggled his way into the seat. When I reached out a hand to grab his arm to help, he froze.

"If she can help you, so can I," I said, and my grip tightened. After a brief hesitation, he consented, and I pulled him into the car as his hands gripped the seat. He shuffled his slack legs in place, then looked behind him.

"What," Henry exclaimed, "is that?"

I followed his gaze to where a wagging pink tongue

bumped my nose, and big brown eyes shined. I grinned.

"I found her on the road on my way to tell Evie to cancel the party."

"You told her to cancel?" he asked, surprise in his voice.

"I-I'm not coming back, Henry."

He stared at me, but not really—as if he were seeing past me into nothing, or something else entirely.

"Right," he said.

I pushed past the closing atmosphere and started the car, driving with no particular route. "Anyhow, I saw her on the side of the road just sitting there and stopped the car to see if she was lost or something." I looked to the beauty with her black and white silk face and matching body. "I don't know what kind of dog she is, though."

"Border Collie," he replied, looking at the animal with slight aversion. He then returned his focus to me, and the road. "Do you know where you're going?" he asked with his rude tone, and I only rolled my eyes at the familiarity, knowing it was all charade.

"No. You?"

I made a left onto the highway.

"Well, for starters, you were supposed to go right."

CHAPTER THIRTY-EIGHT

Three hours later, and my first yawn escaped—the only sound for a long time. Ever since we got on the right side of the highway, Henry remained silent except for a few directions here and there, letting the passing sounds of puddles, rain, and wind, take the air. But I knew this couldn't last forever, not if it was the last.

"Mr. Wilson told me your parents died when you were little?"

That is a perfect way to start an opening conversation, I yelled at myself. Too late now.

Henry adjusted the air condition for the fifth time in two minutes. "Yeah, my dad was a cop too. Got shot in the line of duty, James was his partner. My mom died earlier."

I knew age-old condolences would give no aide, so I discarded them at once. "I didn't know Natalie was his daughter," I confessed more lightly, wondering what his reaction might be. But when no response came, I pushed harder, my grip on the wheel sweaty. "You two seemed to warm up to one another. Do you like her?"

154

"I had to tell them, Prue. The truth."

I gritted my teeth. "Was part of your reason because you had to, or because you really just want her to know that this marriage isn't real?"

"No," he said defensively. "Brandon told me that even though they caught the guy, people could still be after you. And then you foolishly went off twice now!"

"Yes. I am the fool."

"What are you talking about?"

"Nothing, Henry. Let's just keep quiet the rest of the way."

"No, Prue. You need to talk to someone, and I'm the only one here."

"About what?" my voice cracked, hitting a high note in the middle, giving me away.

"You're going to have twins," he said, as if hearing the news for the first time. As if he never grabbed my hand in the first place, hurting me more than he could ever know. And I was the one who told him to start acting like he cared. That sure bit me back hard.

"I know that." My nose was beginning to clog and I had to breathe heavily through my mouth, obvious now that I was crying. "Juliet said multiple births were possible because of the three eggs." I sniffed like a brave little girl, letting her teddy bear float away from her down the dark river, never to be seen by her eyes again. "I was warned."

"Being warned about something, and it actually happening, is very different." Henry spoke with passion, and this new attitude surprised me. "Talk to me."

But I could only keep silent, or else everything would pour out of me like the very rain around us. His knuckles slammed against the dashboard loudly as he punched with all his might.

"The one time you finally shut up," he muttered.

My eyes narrowed. "It isn't like you are saying much!"

"What would you like me to say, *Ms. Collins*?" he asked, and I could have smacked him for it.

"Why did you stop going to church?"

That cut him off. At least for a few seconds, and he was more solemn when he spoke again. "I blamed God for what happened to Sylvia."

"And now?"

In the corner of my eye, I watched as he looked down to his hands, his dead legs, and stared aimlessly. "I don't know. I feel I should be angry at someone for what happened, but can only think of myself, and if I do that . . . I don't know what I will do for justice. I almost killed that driver."

"Maybe . . . ," I said slowly, treading the waters with care. "Maybe God didn't let you kill him because He knew you would never be able to come back from that."

"He let him kill my wife."

"God gave man choice. Free will. That driver got drunk and went out on the road because he didn't care about the people around him, did not stop to think that just maybe he had one too many. Probably thought he could handle it. But you, Henry, God knew that deep down in your heart, you did not want to kill that man. He knew that your anger was powerful and could control you, so perhaps He stepped in so that when the anger died down, you could make a conscious choice. Perhaps He knew that if you murdered that driver, it would ruin you more than the death of your wife."

"I didn't have a choice to kill him. When my '*anger died down*' my legs were already paralyzed."

"So, you blame Him for that, then?"

"You don't think he did this to me?"

"No, Henry, I don't think God crippled you. Your choice did."

A strange flicker of emotion crossed his face before disappearing. "To save my wife, Prue."

I brushed past the thoughts of how that sentence could sound. "But perhaps He did use what happened to you for something better. It is known that God uses our own mistakes and mishaps, and misfortunes—not caused by Him—to teach us things we could not have learned like others. I once heard that heartache makes the best of artists."

Henry didn't comment.

"Maybe He wanted to humble you, Henry. Humble that anger out of you, see if you could let it out instead of sulking in it as you sat in your dark house in your confined chair. Maybe He is waiting for you to defeat this—maybe He is waiting for you to call for His help."

"So not once did you blame God for your sister's death?"

"No," I said firmly, and without doubt. "God does not cause disaster. His plans are to prosper us, give us hope and a future. I am upset about what happened, I am hurt—but this world isn't perfect, it isn't how it was supposed to be because God gave man choice. I don't know why He let that happen to my sister—but I do know He intervened for you."

"I'm still in a wheelchair."

"Which you can get out of," I countered. "But God never promised us a life free of pain or heartache. Jesus told us He will be with us through it all. Even *warned* us, we would face pain and persecution. It makes me sad, Henry, when I see people in the world who are lost and who deal with greater pain even than I do, who have no comforter, while I have a Savior who comforts me. And so do you, Henry. One day, if you do want to get up and walk, if you want that from God, I believe it will happen. But it takes faith, Henry. Or even sometimes you just have to finally admit that there is something bigger than you out there. Sometimes, you just have to surrender."

He turned his head to the window, saying nothing. The rain continued to patter as I wondered what best to do next—drive, or wait until he talked to me again?

He spoke against the glass. "What's her name anyway?"

The corner of my mouth slowly rose in a smirk before turning into a smile. "Sheridan."

CHAPTER THIRTY-NINE

"Let's stop for pancakes," I suggested, my belly growling. We had just past an interstate, and I needed some food. Plus, Sheridan kept whining in the back and I didn't think Henry would like his car smelling like dog urine.

"There is a diner up there," Henry pointed toward a small building with big windows and few cars—any normal weekday rush. I made a quick turn inside the parking lot and swiveled for a spot. Henry got himself out from the car and into his chair as Sheridan twirled in a circle before picking a spot. We kept the windows down for her, and requested a window seat so we could watch her from inside.

Our waitress came and had a glint in her eye that gave away her attraction to Henry. I almost laughed out loud. Always funny how girls fall for a guy's looks but would probably run at his quirks. Who knows, maybe the whole *'wheelchair'* thing turned her on.

"Can I start you off with some coffee?" She was looking at him, but then slid her eyes to me. "Milk?" They scanned my belly, and I guessed she saw no wedding ring for either of us.

"Coffee, black," Henry said, his eyes down to the table as his hand wiped the cool surface of invisible crumbs.

The girl, 'Rhonda' by her nametag, wrote quickly on her small notepad, then looked to me once more.

"The same," I replied lighter than I meant to, and a wave of nausea washed over me, my stomach suddenly sour.

"Prue," Henry said, stopping the girl before she could leave with a touch of his hand to her wrist, and her eyes shined. But he wasn't even looking at her, he was watching me. "You can't have coffee."

"Why not?" I snapped, not meaning to do that either, but the spinning room was getting on my nerves, and so was this waitress' presence.

"She'll have a glass of water," he told Rhonda smoothly, but his own eyes continued to stare strangely at me. When she left, he finally spoke. "Are you okay?"

I shook my head. "I just need to eat something." I grabbed the plastic menu and started scanning down the variety of pancakes, eggs, and hash browns—I was never one much for bacon.

"How are you going to do it?" Henry asked, his voice almost too low to be heard. I looked up from my menu, confused.

"Well, I figured I order the pancakes first."

"I meant," he said with held sigh, "how are you going to raise twins?"

"Two at a time?" I chuckled weakly, then sighed when he wouldn't take that as an answer. "I just will, I guess."

"But how?" He leaned closer to me. "That is more than you bargained for." He acted as if I didn't know that.

I dropped the menu back on the table, and crossed my arms with a second sigh. "I'll just have to, Henry. I'll get a real job, work more hours than needed, come home and care for the two babies with all my heart." I bit my lip. "It's not something I could ever say no to. I just wish . . . that I had . . . maybe *someone*—"

"Here are your beverages!" Rhonda announced, instantly at our side with a glass of water for me, and a mug for Henry as she slowly poured the coffee from her tin pitcher.

"Are you ready to order?" she asked.

"Go ahead, Henry."

He didn't even look at the menu. "I'm still thinking."

I wanted to roll my eyes, but only looked more kindly to Rhonda. "I would like three buttermilk pancakes with two sunny-side up eggs, hash browns, and a side of peanut butter."

"Any bacon?" she pressed, her eyes discriminating.

I smiled threateningly. "No."

She turned to Henry, a cock to her hip and smile to her glossy lips. "And for you?"

"Three pancakes, scrambled eggs, hash browns and bacon." Rhonda wrote it down, and then grabbed our menus.

"All right, you guys need anything else before I go?"

We shook our heads, and finally, she left.

Henry looked at me. "Peanut butter?"

I smiled. "You'll see."

The corner of his mouth rose, a challenge for his face at times, but that was it, and his lips soon disappeared as he took a sip of his dark coffee. I was reminded of the Marthas' chocolate coffee and a pang of longing took over my trying nausea.

"I will miss them," I said quietly. "Everyone."

Henry stalled with another sip of coffee.

"Will you and Natalie be seeing more of each other when I'm gone?" I asked boldly.

He choked. "What? Why—why would you ask that?"

My smirk was pure disdain, but he didn't know that. "I just wondered. I was told you proposed to her." *Wasn't I always the suave conversationalist?*

Maybe it was the fact that I was leaving Henry forever, or just that the hormones were in overdrive. Either way, I felt great with scorn masked as mockery.

"I did," he said, setting down his mug.

"And she turned you down," my voice lowered with some respect; our food was coming. I had to get one last thing in before Rhonda came bumbling in. "Is that why you married Sylvia?"

Rhonda set a plate of pancakes and eggs before me.

That did not mean I didn't catch the expression that washed over Henry's face. His brown eyes met mine with darkness—a darkness found when it thought to be so well hidden.

"Here you go." Rhonda smiled, offering Henry his plate with awe and setting down a ceramic bowl of peanut butter for me as she poured him more coffee. But his eyes could not tear away from me, no matter how much she tried to gain their attentions.

"Anything else I can get you?"

I met her eyes briefly. "No, thank you." She looked to Henry but with no victory, and left without challenge. *This girl wouldn't last a day with Henry.*

I grabbed a knife and the bowl. "You see, I like to put the peanut butter on my pancakes first, *then* pour the hot syrup on. I only like the original stuff, nothing fruity." I spoke lightly, and emptied the bowl within minutes. I said a prayer over our food and began carving away.

It took a few minutes for him to speak to me again; I had just moved to my eggs.

"You don't like the yolk?" he asked as he stirred his fork

into his scrambled eggs.

I shook my head as I picked carefully around the yellow liquid. "No, I only like the whites. You didn't answer my question." My eyes roamed up to his, and surprisingly, he was watching me.

"Sylvia," Henry toned slowly, carefully, seeming to wonder if he could truly trust me with the truth. "Sylvia was . . . Natalie's sister."

My fork slipped through my fingers before I could truly register Henry's words. Before the missing pieces of Henry's puzzle came into focus, and though I still lacked about three more, it was enough to answer some questions.

I picked up my slacked jaw, and said, "The person you had a fallout with . . . was Mr. Wilson."

Henry sighed, and I could hear his lungs expanding with next breath. His hands held the sides of his face now, and it looked like it was the heaviest weight in the world.

"In high school, Sylvia had a crush on me, but it was nothing serious. Besides, I liked—*and dated*—her older sister, Natalie. After my parents died, and James took me in, I grew up alongside them both. A sort of triangle occurred." He paused, looking at me.

"But Evie never mentioned—"

"Evie will never mention Sylvia," Henry confided. "They were more of sisters than Sylvia and Nat, and Evie doesn't like to think about her. After Sylvia left town, she grew closer to Natalie, and when Sylvia didn't return, it was too painful for Evie to talk about." He then added more quietly, "Only to James does she truly confide in now about those things."

I picked my fork back up silently, and forced my shaking hands to cut the food; forced my mouth to open, my teeth to chew, and my throat to swallow. When Henry stayed silent for a moment, my thoughts ran wild. All I wanted to do was hurry him up, get the story out, and know everything, and yet I still felt the sting about Evie, and how she must really feel.

"Sylvia liked me because—I don't even know. But Natalie liked me because I had plans that didn't involve this town. The colleges that accepted me ranged from New York to Boston, and Natalie was always the dreamer." Henry paused again, the memories causing obvious pain to resurface. "When I decided to remain here in Oregon to become Sheriff in James' footsteps, I also wanted to settle down and get married. I proposed to Natalie on the spot thinking it was me she really loved, but I was wrong. She only wanted the escape, and when she realized that I wasn't leaving, she said no."

"But why did you marry Sylvia?" I asked. "Just in spite?"

"In part," he confessed shamefully, and I shook my head in disappointment. *How could someone do that? Use a person like that? How could I even want—?*

"Did she know?"

He nodded.

"How could you use her like that?" I lashed out suddenly, grabbing the attention from others in the diner, but I wasn't hindered by their stares. "How could you manipulate her love like that?"

Henry only reflected my passion. "I was angry and rejected. I took the first person who would have me, and Sylvia knew what had happened, but didn't care. That's when James got involved." Henry's voice lowered. "He hated how I traded one daughter for the other but couldn't stop Sylvia from marrying me. We fought outside the station until we bled and other officers had to pull us apart. Laura had just found out about her cancer and he didn't want Sylvia to be away from her but I had to get away from the gossip and the scandal, the rejection. And Sylvia went with me."

164

"But she loved you!" I said. "And you didn't even want her. You wanted her sister!"

"I was a kid, Prue. Angry. I liked Sylvia, we got along well, and I knew she really loved me. But you see . . . even though I wanted Natalie, over the passing weeks, months, with Sylvia, I grew to love her." He slowly smiled, and it was genuine, causing a conflicted flutter in my chest. "She cared for me with much more depth than Natalie ever could. Natalie and I were—*are*—much alike; cold." Henry's eyes darted up to mine then fell again to the table.

"Sylvia got me back into church, encouraged me on my bad days at work, the days someone who did not have to die, did. She cooked me some of the worst," he laughed, "*And* some of the best, foods I ever tasted. The months went by and turned into years, and we were happy." He sipped his coffee, pausing, thinking something over, something from the past. "Then the day we fought . . . ."

"What did you fight about?"

Henry shook his head, shaking free of thoughts and my question, and ate his food without another word. I decided to give him the break.

"Peanut butter is the best on pancakes," I chimed. "My mother started the trend, though Hannah never got into it."

Henry only eyed the concoction, wary. Or just annoyed. One could never truly tell with him.

"Speaking of which, you will be seeing your parents soon," he said.

My ears perked. "I will?"

"Once you identify the man, you will be free to go home, and I assume that is to your parents?"

So he was sending me away. Or letting me go, which ever.

"Oh, right. You'll meet them," I said with a little too much enthusiasm, and then quieted at the sight of his sparked eyes.

". . . . Won't you?"

"Maybe. If they're at the police station," he said tonelessly, then hesitated. "Can I ask you something?"

I nodded. Anything.

"After you have the twins . . . would you still want to get married someday?"

A blush rippled across my cheeks, and I tried to joke, "Polygamy is illegal in most states, right?"

"Prue, I'm being serious."

I knew he was, and I sighed, slouching against the booth. "Yeah, someday," I confessed. "If I find the right person."

Rhonda came by to check on us and I couldn't take Henry's gaze any longer.

"Check please."

CHAPTER FORTY

Chief Brandon and his son were first to greet us at the police station, followed by Officer Lee and Officer Virgil, their eyes directed instantly at my growing stomach—almost the exact size of a basketball. With twins, no wonder I was so big so fast.

"Haven't you ever seen a pregnant woman before?" Henry snapped, and their eyes averted. I grinned, glad he was still on my side here.

I kept my head low as the Chief led us to a darkly lit room with a line-up wall facing us through a one-way mirror. Henry sat at the far corner of me, shadowed and sullen in this lighting.

"We're going to bring out one man, and I want you to tell me if he the same one you saw at your sister's house."

I didn't respond.

"Ms. Collins?"

"Clay," I said.

That gained a few more looks than the belly, but I ignored them and kept my focus ahead, my cheeks burning with the swift corner glance at Henry. "What about the man behind the murderer?"

Brandon spoke carefully, "Prue, we don't have Mark Brooks. Once you identify this guy we can try to make a deal to get him."

So even this didn't insure my safety.

My hands rolled against my belly and I let out a deep breath. "All right."

Officer Lee walked out of the small room, only to quickly return in the opposite with a handcuffed man in her grasp. She set him to the middle of the line-up, and waited.

"Is that him?" Chief Brandon asked.

My eyes trained ahead, but didn't have to strain for long. It was him. The squished bulldog face, the visible scars from Hannah's fingernails.

I shuddered at the remembrance, and turned away. Henry came to my side like a purring cat, and his darkened eyes looked up to me.

"It's okay, Prue," he said.

"It's him," I gasped, and tears swelled my eyes.

"I know."

"He's going to find me, isn't he?"

"No, he's not," Henry said, rolling closer, and I realized I was trembling. But our intense atmosphere was broken by impatient words from another.

"Is that him, Ms. Collins?" Virgil pressed.

The choice of words brought me back and I looked to the Chief. "Yes."

I fled the room and rushed down the hallway, stopping near the entrance, gasping for breath. Henry was soon at my side again.

"Are you okay?"

"No, I'm not," I said. "I'm still pregnant. Now an only child.

A soon to be mother with no husband. . . . I'm alone." My eyes stung with new tears. "I'm just peachy, Henry."

"I'm sorry, Prue."

I sniffed, searching my purse for an old tissue. "Only three people know how I feel."

"Me . . . and your parents."

"Them too." My eyes flickered briefly to his gaze, enough to catch his confusion. "God. Jesus. You. And my parents. So five now."

"I'm sorry, Prue," Henry said again, and I realized I didn't catch his words the first time, and my heart melted at the sincerity in his voice; the compassion there I never thought he was capable of. The tears had to fall at that, and I quickly wiped them away.

"The man," I said, clearing my throat, and forgetting my purse. "The one behind the murder, Mark Brooks, is still out there. Can the police arrest him if no deal is made?"

"I don't know," he confessed. "But they'll find something. Sometimes it takes baby steps."

"I don't feel safe here," I said, panic filling my voice. "How can they protect me when I'm so close to him now? Even if this man is locked up, Brooks will still be looking for me, I know it. And if he finds out that I'm pregnant, he'll kill me."

Henry seemed to think over my words, his eyes watching me with care. Then he said with so much ease, I almost didn't believe him, "Then come back with me."

"What?" I looked at him in shock.

"If you don't feel safe here, maybe at least you will back in Oregon. Brooks won't be looking for you there, and I'm sure the Chief will agree. What do you say?"

"Will they let me?" I asked, my chest filled with sudden warmth—and hope. "If the trial is so close, won't the cops want me to stay somewhere closer?"

Henry shrugged. "I don't care. The choice is yours."

My decision was instant. "Fine. I want to go back with you."

His mouth lifted in a half smile. "Let's go."

CHAPTER FORTY-ONE

"I just want to stop by to see if they are home," I said as I led the way to my front door. Though Henry said he'd take me back to Oregon, I couldn't miss the opportunity to see my parents again. There was so much to show and tell.

I unlocked the door with a spare key I had kept in my purse. Once inside, I ventured to the kitchen, Henry beside me with Sheridan at my leg.

"Hello?" I called, wondering if they might be upstairs. "Mom? Dad?"

No answer.

A clock with a painted grape vine chimed, and I smirked to Henry. "One Mother's Day, I gave my mom a clock with a painted rooster." I laughed. "I loved it, thinking it was so pretty, but she returned it for the grape one. I guess it didn't go with the fruity flow."

Henry grinned. "I gave Sylvia slippers."

My brows rose. "For Mother's Day?"

"No," he said, shaking his head, "Her birthday."

Sheridan nudged my hand when I stopped scratching

behind her ears, and I started my trek around the island countertop. I spied inside the fridge and my stomach rumbled at the sight of very little options.

"I guess my parents are still away," I said, moving along to the freezer side. *Ice cream!*

I grabbed a half gallon of original chocolate and closed the door with my hip, looking for a spoon drawer—too used to the lake house and its contents' locations. Finally, I found one.

"You have a message," Henry said as I pried the tight lid. "The light's blinking."

I pierced the soft chocolate with my spoon and took a bite, enjoying the taste immensely. "Yummy." I grinned.

He hit play.

Juliet's voice was foreign to me, but I remembered the words well. "That's when she wanted me to come to the office to see the blood test results," I explained through another spoonful.

But I was not ready for the next voice that came up.

My heart broke at once and I dropped the ice cream, my hands numb, the wind knocked out of me. Cold chocolate splattered my ankles, smearing the floor, and Sheridan was quick at my heels to clean up the mess.

I didn't know there was another message.

I didn't know she had called.

"Hey sis," Hannah's voice chimed on the answering machine. "I'm on my way home from the store and you will never guess what I just bought! Well, *two* things!" Hannah laughed, and I sank to my knees, my fingers gripping the cabinets till the nail beds threatened blood. "I was back in the baby's department as usual and then just as I am about to leave, something catches my eye. These two beautiful lockets—" The line went dead.

Hot tears spilled down my cheeks as my breathing sharpened. Sheridan was crowding me and soon, Henry wheeled in front of me as well. His eyes stared with open shock and did not blink; I knew this because neither did mine. I jumped when the next message played.

"Sorry, I accidently hung up when I got out of the car. Anyway—it's this locket. It's heart-shaped, but the cool thing is, you can pull the sides apart and make the one locket into two—each one holding a picture. I'll have to show you to explain it. I even went to the photo place and had pictures of Jacob and I fixed to fit inside the small frames. It didn't take long . . . ." A pause erupted on the other end.

"That's strange . . . ," Hannah murmured to herself. "Jacob must have left the front door open . . . Prue, I'll call you back. Later we can finish planning the baby shower when we go out with Mom. Love you."

The line cut.

The kitchen started to sway around me, bile rising in the back of my throat. I wanted to scream to her. I wanted to shout not to go inside, to go back to the car. I wanted to tell her I was sorry she didn't get to see the blood results. That I didn't come to her house soon enough. That it was all my fault she died. It was me they should have been looking for. That she never got to meet Henry, that because of her, I met him.

The anger inside of me grew and grew and turned into something darker, uglier, and oh so much more cruel. The victim had no idea what awaited him.

My hard gaze shot to Henry, and the venom in my words burned my lips. "I would trade you for her," I said through clenched teeth. "I would trade ever meeting you just to have her back! If God gave me the ability to pick, you would be but a blink of an eye that I never thought twice about!"

I was sorry the moment I said it. The moment the vile words came out. But they were true. It was all so true.

Henry promised me nothing, never even gave a true hint to something for us—but my sister, *my sister!* She was connected to me forever, is connected. I had her friendship, her loyalty, her love, everything. There was no promise from Henry, no bond to keep us forever united. And the one bond I had with my sister was ripped away by the bloodied hands of another, whom I wondered if I could forgive, if I had already forgiven. I hadn't even thought of it.

I looked down to the mess beneath me, my eyes puffy and my soul drained. I pushed Sheridan away and she ran to the couch with sticky ice cream melted into her coat and whiskers. I scooped up the thawing chunks, the cold nothing to me now. Henry's hand cupped my chin suddenly, forcing my eyes to his.

"I am so sorry, Prue," he said, his own eyes watery.

My fingers trembled as they reached out and brushed his lower lip, barely able to contain the emotion, barely able to take the rejection, but somehow able all the same.

"Me too," I said.

We sat in silence a moment, my fingers thawing. Finally, Henry spoke,

"You don't have to come with me."

I could understand why he wouldn't want me to. Recalling my previous words, shame reddened my cheeks as guilt filled my chest. I pulled away.

"If you don't want me there, I understand," I said, looking down. He dropped his hand as well. "But I do want to go."

"I don't know," Henry said lightly, startling me. "I think there's someone else you might want to consider before making such a big move."

I looked up, my chest feeling less heavy now. "What do

you mean?"

"I saw the look in the younger Brandon's eyes. That boy would drive through ten storms to share another car ride with you."

"No way," I laughed and slapped his leg without thinking. My jaw dropped at the realization of what I had done.

Henry's eyes were wide, and I knew I would never swim in a freezing lake or taste delicious chocolate coffee ever again.

"These," Henry bit back a laugh, "are my favorite jeans. You owe me big."

I giggled. "What are you going to make me do?"

"You will just have to wait until we get back to the lake house."

CHAPTER FORTY-TWO

There was only one last stop to make before we could go back to Oregon, but first, I needed confirmation on something.

"Henry?" I said quietly outside Juliet's office building.

"Yeah?"

"Back there," I said, "It was pretty emotional." I recalled touching his mouth and blinked the thought away.

"Being vague again," he teased, his eyes lighter than I've ever remembered seeing them.

"Be honest," I said. "Are you okay going back to Oregon and pretending we're a couple again? Despite Mr. Wilson and Natalie knowing the truth?"

"It isn't going to ruin my day, if that's what you're asking."

I sighed, seeing this wasn't going anywhere.

"As a police officer," he then added more seriously, "I would advise it the safest place for you to go. I think it's the right decision."

"And as a friend?" I said, his gaze almost too much, "how would you respond?"

"As a friend," he toned, baiting me, "I would feel more comfortable knowing you were safe, back in Oregon, where I could keep an eye on you." The corner of his mouth then rose ever so slightly as was his charm. "Unless of course, you think Chief Brandon Junior could do a better job?"

I laughed. "I don't."

If only Sheridan's constant whines were not so interrupting, I could enjoy our light moment a little longer, but with an enlightened sigh, I turned off the car, and we entered the clinic.

"Prue!" Juliet's squeal shook my shoulders and even Henry cringe at the enthusiasm. Her arms squeezed me into a tight hug, and I only half returned the embrace. I soon wriggled from her grasp though, the human contact too much for me at the moment, and I looked to Henry.

"Juliet, I would like you to meet Officer Henry Clay."

Juliet's eyes sparkled only to snuff out, and I didn't understand their strange reaction. Nevertheless, she held out her hand and was polite.

"It is nice to meet you—Officer Henry?" Her voice held a tinge of disapproval.

He gripped her hand firmly, a mischievous grin to his lips. "Well, not anymore—they took my badge away after the accident. But if it makes everyone feel better, then sure, I guess I am," his eyes scanned toward me teasingly, "Prue's officer."

I held a laugh behind trembling lips and watched Juliet's upturned nose as she turned and led the way to her office. I jabbed my elbow into his shoulder playfully.

"You still have your badge," I said with a roll of my eyes. I saw it along with the pressed police uniform he kept sealed in his closet.

He only shrugged.

"How are things, Prue?" Dr. Hayward's voice muddled into Juliet's social one, and she took her seat behind her desk. I moved Hannah's chair numbly so Henry could take its place. Nothing missed Juliet's eyes, though.

"Good. I just wanted to come here to make sure everything's okay."

Henry spoke up. "She wouldn't go to the town doctor because of a certain mishap, but she has been taking her vitamins."

Juliet watched him closely then, as if she had forgotten he was even there. "What about nutrition?"

Again, Henry spoke up. "I'm the cook, so that makes the food non-hazardous," he joked and I grinned as well, but Juliet's icy stare ceased this folly. "But, yeah, uh," he coughed, "she takes the pills, eats right—except for the occasional donut." He looked at me quickly as he teased and I smiled encouragingly. "And like Prue said, w-she just wanted to make sure the babies are healthy."

Juliet's eyes widened. "Babies?"

"Yeah," I said nervously, feeling as if I were in the principal's office getting caught for liking the bad boy when really he was good. "I'm, uh, having twins." I tried to sound excited, instead of scared.

Twins. *Could I do it, God? I know that You never give us a task or challenge we can't handle . . . but this? And alone?* My eyes slid slowly to Henry, and my heart fluttered too many times in a row.

No response came that I could hear, but the jitters in my chest eventually calmed.

A half smile crossed Juliet's pink lips, as if she wasn't sure whether to be happy, or grief-stricken. After all, this miracle did come with a price.

"Well, I—well there *were* three embryos." She laughed more nervously. "There always was that chance, but still, that is . . . exciting?"

"I guess that's why they call it a surprise." I smiled. "Hannah would be delighted to know if she were . . . here." Finally, I dropped the happy façade and let out a sigh. This place was bringing too many emotions, bringing back too many memories.

"I'm going back to Oregon," I confessed. "So, like I said, I just wanted to do a check up." I began to stand, and she followed suit, but when I felt the warmth of a hand pressed against my lower back for support, I froze a second too long. My breath caught as Henry applied more pressure, and helped me to my feet.

"Of course, Prue." Juliet's gaze scanned down to Henry, and she cleared her throat. "Henry, would you mind letting Prue and I speak in private? Just for a moment."

The tension between them was an invisible yet heavy fog. Henry pursed his lips before nodding in agreement and leaving us alone, and I felt the draft.

"Something wrong?" I asked.

"Prue," she said, "I cannot believe what I am seeing."

I kept silent, playing innocent and giving her the benefit of the doubt.

She leaned into me, her hand on her hip, her voice a sharp whisper. "You mean to tell me that there is nothing going on between you and that man?"

I didn't like how that sentence came out—*that man*? Who did she think she was, my mother?

"Don't be so vague," I snapped.

Juliet inhaled deeply, dropping her hand from her waist, noting my hostility.

"All I am saying Prue, is that you have been through so much along with being pregnant and are surging with hormones, that it would be easy for you to fall for someone right now—even a complete stranger. I don't want you—"

"Henry is not a stranger."

Her brow rose. "So you do have feeling for him?"

When I gave no response, she continued, "At most he is using you, Prue. Why would a man in a wheelchair be in love with a girl who is carrying someone else's children? Think about it. You are a kind soul, and I think he is taking advantage of that."

"Forget the check up," I said, grabbing my purse, and I reached for the doorknob, defeat trying to crawl its way into my mind and my heart.

"Prue!"

I gave in, looking back. Her shoulders were slumped and her features slack as she spoke in too soft a voice. "What would Hannah say?"

I scoffed, shaking my head at how little she knew my sister, and replied, "She'd ask why I ever came back to Arizona."

Chapter Forty-Three

I never thought I would be so excited to see the lake house again, and could not deny the rush that swept through me, pounding my senses as I parked the car on the rough driveway, and hurried to get Henry's chair. With neither of us speaking just yet, I helped him inside and shivered quietly in the cold house, soaking it all in.

"It's late," Henry said. "We should get some sleep."

I nodded in response, then bit my lip. I wasn't going to ask him permission. I was just going to do it. Because I knew if I asked, he would refuse immediately and push me away. As Henry neared the steps, locking his brakes in place, I scooped my arm around his waist.

His body tensed, a jolt of shock coursing from his nerves into mine, but his gaze stayed low. In the corner of my eye, I saw his swallow against his throat, I heard the gulp, was sensitive to his sharp inhale. But he didn't refuse.

My fingers gathered their grip and I pulled his right arm around my neck. *Was I sure we could do this?* Yes, yes I was. But it would take the both of us.

Henry took his hand off the banister and I almost buckled under the weight. With his free hand, he picked up the first knee and set the foot carefully on the step as I followed suit with my right; then the next foot. Sweat lined my palm that held the railing as each new step became harder and heavier. At the seventh step, one of us slipped and we both fell forward.

My knee scraped against the wood as Henry's elbow caught the weight of us. We both breathed heavily, looking to one another, and I gave a nervous laugh.

"Are you okay?" Henry asked, one arm still around my shoulders as the other reached for my belly.

My cheeks burned. "Yeah, yeah . . . I'm fine. We're almost there." I forced myself up, along with Henry as he climbed against the staircase, reaching a hand to the railing.

We started again.

It took some time, at least twenty minutes, but we made it. Exhausted and ready for sleep, I helped Henry into his chair upstairs, and pushed him into his room, but knew helping him into his bed was a definite no. His shirt was soaked with sweat at the pits and chests, his brow just as perspired, but he seemed happy enough. I told him goodnight, and went to bed, only to be woken up hours later by a blood-chilled scream.

I sat straight up in my bed, a cold sweat clinging to my skin, and my hair knotted against the back of my head. Shuffles and clatter from outside the hallway erupted and chills ran up my spine, my heart thundering with fear. The door swung open, banging against the wall with a loud smack, and I stifled my next scream.

"Prue!" Henry gasped, his hair disheveled and his eyes wild. "What's the matter? What happened?"

My breathing was shaky, and I realized it was I who had

screamed.

"I had a—I had a nightmare . . . about Hannah." My nose ran as the sob escaped. "She was trying to call me but I couldn't answer the phone to warn her. I was so close to picking it up, but I just couldn't reach it." My voice broke again. I tried to shake the memory of the dream away. "Then the man was chasing me in an alley and I couldn't get away. He got me. He got them." My hand pressed against my stomach, the round swell giving me soft reassurance.

Letting out a relieved sigh, Henry locked his chair against the wall, resting his head back. "Everything will be okay, Prue," he said.

"How do you know?" I said. "How do you know that everything's going to be okay?"

"That's what faith's about, isn't it?" he said with a light chuckle. "I'm not going to let anyone hurt you." He closed his eyes and I realized he wasn't going anywhere. "Now go back to sleep. I'll be here to tell you it's just a dream."

"But it's not," I said, wiping my nose with my sleeve. "It's real."

He sighed, eyes still closed. "I'm sorry, Prue," he said, and I sensed it was because there was nothing else one could say. At least if they were honest.

"Did you have dreams about Sylvia after the accident?" I asked, feeling my cheeks tingle at once.

His eyes opened then, the moonlight through the window giving some clarity to his face. "Every night," he said.

A pang hit my chest. "Does it get easier?"

"I don't know."

I paused, studying his face. "Thanks for letting me come back," I said. "Goodnight, Henry."

"Better dreams, Prue."

"You too."

CHAPTER FORTY-FOUR

The sunlight coming through the windows woke me, and I shielded my eyes, realizing I wasn't alone.

Henry was asleep, his head tilted back against the wall and his mouth slightly open as he breathed. Pulling back the covers as quietly as I could, I got up from the bed, thankful the floorboards didn't creak as I stepped in front of him.

He wasn't clean-shaven anymore, thank God. The salt and peppered hairs that played along his chin, cheeks, and jaw, gave him brooding character, and . . . I wondered if one were to place their mouth against his cheek, if the coarse hairs would tickle like when my papa would kiss me with his big mustache, or . . . would such a thing send a different reaction coursing through me?

I almost leaned in.

Almost.

But didn't.

Too risky.

So I pulled away. And knew it was for the best.

Hoped, it was for the best.

Sunnyside-up eggs sizzled on the stove as I flipped the pancakes for the first time and turned the bacon over once the microwave beeped. A light rain prattled against the trees outside and I felt the soothing cold creep in through the gray robe I wore, the soft wind of the open screens wafting the scent of fresh black coffee against my nostrils.

"Good morning," Henry said behind me, but I wasn't startled. I had heard him coming down the stairs and the hairs on the back of my neck were already up again.

"Morning."

"Smells good."

I pulled the eggs from the pan and onto a plate; next came the pancakes; and finally the bacon. Henry grabbed our cups and filled them to our likings, and I followed him to the table. When I sat down, I reached out a tentative hand out to him.

His eyes looked down in forced confusion.

I only waited.

He didn't sigh like I thought he would. But I did note the pursed lips, clenched jaw. Nonetheless, he took my hand, I bowed my head with eyes closed and prayed over the food.

As he tried the eggs, I said, "What did you mean?"

He choked on his fork. "W-what?"

"At the house, after I spilled the ice cream on your pants—you said I would owe you?"

He relaxed back, finishing his bite before saying with a grin, "I'm still trying to come up with the best punishment."

"Oh, really?" My enthusiasm was forced, though.

How could I do this? I wondered painfully, looking to him as I fought the onset of tears. *How could I keep inside the reason I came back here? Why couldn't he just be the first one to admit something . . . unless, there wasn't anything for him to admit.*

"Speaking of which, where is Sheridan?"

I instantly jumped to my feet, my eyes searching the room. "I haven't seen her all morning."

"Where did you last see her?"

"When we got home," I answered quickly, sprinting out of the kitchen and into the living room. "Before I went to sleep."

I checked near the banister, then ran up the stairs and still no sign. I hurried to my room, wondering if she wandered in there last night. No sight of her.

"Prue!" Henry hollered from the kitchen and I sprinted at the sound of his urgent tone, reminding me much of my mother's not too long ago. By the time I made it to the back porch, I was panting heavily.

"What is it?" I asked, coming to his side, then gasped. "Sheridan!" I knelt down on the splintered wood where Henry was leaning as he petted the dark collie. A pile of old vomit laid next to her head and my heart leaped when her eyes didn't open. "Henry . . . ." I whispered, a sob in my throat.

"Prue, I need you to go into the kitchen, make sure everything is turned off, then start the car."

I nodded like a good soldier and ran to do as he ordered. Minutes later, the engine roared to life and I waited helplessly for Henry to come outside. He soon rolled to the porch steps and I dashed out of the driver's seat to meet him.

"Here," he said, handing Sheridan's limp body to me. "Hold her so I can get in the car."

I reached out my trembling hands to his that were so strong in comparison; so secure in their holding; and for a brief moment my thoughts began to wander.

"Prue," he said sharply, and I jolted to life, scooping Sheridan in my arms and waiting as he got inside the car. My heart started to beat again when I felt her chest expand, but her eyes remained closed.

I watched as Henry scrambled down the porch and to the car, lifting himself inside and knocking the chair away so I could slide Sheridan gently onto his lap.

I hurried to fold his chair and as I leaned into the car, our faces became close again; his breath heavy against my cheek; and my eyes couldn't help but look into his. A mistake.

Fresh tears came, and once again, I couldn't move. Didn't want to, this time. We were so close . . . I knew he felt it too. At least, I knew he felt the lack of space between us now, the closed-in tension.

"Prue," he said slowly, his breath tickling my nose, "We need to get Sheridan to the vet as quickly as possible. You need to concentrate."

I shouldn't be so selfish.

My mouth moved to speak, but no words came, and I was forced to do as told again, my heart torn two opposing ways. I pulled back for the second time that day, because it was for the best. Which caused me to wish I were edgier, bolder, than I was.

I shut his door and sprinted to the opposite side, sliding in. I held onto the steering wheel and pressed the gas pedal. The trees blurred together, red and gold against a raining sky. Life against stillness, serenity, and I wasn't sure what would happen.

All I knew was that next time, I wouldn't be the one to pull away.

CHAPTER FORTY-FIVE

My foot tapped against the gray carpet, my teeth pulling the over-chewed skin of my lower lip, a metallic taste staining my tongue.

Henry sat completely still with his hand holding his face as he stared at nothing, entranced it seemed, by the very carpet I beat against.

"It was all that chocolate," I mumbled, ashamed. "I was too focused on my own crap that I didn't even think about what she was eating till it was too late."

Henry didn't respond. Didn't even look my way, infuriating me more and causing my chest to rise with heat. My mind tumbled with angry thoughts, thoughts that tried to get me to cut him off, keep me from speaking to him, until he finally spoke. "What caused you to let Sheridan in the car?"

I paused, surprised, and said honestly, "She reminded me of you."

He looked at me, and I answered, "The first sign was her color—black and white a definite for you—but when I really took a look at her, I saw it. She was just sitting on the side of the road, unlike most dogs who would wander, and you wouldn't believe what she was looking at on the other side." I paused for effect. "The lake. Her eyes ignored the passing cars and trees and saw into the lake. Like you."

"How'd you know she didn't have rabies?"

I smirked. "There was that possibility, that risk of getting too close only to get bit back in the hand," I said with precision and indication, "But some risks are worth taking."

"She seemed friendly enough when I got in," he said, averting the underlined subject.

"Until you got in the car she was a little reserved, but once you sat down she was right against you. She trusts you, Henry."

"Like you," he said with a soft grin that quickly disappeared, and his eyes looked down again.

My hand reached to his and gently brushed his knuckles. "Like me."

I knew I was being too open, being too comfortable with him. He had to realize by now—*see what was right in front of him.* He had too—we only had so much time.

His fingers tensed, about to pull away, as his mouth opened to speak. "Prue, I—"

"Mr. and Mrs. Clay?" the veterinarian called as he approached us.

We both looked to him as Henry started to pull away, but I gripped his hand, needing his support. "Is she okay?" I asked.

The vet sighed, and it was a knife to my chest. "It wasn't the chocolate ice cream that caused Sheridan's sudden stupor, or illness," he said, then a smile lit his lips. "You see, Sheridan is pregnant, and because she is malnourished from what could be years on the street, that is why she fainted."

My face broke into a smile and I stood from my seat but did not let go of Henry's hand.

The vet continued. "Now, I am going to give Sheridan a few needed shots and will give you a list of foods to feed her over a period of time so she can gain her strength back. You can take her home with you in a few minutes." The vet smiled once more and then left us to our excitement.

I sat back down, washed in relief, and turned to Henry as the ecstatic news soaked in.

But his face was blank of all expression as he sat slouched in his chair, his grip slack as he scoffed at it all. "You have got to be kidding me."

CHAPTER FORTY-SIX

"I guess you were wrong," Henry said as I parked the car in front of Mr. Wilson's shop. The sight of it made me uneasy, but Henry said he needed to call Chief Brandon and let him know we arrived, and wanted to ask questions about the trial.

I gave a curious look to his comment and he added with explanation, "About her being like me."

I chuckled, shrugging my shoulders innocently. "It's exciting, don't you think?"

He rolled his eyes, a retort on his lips, but I was out of the car and getting his wheelchair before he could say anymore.

One of his hands held onto the inside door handle as the other gripped the car, and I weaved my arm around his to help him. For a split second, he froze, but then, as if he had to think a moment, he relaxed, and I supported him the rest of the way.

"I think I will go to the bakery," I told him, breathless. "To see the girls."

"Try not to overuse my tab."

I chuckled as I headed in the opposite direction. My eyes peered past the gray-blue world and down to my belly, my knitted sweater cropped against it and my hands stuffed in the pockets, feeling the warmth from within. My ballet shoes padded across the pavement lightly and I took a deep breath of crisp air before entering the bakery.

I stopped in my tracks.

"Prue?" Mr. Wilson asked quizzically, rising from his seat at the counter. Evie's eyes were wide with wonder at the sight of me. He must have told them I wasn't coming back.

I was angry then. Like I was now.

I turned on my heel and pushed the bakery door back open.

"Prue!" Jim called as he came after me, and after a short breath and five feet down the street, I turned around to face him.

"What do you want?" I said.

"Did Henry tell you everything?" he asked. "About me, my daughters?"

I could barely nod in response, my throat closing with emotion, but I pushed against the hurt and asked, "How did you forgive him. I mean, you treat him as if he were your best friend—and he treats you as if you were his *only* friend. How?" I glared at him, thinking of how it would come across in my eyes if some young man took my daughter away to never be seen again.

"I saw what it did to him," he said, his eyes somber. "The very thing it did to me. It broke him, Prue. When Henry came back, he had aged ten years. When I first heard he was coming back, I was so angry and thought that once I saw him I would kill him. But . . . that day when I went to the lake house to face him, I only broke down and cried in grief. It was like looking in a mirror when I saw Henry." He paused, watching me closely, then said with care, "He asked me if I had brought my gun, and I told him I had. He then asked if I would shoot him—kill him for killing her. Rumors were flooding that Henry killed Sylvia in cold blood for trying to leave him, and the town didn't care about knowing the truth, but I knew."

"What did you say?" I asked, my arms crossed to keep the nerves out. "When Henry asked you to shoot him?"

"I said that I came there with the very notion of killing him, but that the moment I saw his face I realized my own anger and bitterness was no better than the very man who killed my daughter. That I was no better than Henry, and could not pass judgment just because I thought I was righteous enough to take it into my own hands."

"What did Henry do?"

"He told me he was sorry for taking Sylvia away, for everything he did. I sat there with him in silence, and slowly, a new bond formed between us, thicker than friendship. Pain can do that. *God* can do that, and most of the time, He does. I was finally able to forgive, move on though I still felt the loss of my baby girl . . . but Henry . . . he just couldn't move on."

"Why? Why does he blame himself so much?"

"He blames himself for the fight. That if he had not started it, Sylvia would still be alive." He shook his head in disbelief. "But I told him the fight was inevitable and would have happened down the road anyway. The problems between them were much bigger than realized."

"What was the fight about?" I pressed, hoping to catch him off guard enough to reveal the 'big' secret to me. I didn't believe for a second Henry forgot.

"I don't know all the things said, but you can guess what the subject was," he said more coolly, though I was confused, and he then added, "for months after the accident Henry barely said a word. He just sat, thinking of all the bad things that had happened and replayed them over and over again in his mind. No one could reach him, not even me. He was dead inside. But then you came here, Prue," he chuckled, light dissolving the pain in his gaze. "You, with your growing belly, bold spirit and—"

"I'm not bold," I said, shaking my head as a blush heated my cheeks and my eyes went to the pavement. I wasn't bold, I was scared. And sometimes that could come across as such when the walls closed in.

"You are with Henry," he said. "But you also gave him something none of us could."

"What?" I looked up at him.

He leaned in close, like a grandfather telling his granddaughter the reason why the geese flew in V's.

"The very thing you carry within you," he said, touching my belly. "Life."

A ripple flowed against my face as a hope rose within me like the morning sun, only for dusk to come too quickly. "That's nice to know, but . . . Henry and I aren't really together. Sure, we're married—*under a fake name for me*—but that was so no one could find me."

I heard Mr. Wilson's deep inhale, and realized that all of us had been taking more breaths of late; as if we had forgotten to breathe in the first place. Maybe we had.

"You know," he said playfully, "I invited Henry to church every Sunday, but he always turned me down. When you told me to save a seat, I had my doubts." He then laughed out loud "But then, I see you pushing him down the aisle—it took everything for me to keep it in!"

"I didn't really invite him," I confessed sheepishly.

"Exactly!" he exclaimed. "Everyone here is waiting for Henry to come back. But you—*you*—are the only one of us to make him. You force him to realize that the world is still spinning, that he is still alive. That is why he treats you as he does. Some days with respect, and others with disdain."

"It's not fair."

"No, it's not," he agreed. "But it is necessary."

I took a step back, looking to him for answer. "And what do I get in return?"

"You get to be the one who brought him back." He took a step closer, reaching for me again.

But I pulled away, looking to the other figure in the background who had been sitting next to him in the bakery.

"And she gets to keep him."

Jim turned around, and before he could look back, I was gone.

CHAPTER FORTY-SEVEN

Sheridan slept in Henry's lap on the ride home, her head resting on his arm nearest me, very content. The IV the vet gave her made improvement, and tomorrow Henry said he would get the right foods and vitamins for her while he grocery shopped with Mr. Wilson. I didn't know what I was going to do, fatigue was coming more easily these days.

"Prue?" Henry's voice came out sudden and sharp, his head up against the window.

"Yeah?"

"Speed up."

"Why?"

"There's smoke in the woods."

Henry was right. A gulf of black and gray smoke danced above the treetops, but it didn't seem to be a forest fire; too a-line of a trail. Then the word escaped me. "Oops."

"What was that?" Henry snapped, his voice hard.

My grip tightened on the wheel as I pressed harder

against the gas pedal, keeping my lips sealed.

"Did you turn everything off like I told you to?"

"Let's not jump to conclusions," I said.

"Jump to conclusions?" He slammed his hand against the dashboard, startling me and Sheridan as we both jolted in our seats. "Just great, Prue!" he said.

I held my breath until the lake house came into focus, and didn't let it go. Not even when I saw the man with the bucket running to the back of the house.

CHAPTER FORTY-EIGHT

The house was fine, only the stove burnt with black scorch marks and smoke, the kitchen stuffy with the smell, but nothing too bad. Henry had left the back door open after carrying Sheridan, the reason all the smoke came out into the woods. I was thankful nothing permanent was done, but Henry acted as if the entire place was in rubbles.

"I'm sorry, Henry," I said. "I was just so worried about Sheridan that I didn't look close enough to make sure everything was turned off."

Henry shrugged me away, and looked to the young stranger before us, panting with sweat-soaked clothes, the bucket discarded at his feet.

"Who are you?" Henry said, his eyes slits under his dark brows, his sitting stance that of a panther ready to strike.

"Henry," I chided, slightly embarrassed by his rudeness. "You should be thankful that this man was kind enough to stop the fire."

Okay, so yes, there *was* a fire—but only a few curtains got in the way, and the stove, nothing too awful.

"Don't tell me how I should act," he said, and my cheeks burned with hurt.

"Henry," I tried to play along, "As your *wife*—"

Black eyes shot at me, killing the words off my lips. I willed myself not to cry, willed the tears not to brim, my hormones gaining on me, and took a sharp sniff, then reached out a hand to the stranger who returned it kindly. He looked vaguely familiar, pale eyes and light brown hair, but I couldn't place the face or name.

"Thank you," I said, trying to smile. "For putting out the fire." I retrieved my hand and pulled my sweater closer, taking the quiet steps inside the house without another word.

Ten minutes later, Henry rolled into the kitchen as I pulled off charred curtains.

"Who is he?" I asked, wanting the tension between us to cease.

"*He says* that Dr. Hayward sent him when she realized you were coming back to Oregon. She asked him to be your personal physician and make sure everything went smoothly." His voice then turned dry. "I can send him away if you want."

"You mean if you want?" I scoffed, then shook my head. "He looks familiar. I guess I must have seen him in the office a few times. If Juliet sent him, then it should be fine." My heart then squeezed inside my chest. "Did he check with Chief Brandon first?"

Henry looked slightly annoyed. Actually, completely annoyed. "He said he talked with the Chief and they cleared him and that's how he got the address here."

"But you don't trust him?"

"Is that such a surprise?"

I shrugged. "I guess it would be for the best then, if he

stays." Then I added, "Juliet obviously trusts him enough to send him here."

"Great!" A cheerful voice jumped out from the living room and was soon followed by the lean, young man. *Yes, I must have seen him in the office—but why didn't I notice him more with that cute face?*

The thought popped into my brain without warning and I blushed. The man was cute, yes, maybe in his twenties, but my heart only barely gave a second glance. "Now I just need to find a place to stay."

Henry rolled his eyes to him, distrustful like always. "There are no hotels here, only an inn at the edge of town."

"But what if there is an emergency?" I piped up, gaining both of their full attentions.

"We can call him," Henry said.

I placed a hand on my hip, condescending, and I didn't know what brought it out of me—perhaps the idea of my water breaking and having only Henry to drive me to the hospital.

"We don't have a phone," I said. "And it's not like you can very well drive to the hospital if my water suddenly broke, and I couldn't move."

His jaw clenched. "Then we'll get a phone."

I almost laughed, not believing him. "Yeah right. You hate phones."

"It will be the first on my list of things to get tomorrow." Henry was serious.

I relented, Henry's animosity heavy on my tongue. "Would you mind?" I looked to the man, "Mr.?"

"His name is Todd," Henry replied before the man got the chance, then turned on me guardedly. "Or, didn't you know that?"

I sneered at him. "We've never been introduced."

Todd smiled nervously, the corners of his mouth higher than the forever slopes of Henry's, and he seemed to carry life, opposite his counterpart who despised it at times.

"That's fine," Todd said brightly, "I can stay at the inn. But I will need to come over to do checkups, and monitoring."

"That's fine," I agreed.

"How often?" Henry said as if I had not spoken. "Once every few weeks?"

The smile left Todd's mouth instantly, and a serious professionalism took over. "Oh, no, more frequent actually." He then looked to me. "Juliet said that your blood pressure levels may be too high, and with the added stress of past events, it could do harm to the baby."

"*Babies,*" Henry clarified sharply.

Surprise crossed the young doctor's face, but he then quickly smiled again. "Juliet forgot to mention that happy fact. Congratulations!"

"Thank you," I replied, a little nervous.

"Though," he added, "I am very sorry for your loss as well." My smile waned and I could only nod in response.

"It's getting late," Henry said, though the sun had barely even set.

"Oh," Todd hesitated, "Would you mind giving me a ride to town then? I took a cab from the airport here," he explained, then looked to Henry's stone cold face. "Or I could just sleep on the couch tonight and wait till the morning when it's lighter out?" I noted the humor in his voice.

Henry grabbed the keys from the table and flung them at me. "We'll drive you."

We drove in silence, Henry in the passenger seat (with no help from me in front of the newcomer's presence), and Todd in the back breathing quietly out of his nose. The town sign eventually came into sight and I forced words out of my mouth.

"So, how long have you been a doctor, Todd?"

He seemed thankful for the question, and answered readily. "Only a few years now, but I was top of my class, so don't worry."

"They sent an intern to take care of you?" Henry mocked, but kept his gaze out the window.

I ignored Henry. "I will have to show you around town tomorrow so you can get acquainted with some of our friends and not feel like a complete stranger."

"That's what he is, Prue," Henry said rudely, "A stranger."

"Henry would love to introduce you," I teased.

The brooding man glared at me, not amused. "I have errands to run."

"And just how do you think you are going to go about doing these errands without me?" I should have known that was too much of a punch below the belt, and I didn't know why I kept pushing him with every sentence coming out like flying daggers.

"I asked Natalie to take me."

My breath caught, and I had no returning remark.

He knows then, doesn't he? My heart began to ache with my coursing thoughts. *Why else would he use Natalie as a jibe to hurt me? Or was he just guessing, playing with whatever embers he had to burn me with, not realizing the forest fire he had already created in my heart?*

Maybe I was just a foolish, pregnant and hormonal girl. A girl who couldn't see that sometimes, when you are the one to give life to someone, you give even more than you realize. You give them the very thing that takes strength to keep. And you are foolish enough to think that they'd give it right back.

CHAPTER FORTY-NINE

The ride home was worse than the one going. Once parked outside the lake house, I turned my entire body toward Henry, my legs crossed.

"What is wrong with you?" I said. "Why did you have to interrogate Todd?"

Henry's eye twitched, and he lashed back with just as much stamina. "I'm a cop, Prue. This is what I do. Why are you so naïve? You just keep opening your big mouth, saying anything, and not once looking at whom you're talking to. I mean, did you ask your sister's killer if he needed a towel to wipe his hands?"

I slapped him. I slapped him so hard my hand stung from palm to fingertip, but I didn't care. The pain fueled my fire.

Off guard, Henry kept still and I breathed heavily, shocked at my own actions yet still angry at his words. A red print formed on the left side of his face.

He let out a small breath, not meeting my gaze. "I didn't mean what I said. You just make me so angry—you talk to anyone and everyone, and tell your life story to them—real or not."

"Is this your way of apologizing?" I asked, surprised I even gave a response. Then I wondered, *Was I so naïve?* I didn't mean to be, though ever since I was little I was always so trusting of people. *And was there something to worry about Todd?* I didn't know if my heart could take it anymore. And then I just realized how easily I forgave Henry. *Ugh.*

His voice softened as he look at me. "I am sorry for what I said, Prue. It was way out of line, and wrong of me. I just—I just don't know why—"

"I do," I said, shaking my head. "You don't trust me, Henry. You keep pushing me away instead of opening up. And until you do, there will always be this exploding tension. So stop lighting the dynamite."

He stared back at me. "Stop giving me the fuse."

CHAPTER FIFTY

The burnt smell was pretty much gone by the time we got back, and replaced with musky dew from the back door being left open, along with all the windows. Dinner was silent and so was our ascent up the stairs. He filtered to his room as I went to mine.

I did have nightmares that night. A mixed variety of Hannah and the murderer, with a few doses of Henry that forced me to wake in a cold sweat as a scream died on my lips.

"Are you okay?"

I jumped at the sound of Henry's voice as he appeared at my door. I tried to calm my rapidly beating heart and answered without thought,

"It seems like you're always asking me that."

"I guess I'm waiting for the right answer." He rolled close to the bed where he had slept before against the wall.

"I had stopped having nightmares . . . but ever since seeing his face again, they came back."

Henry kept silent for a minute as I stared at the ceiling,

noticing a crack in the corner. Then he spoke up, his voice strangely light. "I guess I don't need to worry so much about you now. You have a good slap."

A smile rose to my lips. *Henry worried about me? Did he even realize his confession?* "I'm not sorry for that."

"No, you're not."

I smiled again, and said, "You could have made my water break, you know, coming in out of nowhere, in the middle of the night and into my room."

Henry laughed. And there it was again. That rush of bubbles except with a firmer current that time. Harder thuds. Like my own personal spa with the exploding jets. A surge went through my skin and I felt the glow come to my face instantly as I cradled the swell beneath me. "I'm sorry you had to wake up to screams."

"It wouldn't be the first time," he said and my brows furrowed, wondering his meaning. "At least when you wake up, you don't have to be alone."

Surprise hit me at his honest words and I wanted to ask, *how many nights did you wake up screaming after Sylvia's death? With no one there to comfort you?*

"Thank you, Henry."

"Just doing my job," he said. But I didn't believe him, my heart wouldn't. "Now, get some sleep. If I happen to snore, don't wake me."

I chuckled, forcing my eyes to close. I soon fell asleep, having no dreams, only deep rest. When I did wake, I turned to face the sleeping Henry, his head rested back against the wall. He looked at peace, and younger, the weight of world gone for now.

My heart fluttered in my chest, surprising me as I thought I could rest here forever, and once again, I wasn't prepared.

It was so strange, this feeling inside. I had never loved

anyone before.

Love.

Was that what it was, then? That burst through my chest whenever I caught him looking at me? The kicks in my stomach every time we touched or he laughed? I didn't want to be anywhere but here. But was that it? Shouldn't there be more?

I feel safe whenever he's around, and I know there is something between us, though perhaps only tragedy as its bond. Still, there could be more, if he were willing to let down those ancient walls.

I knew the day was coming when I would reveal the truth, the obvious. For him to either accept my imperfect heart, or ram it back inside my chest, losing me forever.

Until then, I would let myself have this, this time here in Oregon, no matter how short. And with a sigh, I closed my eyes.

CHAPTER FIFTY-ONE

Scrambled eggs and brewing coffee waited for me downstairs as usual, and a smile could not leave my lips for anything. At least, that's what I thought, until I entered the kitchen and saw things for myself.

"Good morning, Prue," Todd said, a smile to his face. I sat next to Henry, and poured myself a cup of coffee. As I reached to take a sip, Henry's hand clamped over the rim and pulled it away. I made a face, which he ignored, and I watched in annoyance as he poured me a glass of orange juice.

The next speaker was not so welcomed.

"Todd was just telling me how he was sent to make sure the pregnancy went smoothly from now on," Natalie said with a smile to me, but I barely returned the gesture. "He also said that you were going to show him around town today?"

"I guess so," I said with fake cheerfulness and implied annoyance. Henry's gaze shifted toward me slowly, picking up on my tone. I stuffed a piece of bacon in my mouth, regretting it at once. "Where are you and Henry off to?"

"Why are you eating bacon?" Henry asked before Natalie could respond, drawing my attention. His shadowed eyes scrutinized me, and I hated it.

Why did he keep doing that? Sizing me up when he and I both knew I would fall short?

"Cravings," I excused dismissively, then returned to the blonde, my brows raising with an unanswered question.

"Henry and I are going to—"

"You don't like bacon," he interrupted more rudely, completely ignoring Natalie, and I admitted to feeling the thrill of his smite. Both Todd and Natalie gave us looks, but my eyes stayed on Natalie, widening with *'interest'*.

"You and Henry are going to . . . ?"

"Um, to the—the uh,—" Her fingers snapped for the word. Any word, and her brow rose to Henry.

"The city," he said.

My ears perked at once. *Why were they going to the city? For a date?* No, no, Henry isn't going to date anyone—he is too involved with himself and his troubles to take true care of another's. *No*, I thought firmly, *they are not dating*.

"Why are you going to the city?" I asked, my voice rising an octave as I pretended to be enraptured by my scrambled eggs.

Henry sipped at his coffee, and I barely noticed the uncomfortable-looking Todd.

"Shopping," he said.

"Shopping?" My voice squeaked to a crack. "For what?"

"Oh," he murmured lucidly before the next sip. "You know."

He's cheating on me! Heat rose up my neck, burning my cheeks. I then yelled at myself. *He can't be cheating on you, you're not dating!*

"Well," I tried to scoff lightly, failing incredibly. "Have fun,

I guess." The bacon soured in my mouth, and I didn't know why I even ate it except for the fact that Natalie had some on her plate, as did Henry. I swallowed some juice and turned to Todd. "Did you like your room at the inn?"

"I got homesick the moment you left." He chuckled and I returned a grin. A light bulb went off in my head.

"You know," I said, leaning forward a bit, "There is an available room just upstairs, you could use it if you'd like."

"That wouldn't work," Henry said, and I was quick on my feet.

"The attic, then?" I proposed, my eyes fully trained on his gaze now, challenging him. "Sweetie?" I hummed. *Didn't just a few hours ago I thought I was in love with the man? How did I get so angry at him so quickly? Why did this thing between Natalie and him irritate me so much?*

"No," he replied firmly, eyeing Natalie at once. "Neither of those rooms will work."

"Fine," I declared, scooting my chair back, my focus evidently on Henry. "I am going to go change, and then Todd and I can take a tour of the town."

I walked out of the kitchen seemingly peaceful, but fumed inside the entire way. A while later and I was dressed to go.

Todd started out the door but Henry caught up to me before I could make my escape.

"Before Natalie and I leave town, I'm going to talk to Brandon and make sure this guy checks out." His gaze wandered to the open door. "Perhaps you should hold off on this tour until we know for sure."

"Chief Brandon wouldn't let him come here if he didn't check out. So unless you want to call off your shopping trip, I am going to take Todd to meet the Marthas' and have a coke with Jim."

"Jim?" Henry's eyes widened with surprise.

I nodded. "We talked, and I can't ignore him forever." I began to leave, my eyes shifting from Natalie in the background to Henry again. "Besides, I figure I just have to get used to some things."

"I think you will really like this town, Todd," I said as we walked down the main street that led to every shop and store. "And the people here are really great."

"I believe you," he said. His eyes shined at me, and I had to look away and keep my focus to the ground, my head beginning to throb. "You know I know you and Henry aren't really married, right?"

My head jerked up in surprise. "What?"

"Well, you called him sweetie at breakfast, but I know you two aren't really together."

"Oh," I shook my head. "That was just a jibe, I guess you could say. I know you know," I said with a forced laugh, suddenly remembering that Natalie knew too.

I wonder what she must be thinking, or telling Henry.

"Then why—"

"It's complicated," I said, ending the conversation and increasing my speed.

"I'm sorry for prying. I just noticed, that's all." He touched my elbow, and I involuntarily inched away

"It's fine." I shrugged, a cold shiver from the wind coursing up my spine. I reached for the bakery doors, a grin spreading across my lips, and his mouth soon formed the same upward line Henry could never grasp. "Have you ever had chocolate coffee before?"

"And it's not hot chocolate?" Todd asked in disbelief,

taking another gulp from his second cup of the delicious brew.

Evie shook her head happily from across the counter, her black curls bouncing. "Nope. It's pure coffee *and* chocolate. With only a dash of heavy whipping cream."

Todd guffawed playfully, and I laughed. It had been two hours already and we still had yet to see Jim. Evie and Martha took the privilege of momentarily closing the bakery and showing Todd the hotspots of the town—all within walking distance of each other. Evie handed me a small box of donuts as we went out the bakery doors, laughing still.

"You really like those, huh?" he asked, holding my cup of coffee for me.

I smiled, leading the way to our new destination. "I hope it isn't too bad for them," I indicated toward my stomach that helped keep the box aloft.

"No, I think you're fine as long as you take steady doses."

"So are five in the afternoon pushing it?" I had already had three while we were in the bakery, and two more when Evie told Todd the hilarious story about her date with a mortician. She had felt bad for the guy and even admitted to being slightly attracted to his strange, isolated behavior. That was until he crossed the line by asking for a lock of her hair. I think she made the whole thing up but it was still hilarious how she told it.

Todd reached over and lifted the lid of the box, looking inside. "Well, I do see some plain ones, so you must have some restraint."

My cheeks heated. "Actually, those are for Henry. It was his tab after all."

Todd put his hand to his heart dramatically. "Which I would have happily paid for if you'd let me."

I rolled my eyes. "Nonsense. You're a guest."

"Where are you taking me now?"

"To meet another friend of mine," I said, nearing the swinging porch, ready for a refreshing coke and the calm wind on my face.

"Hmmm."

"What?"

"Isn't there a lake around here that you could take me to?"

My answer caught in my throat and I knew it couldn't be a yes. That was Henry's lake. And it wouldn't feel right being all alone with Todd in such a secluded area where ideas could be made.

"What is it?" he asked, reaching for my elbow again, and I drew back from his touch.

"Nothing," I said and entered the warm shop. Jim must have seen us coming, because he had three coke bottles ready.

"Who is your friend, Prue?" he asked.

Todd held out his hand. "My name's Todd."

Jim handed him a bottle instead, opening up mine for me like always. I could never get the caps off without drawing blood, and Jim laughed at me the last time I tried. I noted how his eyes kept with Todd's carefully, like a watchdog studying its intruder, and then I remembered he was a cop too. "And uh, how do you two know each other?"

"Todd is my doctor," I said, taking a quick sip of coke and regretting it at once when fizz went up my nostrils.

Jim eyed me. "Is Henry okay with this, Prue?"

"Boy," Todd said, "Do you always have to consult Henry with everything?"

"When it comes to her safety," Jim said firmly, "yes, she does."

I sighed, the tension seeming to have returned from the house. "Henry is figuring that out."

"And you?" Jim's eyes watched mine closely, and I felt the walls of my heart closing in.

My own gaze flashed at him with confusion. I didn't understand. And he didn't clarify, only turned his focus back to Todd with guarded eyes.

"I assume you have met Evie and Martha already." He nodded to the coffee cup in his hand and box of donuts in mine.

"Yes," Todd said. "They are very nice."

"*And*," I added more cheerfully, "Evie told me how instead of my welcoming party that I had to cancel, she is just going to throw a Christmas party for us instead—inviting the whole town!"

This cracked a grin from Jim, and his eyes twinkled at me. "I am sure she will. All two hundred of them," he laughed, seeming to settle. "Got anything in there for me?" His curiosity was like a child's, making me smile.

"Of course!" I said, grabbing him a crumb cake donut.

"What are your plans tonight while Henry and Natalie are gone?"

I froze, my skin electric. My eyes roamed up slowly from the box, widened and ready for attack. "You mean . . . they won't be back until tomorrow?"

Jim's brows creased together in confusion, then his foot shifted at his loss for words. "Well, I—" he cut off, nothing coming to mind or aide.

"Actually, Prue and I were going to have dinner at the lake house tonight," Todd said.

"Alone?" Jim toned darkly, and I wondered what he could be hiding from me about Henry and Natalie's trip.

"Yeah, she was telling me about some secret recipe of hers and I just have to try it. I figured tonight would be best since she'll be all by herself while Henry is in the city."

"Prue, I don't think—"

"Thank you for the cokes, Jim," I chirped before he could finish his thought. "If I come to town tomorrow, I will stop by."

I started for the shop door, Todd ahead of me.

"Prue," Jim called just in time for my foot to reach the outside. If only I had kept going. If only I hadn't stopped. But there was that dang curiosity again with its eight remaining lives.

"Yes, Jim?" I asked, my voice barely above a whisper.

One less life now. One less chance.

"Don't forget Henry so easily."

"Never," I said.

CHAPTER FIFTY-TWO

I didn't know why I was nervous, only that I was. Not like a girl going on her first date, anxious with excitement, but much more like being on a blind date set up by no one.

I couldn't stop thinking of Henry and what he could be doing all the way in the city *'shopping'*. Shopping for *what* exactly? And why with Natalie? I could only roll my eyes and switch my thoughts back to the present awkwardness.

My only skill with cooking was baking, and so we ate very dry herb chicken with lumpy mashed potatoes, and washed it all down with glasses of tap water.

"Have you felt them kicking much?" Todd asked, and it surprised me how different he was with his sunny personality verses Henry's gloomy rain parade.

"A few times," I replied, dry chicken caught in my throat. I took a big gulp of cold water before continuing. "I thought by now it would feel more like a soccer game going on inside of me, but it isn't too rowdy."

"It will get stronger as the weeks go on," Todd said, eating his chicken and potatoes heartily, not even making a face at its strange texture. "At the hospital, the mothers love to talk about the kicking."

"You know, we could have just ordered takeout. I don't want to make you eat something unbearable."

"No, it's really good." He took another bite to make his point. I only laughed.

"Well, I have had enough." I dropped my fork onto the plate and picked up the dishes to take to the sink. Todd followed behind with his plate and glass. "So," I said coyly, "You know Juliet?"

He gave a short laugh. "We, uh, dated."

"What? She never said she was dating anyone."

"Well," he hummed, "It was brief."

Then I understood. "Oh."

He shrugged. "We work together fine. But when I heard she was going to send a colleague somewhere out of state, I volunteered right away. I liked the idea of a vacation."

I dropped the plates into soapy water and emptied out the glasses before leaving it to sit. I sat back down at the table, bringing a bag of cookies with me, offering him one at once. "What made you want to be a doctor?"

"My mom's father was a doctor and she wanted me to follow in his footsteps. I found the medical side of things interesting, so I took a shot at it in college. Turns out, I'm pretty good." He smiled, popping a cookie in his mouth.

"Did your dad approve?" I asked, getting up to get a glass of milk, my mouth already dry.

I gave Todd a glass when I sat back down and he happily drank away before answering. "*He* wanted me to go into the family business, but it wasn't for me, and eventually he understood, I guess. What is it that you do?"

The doorbell rang, cutting off my reply. *Who would be coming by at this hour?* I stood and walked to the door, the living room darkened by the set sun. *Who ever came by here?*

"Hey, Prue," Evie chimed at the sight of me, her cheeks red with cold.

"Hey," I replied unevenly, not expecting anyone at all. I could feel Todd's patient figure behind me, and my cheeks burned.

Embarrassment at being caught? But caught how? True, Evie thought I was married to Henry—and I was, sort of—but she wouldn't think this was a date . . . would she? And . . . was it?

"What are you doing here?" I asked, about to let her in.

"James told me you would be all by yourself and asked if I could stop by to check on you."

Of course he did, I thought. Still, the notion touched my heart.

Her eyes locked onto the young man next to me, striking me with an idea. "Did you need anything?" she asked me.

"Actually," I said, my eyes roaming to Todd. "My *doctor friend* here just had to eat through a terrible dinner made by me and I am sure he is starved by now! So," I eyed Evie mischievously and she seemed to catch on to my glint, "I wondered if you could take him out to the best fish place in all of Oregon!"

"Oh, sure!" She said, stepping in and taking hold of Todd's arm. "I would love too! Bob's got the best catfish in all the states and I just *love* his red salmon!"

Todd's eyes widened a bit, but he looked to me and nodded politely. "It was nice talking to you, Prue," he said as he brushed past me and out the door. Evie let him go ahead as she handed me a plate of fresh cake rolls filled with strawberry and crème.

"Thanks, Ev," I said.

She pecked my cheek. "No problem, I just hope James

doesn't get jealous!"

I waved toward the car as they drove and closed the door behind them. Suddenly, the house seemed so empty and dark, the air too still. I grabbed Henry's robe from the couch and slipped it on as I walked up the stairs.

Now I have my chance to look in the box . . . if I wanted too. While Henry's gone. I chewed the inside of my lip, wanting badly to know the contents, but not wanting to incur the wrath of Henry nor carry the guilt of such knowledge.

I don't know what made me do it. What caused a type of boldness to rupture inside of my chest and force my limbs to move forward, reach the box, and carefully splay out its contents on the floor with trembling fingers. No, I don't know what pulled me to do this. I only knew one thing.

Well, two.

I would never look at Henry the same way again.

And.

If the truth revealed, it would cause everything between us to be questioned.

Chapter Fifty-Three

For once, the sun was not what woke me in the morning.

I heard him come into the room, and I clamped my eyes shut, feigning sleep.

The floor creaked as he rolled to the bedside and I felt his presence before me, still, and breathing with slight heaviness from the strain of climbing the stairs and into his chair. He smelled of old spice, new house, and cloth. It wrinkled my nose, but I let out a yawn to keep up the pretense.

I could feel his eyes piercing my face as they most assuredly watched me. Paranoia hit like an echoed drum as I frantically worried he knew—knew that I knew.

Did I leave the closet door too open? Did I forget to shut the lid tightly, like he had it sealed? Or did he just read it on my face, my fake sleeping face, full of knowing? I could take his suspense no longer, and I slowly fluttered my eyes open like a soap opera actress waking from a sweet dream.

"Henry?" I yawned again, rubbing my eyes and realizing how completely messy my hair was. Like a strawberry blonde afro haloing my face, and I wiped a tangled strand out of my eyes.

"Morning," he replied with an almost cheerful tone, as if he were truly the type to be a morning person, long ago, before the world struck him down, and the weight was too heavy to carry without falling. "I just came by to check on you. I heard you mumbling something."

My ears perked, and I knew my face reacted just as openly. "How long were you in here?"

His eyes shifted. "Not too long."

I didn't believe him.

"You managed on your own for one night easily."

"Todd was nice company," I said, venom left over from yesterday.

"Natalie went back home after she dropped me off," Henry continued on, letting out a loud sigh as he ignored my jibe. "We went to see Jim first, and I called Brandon about your new doctor."

My eyes waited with patience, but my heart was speeding away with anxiety.

"He checks out," Henry said with obvious disdain. "He went to the station explaining Juliet's concerns, and once they went through his background, they let him go. Juliet even personally called in a referral."

"Good." I sucked in my lower lip, slightly relieved as I eyed Henry. "But you still don't trust him."

Henry only shrugged. "Ready to get out of bed?"

My eyes narrowed suspiciously. "Will you and Natalie be having more 'shopping' trips to the city?"

"Maybe."

"Then no," I huffed. "I am not ready to get out of bed."

"Have it your way."

And I did.

Thirty minutes later, I was done having it my way and succumbed to the downstairs. Henry sat in the kitchen, looking out the sliding glass window, into the foggy atmosphere, changing trees, and colder sky.

"Henry?"

He didn't answer.

I took a few steps closer, coming to his side and put a hand to his shoulder hesitantly. "Henry?" I whispered.

"Do you want to see the best view in the world?"

CHAPTER FIFTY-FOUR

Cobwebs were the very air in the attic, along with dust, spiders, and splinters, but not much else. I don't know what exactly I was thinking I would find, but I did have an idea of furniture, pictures and boxes covered with white sheets. Instead, all I got was an empty room with a window overlooking the best view in the world.

I stepped forward, inspecting the sight. Fog painted the tips and edges of the window, giving the entire frame an eerie and beautiful glow. And right there, atop the horizon of trees, the lake lived.

You could see the entire woods, where they spread to and where they ended against the mountains. The water glistened; deep blue and green with white-tipped waves against the yellow shore.

"Why did you keep this a secret?" I asked.

"A lot of memories here," Henry said.

"But Sylvia was never here," I said and the statement made me realize that I did have something to share with Henry she didn't. This house, and I felt guilty for my cruel thinking.

Sorry Sylvia. My stomach twisted from guilt. *Am I so bad of a person? Living with your husband, though nothing happens between us, and yet still having thoughts about him? For you, Sylvia, perhaps I should just leave.* I bit my lip. *I just don't know if I could. He made me stuck, remember? And it is so hard to get loose. Especially when I don't want to.*

"Huh?" I asked when I thought I might have missed his reply.

He shifted in his seat. "This is where I . . . uh, was going to . . . when tried to . . . ."

"Tried to what?" I asked, looking at him.

His eyes wouldn't meet mine. "You know what, Prue."

My eyes narrowed. "Don't be so vague."

He let out a loud groan, shifting his arms in his chair. "Where I was going to kill myself."

My eyes widened and I couldn't believe it, and yet, there it was. The truth.

"Why would you do that?" I gasped. "Why would you take your life so easily?"

"It wasn't easy, Prue," he argued, but I could only shake my head in disbelief. "I didn't do it, all right!"

I moved away from him, looking back to the lake as thoughts ran across my mind. *What would people think of me if they saw my reaction? A stupid girl getting angry because someone had made a choice, their own choice?* But I knew it wasn't that. I knew why I was angry. I could never forgive Henry for taking his own life, and taking from me the chance to meet him.

It was selfish, and immature, but it was the truth. It hurt too much to think of him not being here, of me being shipped off somewhere else with some other family to *'protect'* me, and no one truly knowing what I was going through. No one to grab my hand against their better judgment and inner conviction, and pull me from the very darkness they were once encased with.

Thank You God, for this man! My heart cried out. *Thank You God, for this chance, thank You God.*

But I don't think I can keep this up. I don't think I can keep my heart at risk.

I sniffed, trying to harden my heart against him, but something else squeezed it tighter, forcing the blood to pump.

"And why didn't you?" I finally asked, turning to face him again.

He was staring at the floor. "I planned to either hang myself or put a bullet through my head as I looked out to the lake for the last time. Hanging was near impossible."

I didn't laugh at his joke.

Henry coughed, then continued, evidently catching my hint, "I went with the first. Just as I put the gun to my temple, the doorbell rang. I wasn't going to answer it, but when I tried to pull the trigger, something else was pulling at me when the next ring came." Henry rubbed his eyes, trying to rid them of the past, it seemed, but that wasn't the way to do it. The past wasn't some dirt you could just sweep away. The past was the dirt that clung to your pores and nail beds; made its way into the marrow of your bones; and could only be washed away by something thicker than water.

"I decided to answer it," he said. "It was a struggle to get down the two flights of stairs, one right after the other, but I made it, in a sweat, to the door . . . only to open it to the very man who had the only right to kill me."

"Jim," I said.

"I thought it was God's little joke, interrupting my suicide only to be murdered instead. I guessed even at the end, He didn't want me having my way." Henry scoffed, waiting for my snappy response that never came. "But now, I guess . . . I guess you could say He saved my life."

His confession stunned me, my limbs tingling, and I took a step closer to him, a small smile to my lips.

"Giving me over to James though, wasn't the greatest thing. He was going to kill me, had it all planned out just as I had my own death outlined. But then suddenly, he broke down at my steps, and I realized it's true what people say: God doesn't give the easy way, in or out." He let out a soft chuckle. "Suicide would have been a piece of cake compared to having to deal with James."

"So, you believe in God now?" I asked. "Why didn't you start going back to church like you used to, when Jim invited you?"

Henry swallowed something thick, and I heard the descent. His eyes were doughy as they looked up to me. "Believing and trusting, are two very different things, Prue."

I nodded. "I know that."

"Then you understand."

"But I don't excuse."

"What?"

I marched up to him. "So you believe there is a God, and you leave it at that? You don't even try!" I said. "Oh, He's there—and I'm here, my life sucks—and that's it!" I wanted to scream, but then suddenly my voice lowered, and my head leaned down close to his, my hand resting on his chair. "You are one of very few people, Henry, that know without a doubt there is a God. And one of *many* who do not trust Him."

Our mouths were too close again, I wondered if he noticed, but I pulled back, even though I had said I wouldn't.

"I've always believed in God," Henry said. "I just spent a long time hating Him."

"And now?"

"I hate myself more."

My brow creased as I tried to understand. *Was it because he blamed himself for Sylvia's death?*

Something prodded me to speak, though I couldn't know the point or why. "With God and man, there always seems to be an inner tug-o-war."

"Who do think will win?" he asked, amusement in his voice. But I answered plainly,

"That depends on you."

CHAPTER FIFTY-FIVE

I found him by accident. I wasn't looking for him—only for an escape—and he chose the very same place.

He sat close to the waterline of the lake, the waves smoother today than usual, and I sat down next to him on the sand, saying not a word. That was the day I found the rock most like Henry.

My arms enclosed around my belly, trying to grab warmth from the loose robe I still wore, and I wondered how Henry could be so unbothered in simply a long-sleeve shirt.

A sigh escaped my lungs, out my throat, and I shook my head.

I wished things could be different. Different lives, different circumstance, different beginnings, same people. But some things do happen for a reason, maybe not everything, but *some* things . . . .

"How do you trust people so easily, Prue?" he asked. He kept his face ahead, as did I, but his words were clear in my eardrums.

"I guess because they know nothing about me, so they

can't hurt me."

I took the risk of looking at him, but his focus continued to stay ahead.

"People who know the most about you, know the best way to hurt you. They know how to kill you. But strangers, they don't know what it takes to break you, they don't know." I paused, then tried again. ". . . . I guess I trust people so easily because I see the good in them, Henry, I don't know any bad they have done, any mistakes they have made, and vice-versa." I smiled faintly. "I've never been afraid to trust somebody."

He looked at me, confusion clear in his eyes. "Why?"

"I don't know." I shrugged. "I've been hurt before, my trust betrayed, but whenever another person comes along . . . . Grace, I guess. You can't hold something against someone because of something someone else has done—it's not fair to either party." I paused again, my gaze still with his, then said, "I think you just have to look at trust as giving someone a seed and waiting to see if it will grow."

Henry cocked his head to the side, his eyes a bit wild. "Do you trust me?" he asked.

I smirked, my smile waning as I thought of the closet. "Ask me again when you know the truth of me."

"Don't you want to ask me the same thing?"

"Won't you have the same answer?" I then teased, "I remember not too long ago you being unsure if you trusted me or not."

"Try me now."

But I didn't want to play this game. I stood, ready to leave.

"What?" he said. "Afraid?"

I licked my drying lips, as was my tell; a slight ache in my chest, because I knew.

"Will you be honest?" I recalled when he said he trusted

me as much as he could walk a mile. *Would this time be any different? Why? What had changed?*

"Yes," he said, surprising me already.

I sighed. "Do you trust me, Henry?"

His mouth twitched as his eyes tried very hard to stay within my gaze, sliding back and forth between my irises. At last he kept it, and like a man aged by pain and war, he answered, "You're the only one, Prue."

CHAPTER FIFTY-SIX

The weeks rolled by easily, and my belly continued to grow, though it seemed impossible. Todd said it should slow down soon, since I grew so fast in the beginning, but I was doubtful about that. A girl could only take so much weight gain and emotional swings that shook a mountain. I was surprised I hadn't scared everyone off.

Pumpkins lined the doorsteps of shops and window displays. The Marthas' had me help cook up a storm of cookies for the kids Hallelujah Festival at the church, and now wanted even more help as Thanksgiving neared. I wore red and brown and orange almost every day as I reveled in the fall weather, though the trees bared away as winter came.

The routine between Henry and I changed. We talked more, and I wasn't so threatened by Natalie when she came over for his physical therapy (plus I would usually go visit Jim anyway), and she said he was improving tremendously. Though he still had no feeling in his legs, he at least had a better attitude when it came to exercises.

Church became second nature as it wasn't such a hassle to get Henry to go, and he didn't mind it as much as he liked me to think. I saw how his eyes watched with interest and ears perked with care as the pastor spoke sermons about faith and trust, coincidently.

Todd came at least once a week to check on me, my pulse, mood swings, medicine, and eating habits. No more peanut butter pancakes *was* a suggestion, and I laughed one morning when Henry put a huge container of peanut butter on the table with seven pancakes on my plate. The kicks came more and more, but only at certain and very random times and I tried to ignore the obvious cycle.

We celebrated Thanksgiving on the twenty second, and it was an enjoyable evening with Henry, Jim, Evie, Martha, Natalie, and even Todd. Stories, funny stories, were told from when they were all in high school, and there was no sadness that could be brought. Jim carved the turkey as Evie stood up right beside him to distribute the plates. I had made the mashed potatoes along with a chocolate pie, though Evie's pumpkin pie was all the rage from everyone's lips. Henry enjoyed the company for once and it brought out a new life in him I hadn't seen before, and I prayed every night that that life would thrive.

The next to-do was the big Christmas party Evie had planned and I helped out at the bakery four days a week as we practiced the best recipes for all types of foods that we knew people would love, inventing some for the bakery as well. My peanut butter pancakes were a sensation and even had Jim talking about us opening up a diner to join the bakery—that got the girls and me brainstorming! We also came up with a mint-based coffee with real mint leaves, *much* different than just flavoring squirted in like other places, and though Evie was trying to convince Martha and me that a strawberry coffee would be a hit, we disagreed after a taste of the first trial—seeds included.

Every morning I had breakfast with Henry, and he would read the newspaper as I chatted away about something unimportant, somehow him still managing to catch every word all the same. He liked to sit and think for a while and so I would help him up to the attic where we could watch the best view in the world, sometimes making small comments, doing crossword puzzles, or just remaining quiet. Lately I had been drawing design plans for the diner idea, and he would ask how that was going, though it had barely begun.

A little bit later, the doorbell would ring and Natalie would come inside, then I would leave to go meet Jim where we would sit on the porch swing, drinking fresh cokes or sometimes looking through his collection. The rest of the day changed often whether I went to bake with the Marthas', Martha and Evie having their own designs ready for me to see, or taking Sheridan to the vet for her shots, then coming back home to eat dinner, and sometimes Todd or the others would come over. Henry still didn't trust him, but he tolerated him as I tolerated the awkwardness with Natalie, so neither one of us said much to the other on the subject. Things were good, really good, and I was happy, very happy.

Until Henry announced another trip with Natalie, then all hormonal restraint broke loose.

CHAPTER FIFTY-SEVEN

"What do you mean you're going back to the city?" I said, staring down at Henry in the living room as he told me the news of another shopping rendezvous with Natalie. "And why can't I come?"

Henry gave me that look my parents did when I started sounding immature for my age, even though my intention was to appear the opposite. I didn't like that look, especially coming from him.

"I thought you had plans with Jim?" he reminded, and I remembered the rock I wanted to show him.

"Fine," I groaned, rolling my eyes, very childish. "How long will you be gone?"

"We should be back by tomorrow morning."

I walked with him outside to Natalie's car where she waited in the driver seat.

"Be careful, Prue," Henry said.

"Aye, aye, captain," I retorted.

He rolled his eyes, snubbing my immaturity once again. I walked up the porch steps and turned to watch them go. I felt like the pregnant girlfriend getting left for the secret wife. Once they were out of sight, I hurried upstairs (not very fast when pregnant) and changed into comfy jeans and a shirt with a thick overcoat. Henry's car keys waited in the ignition, and I was off to town.

"So you found one, did you?" Jim asked me from above the shop counter.

I smiled, pulling the rock from my coat pocket, my hand coming forward to show.

"Who does it remind you of?" I prodded, both our noses down to the table. "Breakable like glass, though it gives off the idea of invincibility; dark, but when you hold it up to the light, it shines from within; and very cold to the touch, but after you hold it for a while, it warms up."

Jim eyed me playfully, then held it up to the lamp. Sure enough, the inside glowed to a sparkle, only remains of black crystal at the very edge, like a candle beneath a shade. He then knocked it hard against the counter, and a sharp shard broke off, sliding to the end of the countertop. "I think you found it, Miss Prue."

I grinned like a schoolgirl. "Thought so." I laughed, and he handed the rock back to me before going to grab us each an iced coke from his small fridge. I led the way to the porch swing out front. "I could get used to this," I said, smiling.

"I want to apologize," Jim said, placing a hand upon mine. "For asking about the baby names. I didn't know then, about you and Henry."

I shook my head, sudden tears to my eyes. These hormones were really getting to me.

"No, it's okay. I didn't mind, really. I thought it was sweet you wanted to talk to Henry about it."

"I did talk to Henry . . . though."

"What?" I gasped, then quickly added, "No, I don't want to know." And I didn't. I didn't want to know what he said, or if he said anything at all.

"You could stay . . . you know," Jim said quietly, releasing his hand.

"No," I shook my head for the third time. "I couldn't."

"The friends you have made here, would accept you even after hearing the truth. It's you they love, Prue, not your reason for being here."

"That's not what they did to Henry," I said.

"Is that your real excuse?"

My cracked voice betrayed me. "Excuse?"

His thick brows furrowed into one as he thought a moment. "I will miss you when you leave." I put my hand to his this time and noticed the sparkling water in his own gaze. "You have been a true pleasure, Prue."

"I haven't done much."

"I wouldn't say that. And neither would your sister . . . or Henry." After a moment, and a painful wince from his features, he retrieved his hand and cleared his throat, his eyes back to the sky. "You have this knack, Prue, for connecting people. You truly care about them."

"Your daughter wouldn't say that."

His head shot to me, but kindness held his voice. "Which daughter would that be?"

I didn't know whether he was serious, or merely mocking me. I waited for him to say more.

"You and my daughter have more in common than you realize."

My voice then rose with the same question. "Which one?"

"Both," he said, then smiled briefly, "I guess."

"Why? Because I'm trying to steal a husband from one,

236

and a lost love from the other?" I bit my lip, amazed at my sudden and cruel boldness, and my heart raced as guilt came.

"One knew how to love someone, even if they weren't loved back," he said gently, "And one knows how it feels to lose the closest person in the world to them."

I looked down to my hands as they cradled my swollen belly, feeling the moving grooves of two babies. My chest felt tight and I couldn't release the tension—I didn't want to have this conversation.

"I'm so big," I said, and hoped he didn't think I was being cold, I just needed to breathe right now. I could always hurt later.

Jim chuckled. "You're pregnant. That is a good thing."

"Tell that to my ego," I said.

"A woman with a child—*children*—is a beautiful thing to behold," he said, and I believed him in that moment. "I remember when Laura . . . she glowed."

I smiled at him, watching how soft his features turned when he spoke of his wife.

"I hope that when I get married . . . ." I stopped short, no longer able to speak of my future so freely, I realized. I took a deep breath. ". . . I wish that I had someone to look at me that way, and see me how you saw her. Did you know that I've never been kissed before?" My cheeks burned at my confession.

Jim leaned forward and kissed my forehead, warming the spot with sympathy.

"You will, Prue," he promised. "And when that man looks at you, you will see it in his eyes."

"What will I see?"

He smiled. "Awe."

With that, I leaned against the chair, looked back to the world, and my heart was light.

CHAPTER FIFTY-EIGHT

I drove back to the lake house with Jim's words running through my mind like water on a ledge. Sheridan whined in the backseat, ready to be home after her last shot from the vet. I turned onto the driveway and parked the car, letting the engine run for just a few more seconds before stepping outside.

Todd waited at the porch steps, a bag of groceries in his hands and a kind smile to his face.

"I thought you might like some company," he said, coming to my side as I let Sheridan out. She sniffed his feet, and gingerly moved on, my figure in her vision the entire time. "Evie told me that Natalie was going back to the city with Henry."

I cringed. "Yes, she is. But thank you, that's sweet to come by." I smiled, fumbling for my key in my jean pocket; lately it had been getting stuck more and more. "I appreciate the thought."

"I figured you for a pasta girl."

Think more meat and potatoes, I smirked. *Fish is a favorite, too.*

"How'd you know?" I played along, twisting the doorknob. Sheridan rammed into my leg, rushing to get inside and I lost my balance against the door. Next thing I knew, Todd dropped the grocery bag, glass shattering, and I was in his arms.

"Thanks," I gasped, my cheeks burning. After his gaze became a stare, I leaned up quickly and tried to regain my footing, wiping beads of sweat from my brow.

"Are you okay?" he asked, reaching down for the bag, his focus still on me.

I nodded, eyeing the kitchen. "Yeah . . . . What were you saying about pasta?"

An hour later and I sat at the table sipping iced tea and slurping up creamy noodles. My stomach rumbled for more, and Todd quickly came to my aide with the bowl. "Don't you know I've gained enough weight already?" I laughed, taking another gulp of tea.

"You're as healthy as a horse." He grinned, fully watching me now.

"Nice choice of words," I teased.

He flushed at once and held his hands in surrender. "Not what I meant at all!"

I rolled my eyes. "I'm kidding," I laughed, adding, "The pasta's good."

"I'm glad you liked it." He smiled again, giving me a headache. I wasn't used to such open, good cheer in this house.

I sighed when his gaze deepened a little too much for my taste. "Well, it's getting late," I said.

"Crap," Todd groaned, gaining my attention at once. "You don't have a phone, right?"

I shook my head, clearing the dishes. "Henry conveniently

forgot to buy one." *Bet he wished he had now,* I grinned.

"I told Evie I would call her for a ride after dinner."

"Oh," I said, then chewed my lip. "I'm sure she'll stop by soon anyway."

"Yeah." He nodded in agreement. But the idea of being alone here with Todd did not suit me one bit, and my stomach soured.

"Or, I could just drive you back to the inn?"

"But won't that be too far at night?" he asked. "I mean, twenty miles there, and twenty miles back straight will tire you out. I told you to be careful of how much energy you use. I can just sleep on the couch," he then added at my stunned reaction, "if you don't mind?"

My cheeks reddened. "No, I don't think Henry would like that."

"Right." He sighed. "I'm sorry, Prue, this is my fault."

"It's okay. I can just drive you." I left the dishes in the sink to soak in hot water and grabbed my coat from the green couch. The keys were left on the coffee table as I went to grab them, whistling for Sheridan to come.

"I think she's knocked out," Todd chuckled when Sheridan didn't move but an eye from her position on the floor.

"The shot must have wore her out." I yawned myself, the long day wearing on me as I locked the front door behind us, leaving the lights on inside for when I came back.

"You should really look into getting a phone," Todd suggested as he slid into the passenger seat.

"Henry likes his privacy."

"Would if there was an emergency?"

I shrugged my slump shoulders, ready to be back home already, though his choice of words did send a chill up my spine. "Henry would take care of it."

"Thank you for taking me back to town, Prue."

240

"You're welcome," I said, flicking the lights on and trying to keep myself alert. But the sky was too comforting, the moon too covered, and the air too cold for such a feat. The last thing I remembered was saying goodnight to Todd outside of the inn, ready for home.

CHAPTER FIFTY-NINE

I never liked alarm clocks. Or worse, dreams about alarm clocks. You could never seem to hit that dang button to turn it off, and it would just keep blaring and blaring until you wanted to break the thing into pieces. This was such a type of dream, except it wasn't an alarm going off.

It was a horn.

I tasted blood. Salty and metallic. Like when you bit your lip too hard, or your tongue by mistake. But I wasn't chewing gum.

My head pounded, my brain floating in water, and I tried to breathe slowly, but there was too much blood that got in the way. If only I could turn off that stupid alarm.

Someone was calling my name. I knew it was my name because the voice was familiar, and that voice was the only one that could say it so rashly, so rudely, and with such disbelief. I felt hands shaking me, then a muffled argument whether to move me or not, but I couldn't fully wake up.

Why did they want to move me? Why couldn't I move myself? Or just stay here . . . .

Finally, someone pulled and carried me away. I reveled in how they made the noise stop. They turned the alarm clock off, and I could sleep.

CHAPTER SIXTY

Lights traveled against my closed eyelids, the spidery veins like a map. My senses were clearing and I felt a warm body against mine, a pulse pounding against my arm where someone's heartbeat was.

That's when I started to feel the pain. How badly my upper body felt against the rhythm of hurried motion, my ankle most likely bruised to a plum, and my body sore and stiff—it all made me dizzy. The metallic taste in my mouth didn't help either.

I sensed my fingers grasping for my stomach frantically but with too slow a speed. This forced my eyelids to flutter open, to blink until the blur cleared away. Until focus started to come, and certain images began crossing my vision.

All of Henry.

The firm line that made his mouth set so attentively, the creases above his furrowed brows, and the constant movement of his eyes around the room. I was in his lap, the side of my face pressed against the crook of his arm, cradled securely in his grip though his arms moved with ferocity and determination against the wheels of his chair. We were in a hospital. The sterile smell of clean burned my nostrils as more voices crushed against my hearing, words I could never forget.

I found her off the road.

Car accident.

Almost eight months pregnant.

Extreme blood loss.

Could be in early labor.

Trauma.

We might have to take her into surgery if there is internal bleeding.

I'm not leaving her.

Who are you?

Her husband.

You will need to fill out some paperwork.

Screw the paperwork, I'm coming with her.

Sir, you need to cooperate.

No, you need to get out of my way.

Foreign hands ripped me up into the air and onto a solid bed that gave no comfort. A mask covered my face, suffocating me as something sharp pierced my arm. I whispered his name, I knew I did. They were rolling me away from him, I could feel it happening.

But he had heard me. His hand clasped mine, and he answered back,

"Prue, I'm right here. I'm not going to leave you."

Chapter Sixty-One

I didn't like taking naps, either. Hated, how you felt afterward. Much like how I felt after this particular nap. My mouth full of cotton, my head not all there, my eyes droopy even after so much sleep. Ridiculous, really, how you felt after such a sleep.

I would have rubbed my eyes awake, but I was tied down by wiry, plastic tube-like strings; one sticking out of my arm and another forked into my nose. Funny how I couldn't breathe even with it in me. Perhaps they pushed too far, breaking my nose, or maybe I was just over thinking it. I wondered what would happen if I ripped it out.

"Prue?" he asked for me quickly, firmly. My hands reached for my stomach, sickened to think of it flat. "They're fine," he said and my eyes opened to Henry.

Ragged, deeply unshaven, and eyes full of more fire and water than I could ever think possible. It made my breath catch.

My throat burned with coming words, and a request for water was all I could manage to ask. Henry grabbed a cup from a table beside the bed but when I tried to reach for it, he quickly rested the tip to my lips. After a jolt of surprise, I slowly drank away, amazed at what was happening. *Henry was caring for me.*

"What happened?" I asked after a few gulps. I wanted to rip the tubes from my nose then and there, but a disturbing image of my brain coming out scared me enough not to.

"I found you on the side of the road on our way back to the lake house. Rubber tires were scattered around, and down the slope between the trees was my car, the front crushed against a tree trunk." His fingers raked through his hair, his elbows against the bed, and I wondered if he was having memories of Sylvia. The thought pained me. "You were barely conscious, your head bleeding from hitting the windshield—the airbag didn't go off, thank God."

"Why?" I asked, my eyes having trouble staying open.

"It could have killed the twins. The doctors said you were lucky. You lost so much blood, it's a miracle the twins survived at all after such trauma."

"Oh, my God," I cried, unable to breathe. "I could have lost them." Henry's hand clamped against my fist before I could go into outright sobs.

"Prue, you're all right. The twins are healthy and unharmed, everything is going to be okay. You got a miracle."

"I thought you didn't believe in miracles?" I said, slowly able to take a breath.

"Until I met you, no."

"I remember you telling me, *'it's going to be okay, Prue, it's going to be okay'*."

I thought he blushed, but then he said, "What were you doing, Prue? I mean, you were so cold—you had to of been out there for hours."

"I was driving back to the lake house after dropping—"

I cut short my words, knowing where things would lead if Henry knew why I was out so late. But the anesthesia had already done its damage with my loosed tongue.

"After dropping what?" he asked, anger rising in his voice as if he already knew.

I sighed, too tired for this. "*After* I dropped Todd off at the inn."

"Why were you dropping him off?"

"We ate dinner and he needed a ride. I just should have let him sleep on the couch, but I knew how you would feel about that."

A shadow crossed Henry's face and I realized that he was blaming himself for all of this, though his anger would still be directed at Todd. He exhaled sharply through his nostrils and they flared with intensity. "You are not to see Todd ever again."

"He's my doctor!"

"I don't care. You can find someone else."

"Then you can't go to the city with Natalie anymore." I crossed my arms, regretting it at once when the needle pulled my skin and I winced.

"Fine."

"Because it isn't right that you—w-what?" I stammered, not expecting that answer.

Henry arms crossed more lazily now with control that I remembered vaguely holding me, and a firm line for his mouth. Something was up.

I shook my head, scoffing. "Oh, no! Just because you and Natalie finished doing whatever it was you were doing, does not mean I have to stop seeing Todd!"

"I forbid it."

"And who are you?" I lashed out, hating the way he was acting—like a father to his teenage daughter that was in love with a motorcycle-riding, leather-wearing hooligan.

"A cop."

"*Ex*-cop," I clarified, then added, "And besides, he checked out. This wasn't his fault, Henry."

"Why do you want to see him anyway?" he asked, now the little whiny boy instead of the big bad cop.

I sighed once more, a wave of exhaustion washing over me. "Can we just stop fighting, please? I'm really tired." The pulsing pain was making its return, and I wondered where that red button was that you pressed for painkillers.

Henry's expression changed to a softer, more sincere one, and he reached for my hand boldly, surprising me once again. "How are you feeling?"

My eyes stared down at our linked hands, his firmly atop mine, nursing the bruised and scratched knuckles. I spoke softly, my ribcage puncturing my lungs. "Fine." *Entranced* might have been a better word.

"Well, get some rest. I'll be here when you wake up."

I agreed instantly, my eyes already drooped, but the few moments of peaceful sleep would soon be interrupted by a loud argument.

CHAPTER SIXTY-TWO

Henry was mad. That much I gathered by the anger in his voice upon my sudden waking. My eyes peeked open through their lashes and I saw Todd standing opposite the wheel-chair-bound Henry next to the foot of the bed, a bouquet of flowers in his hand. I listened closely before making my entrance known into their conversation.

"You should have never been at the house in the first place," Henry growled, not once looking the inferior in his chair.

"It was an accident!" Todd said, the flowers shaking in his hand. "I didn't think she would fall asleep at the wheel!"

"That's right, you didn't think," Henry said. "And you obviously didn't think how much your life is in danger right now by you coming here of all places when the only place you should be going to is—"

"Henry," I sang his name, quickly interrupting his next word I knew he didn't mean; or at least, hoped he didn't.

Both pairs of eyes shot to my face, causing a blush to rise instantly at the attention. Henry ignored Todd and came to my side, but with a significant amount of space between us this time.

"You're lucky I don't kill him now," he said. "The only problem is, we're in a hospital, giving him a higher chance of survival."

I rolled my eyes, noticing the lack of a forked tube in my nose. "It wasn't his fault, Henry."

"Like you could even try," Todd murmured in the background, and Henry's head shot backward, venom in his voice.

"Is that a challenge, scout?"

"Depends."

"On?"

"If you consider yourself a challenger."

"Todd, that is enough!" I shouted, my eyes aflame, and the two fighting boys silenced.

Todd looked to me with a strange expression, then returned to a normal mask of calm. Henry remained obviously indifferent.

"Don't even think about coming back to the lake house," Henry threatened, pushing his wheels toward the busy hallway. "I'll be back in an hour," he called before leaving.

Todd came closer to the bed, extending the white flowers. "I am so sorry, Prue."

"It wasn't your fault," I repeated the same earlier line. "I should have just let you sleep on the couch. I know Henry is blaming himself more than you for that."

Todd shrugged, leaning against the cabinet, and I noticed how lean he looked at that angle. "I think I knew from the start we wouldn't be chummy-chummy."

I snorted. "Chummy-chummy?"

"Anyway," he grinned, continuing, "I am going to make it up to you. First thing after you are released, I am taking you out on a date."

"W-what?"

He pulled up a chair and scooted close to me. "Come on, Prue," he prodded. "Don't tell me you haven't felt a chemistry between us these past weeks?"

I kept quiet, still amazed at his sudden bold approach. I hadn't pegged him for an outgoing wooer, and I didn't know what chemistry he was talking about exactly. Did I feel anything for the guy?

"Or . . . am I just making a complete fool out of myself?" he asked.

"No," I said, not quite sure how to handle this. "It's just . . . I am just . . . surprised, that's all."

"Is that a yes?"

"I guess." I tried to manage a smile.

"Great!" He clapped once, rising from his chair suddenly. "I'll have to find the perfect place to eat and make reservations."

To this, I had to laugh, still in shock. "I don't think they take reservations in this town. Anywhere."

Todd only smiled. "I can't wait."

Less than an hour later, a new visitor joined my current triangle.

"Jim!" I cried out with excitement as he walked into the room, his hands in his jacket pockets. Strolling gloomily behind him was Henry.

"Hello, Prue." Jim smiled, the skin around his eyes crinkling. "Everyone at the church has been praying for you. Henry called me once they took you into surgery—he needed someone to keep him from busting down every door." Jim winked, squeezing my arm gently, and I returned his smile.

"Haha," Henry said from behind, remaining in the corner, the shadows playing nicely at his features, adding to his whole *'sullen'* look. But he had trimmed his on-going beard back into the familiar salt and pepper scruff I came to love. "Aren't you going to give it to her?" he added dryly.

My eyes widened to Jim. "Give me what?"

The older man sighed, giving a stern look to Henry who only shrugged, then quickly changing into a wide grin just for me as Jim reached into his pocket and pulled out a small, blue box.

"It isn't a ring," he chuckled as I grabbed at it, my heart pounding with anticipation. Henry only snorted from behind. "You can leave," Jim suggested without looking his way.

I caught the flicker of surprise cross Henry's face, but he stayed put nonetheless, and quiet. I looked to the small blue box, pried open the lid, revealing what I had been waiting to see for a while now.

A pebble most like me.

I had imagined a very pudgy, very oblong and deformed rock colored white—the only thing I thought could resemble me. But this was not what I had expected, thank God.

Jim took the pebble from my hands and held it up for inspection. "Now," he said philosophically, playing the part. "When you hold it this way, what does it look like?"

I gazed at the pale surface, and focused on the silhouette.

"Don't look at it too hard, or you might miss it. Just look closely."

I tried. The height was about the length of my pointer finger. Curved and jutting out from its side was more formation. Not deformed, as I would have quickly judged, but elegant as you saw its pregnancy, matching my own. I grinned. "It's pregnant."

Jim kept his smile. "*But*," he added more thoughtfully,

"When you turn it upward, what do you see?"

The way the rock curved, it looked pregnant to the side, but turned around it became something else entirely.

"A heart," I whispered, tears stinging my eyes.

"Matches you perfectly."

I bit my lip, happy and humbled at this new finding. I took the pebble in my hand, rotating it back and forth, amazed at how the oblong appearance could quickly change into something so much more beautiful.

"Like I told Henry," Jim said, watching me with joy. "You are full of heart, Prue. And part of that comes from the fact that you are pregnant, and the reason why."

"Thank you," I said, eyeing both of them at once.

Henry spoke up, "I never understood your strange fascination with rocks."

"Laura always loved the symbolism you could take from ordinary things. After she died, I could at least keep that part of her alive." That silenced the brooding figure. "Prue will have to show you yours some day."

Henry's brows rose suddenly, confusion evident. I only laughed and continued rotating. The three of us chatted until a nurse came in saying visiting hours were over and the two men, with more in common than wanted, said goodbye as one promised to return in the morning. It was hard to sleep at first, but I was given good dreams in return, one in particular that made me smile.

A dream of Hannah, dancing with her children on a shore of white pebbles.

CHAPTER SIXTY-THREE

The doctors forced me to stay in the hospital for two weeks under close supervision. They were amazed I had no broken bones and little internal bleeding; the twins completely safe and healthy, thank God. The bump on my head slowly healed, and I was cleared for any concussions and brain damage. But the days were dull, and even though I had many visitors bearing gifts of chocolate, flowers, teddy bears, and food— the hospital was not a convenient distance from town. Still, Henry came every day.

Todd came by whenever Henry wasn't in sight and said he found a nice restaurant to take me to, one just outside of town, and he would be the one driving. I had yet to tell Henry about the *'date'*.

Evie was faithfully at my side every morning before opening up the bakery, but I didn't like the idea of Natalie coming along, so I assured her she didn't have to come every day. Surprisingly, Martha visited and we had a heart-to-heart about our lives. I told her about losing my sister—*keeping out certain details*—and she explained about how she came to own the bakery shop. Her husband worked overseas and she was never skilled in anything much, except that she loved to bake, and the months he was gone, that's how she spent majority of her time. One day he surprised her with the shop and wanted her to have something to do while he was gone, something to take care of (she didn't want to start a family until he would be able to spend more time at home) and she grew to truly loving the place.

The day of my release was greatly welcomed and Henry and I waited for the doctor to arrive and officially sign my release forms. Minutes passed until surprisingly, Todd walked in.

"Todd? What are you doing here?" I asked.

"I have the official right to clear you for release." Henry groaned in annoyance beside me, arms crossed more tightly than before. "And, I wondered if you wanted to know the gender of the twins."

My body stiffened, and I didn't know how to answer. I looked to Henry. "Do you think I should know now?"

"If you want to," he said, shoulders shrugged but eyes watchful.

"Or do you think I should wait?" A pang struck at my heart, and I forgot to take a second breath, then a third, and fourth.

"You won't betray her by knowing, Prue," Henry whispered. "I know you want a boy and girl. I know you want to incase Hannah and Jacob in their forms, and that if the truth doesn't match your wish, then you might be disappointed, and you'll feel guilty for it."

He read me like a children's book.

I turned to Todd. "I want to wait," I said, "until they are born to know the genders."

Todd returned my smile more faintly, and grabbed the

clipboard from my bed, signing away.

"Does Friday night sound good?" he asked, keeping his eyes down to the sheet of paper, feigning interest.

"What?" Henry asked sharply.

Todd looked up. "Oh, I was just asking Prue if this Friday was a good night for our date?"

"Date?" Henry burned the word, and then me. "*Date?*"

"Friday's fine," I said, my cheeks red as I looked back to Henry. "Can we go home now?"

"I said he couldn't come to the lake house."

"We won't be eating there," I replied, rising from the bed, my bones stiff from so much rest. By the time my feet hit the ground, I was out of breath, my head pounding as the room began to spin. "Could we just not argue?"

"Fine, Prue." Henry surrendered. "Do what you want."

And suddenly, I didn't want to. But my next response was useless as he rolled out of the room and it was left to Todd to kill the awkwardness. I said my goodbyes to the nurses as I was rolled in a chair with Todd holding the handles, my feet propped up off the ground, and I knew what they were thinking.

Where is the man who rushed through these halls like a maniac with her in his hands? Why isn't he with her, the one who saved her life—fought to be with her the whole time during examination? Why is she with this kid, this boy in comparison? What about the one who feared for her life?

The answer though, was simple.

I was the cheerleader. Todd the captain of the football team. And Henry the stud dressed in black who cared nothing of football, yet still went to every game, watching beneath the bleachers looking for a reason, with a cigarette in his hand that he didn't like to smoke but was his escape.

Except I didn't choose this. I didn't choose to be with the

football player. The stud told me I didn't belong in his world and I was stupid enough to believe him. Stupid enough not to see that I held his gaze through the stands, through the smoke—unable to see that he was daring me to choose him.

Only, I didn't know it was a dare.

I mistook his waiting, for refusal; carelessness.

Not realizing, he cared the whole time.

CHAPTER SIXTY-FOUR

I pulled the sticky surgical tape from my forehead and prodded the tender skin held intact by five stitches. Make up wouldn't cover this, but I didn't mind the scar. I liked the character it added to me above my brow.

"Getting ready for your date?" Henry asked acidly, taking occupancy in the doorway of his bathroom.

I barely gave him a glance through the corner of my eye as I applied mascara for the third time.

"Not much of a date if you don't look nice," I said, annoyed from the fact that I didn't have anything truly outstanding to wear.

I wore stretchy jeans that rode beneath my bulk with no button and a long-sleeved shirt with a jacket. I had washed my hair earlier and wore it down now in natural golden-red waves that haloed my face, until deciding to wear it up again.

"So, the Christmas party has been rescheduled?" he toned, trying to sound interested in making conversation, and I wondered what he was up to.

"Yep. Evie had to plan most of it herself since I was in the hospital for two weeks." I touched my forehead once more, apprehensive. "Does it look terrible?"

"No." He shook his head with a light grin. "You look fine."

I smiled, and brushed past him to grab my shoes from his bed. Simple flats were all my swollen feet could handle.

"And I used to think I had big feet," I mumbled, squeezing my toes in.

"What's the date?" Henry asked, following me.

"Tonight?"

He sighed. "The Christmas party."

"Oh, next week. The twenty-first." I pulled at my top, sweating in winter. "Can you turn the heat down?"

"It's on eighty," he said. "Next week, huh?"

"Evie figured no one was headed anywhere out of town—*which she was right*—and she wanted to make sure Dr. Seymour had plenty of time to prepare for the feast." I waited for him to go with me downstairs, but Henry seemed all too patient.

"Are you coming?" I asked a little too sharply, ready to lie down.

"Tense much?" he countered back but finally reached for me and down the rickety slope we went, step by careful step. I didn't like going *down*stairs.

"You know," he said. "People may talk when they see you out with your new doctor instead of your husband."

My eyes rolled. "We're just friends, Henry."

"Oh, *I* know that," he teased. "But how does your pretend husband feel?"

For some unknown reason or urge, I shot my gaze to his daunting eyes, and my breath caught at once.

"Jealous, Henry?"

He breathed against my lips and I knew it was on purpose. "And if I was?" he said.

260

I knew he was teasing me, I knew he couldn't be serious, and what happened next was pure accident—a reflex, really.

Basically, I dropped Henry.

My hand shot to my mouth, muffling my gasp, as I watched Henry tumble down the stairs and land at the bottom with a hard thud. His loud groan broke my frozen state, and I ran down to him.

"I am so sorry!" I said, not sure what to do, my heart racing inside my chest. He laid there a moment, eyes shut, and then slowly took deep breaths that did nothing to settle me. "Are you okay?"

"I'm fine," he said through clenched teeth. "Just . . . help me up."

A laugh escaped me. I knew it was a stupid thing to do, but really, how could I honestly control such a reaction? And second reaction? Was I supposed to wait the twenty years later when it became funny to both of us, or finally let escape something barely captured these days?

I chose laughter.

And so did he.

I bit my lower lip to keep the outbursts from taking full rein, but surprisingly, Henry began to roar with laughs of his own, his chest heaving up and down, and only his chest; his legs motionless in the corner of my eye.

"Sorry," I said again, helping him rise to a sitting position. We were but breaths apart, our arms touching briefly.

My hair had escaped from its tight headband that already was causing a pulsing to my brain, and Henry, without second thought it seemed, reached his hand to gently brush against my cheek, and tuck the strands behind my ear. His mouth then opened to speak, and I awaited the coming words with a heavy heart dreaming to be lifted up, wishing he would kiss me, when we were suddenly interrupted.

"That's Todd," I said quietly after the doorbell rang a second time. Cautiously, not wanting to lose eye contact with Henry, I pulled over his wheelchair and helped him into the seat. "I shouldn't be back too late."

"Have a good time," he grumbled.

"Don't say that," I chastised lightly. "Don't lie."

"I have something to show you when you get back," he said off-handedly as I got up to go to the door. I nodded in response, not wanting to leave this moment, but another knock came and I answered it.

I left him there, sitting in his chair, staring out at me as I went, his eyes waiting. Waiting for me to open that door again. The dark stud daring me to leave the jock to his game, and go for a real ride out. To take a chance with him despite all the rumors and charred reputation.

But I wasn't going to be the first one to say it.

CHAPTER SIXTY-FIVE

The drive to the restaurant ten miles outside of town was filled with awkward silence. Todd borrowed Evie's car for the night since Henry's was still in the shop.

I tugged my jacket close and kept my focus outside the window, bare trees blurred by speed, until finally Todd broke the ice.

"I hope you like this place," he said. "And, I wanted to apologize again for what happened."

"It wasn't your fault. Besides, things happen sometimes." My heart convulsed at my statement and I winced, but quickly pushed against the hurt with more distracting words. "So, even though your mother wanted you to be a doctor, and your dad wanted you to go into the family business, what did you want to be?"

He winked. "A hit man."

I flinched at his choice of words, trying to force out a laugh as my eyes stared hard.

His expression then showed concern, "Prue, are you okay?"

"That is an interesting field." I said, forcing the bile back down my throat. "Why a hit man?"

"Prue, I was only kidding. You look like you've seen a ghost. No, I wanted to be a doctor for a long time, it was just that my mother wanted it for me as well, or else my dad would have never allowed it."

I nodded, my heart regaining normal speed. Thankfully before either of us had to say more, the restaurant came into view.

He was quick to get out of the car and open my door. For a split second, I thought of reaching for the wheelchair, but then remembered Henry wasn't here, he was back at the lake house. I gave my head a good shake of thoughts, then politely followed Todd inside, ready to get back home; wondering what in the world Henry had to give me.

Returning home caused my building fatigue to fade as curiosity burned, and I swung on my heel to face Todd, a smile to my lips that wasn't for him. He had walked me to the front door, and I wondered when he would walk away.

"I had a good time." Todd's teeth flashed beneath his smile, his expression and words causing heat to rise to my cheeks. I supposed that was my queue to agree, or something.

"Yeah." That was all I had.

Todd's hand reached up and slid against the side of my face without warning. His face came to mine, his eyes closing, but I pulled back just before his mouth could do its damage.

"What are you doing?" I gasped, inching farther away, my back against the door. My first kiss wasn't going to be with him. Or like this. I was too much of a dramatic romantic to want something so original. I wasn't sixteen, and even though this *was* my first date, tradition still did not apply.

He stopped, his face a little disgruntled. "Well," he said, a slight chuckle to his voice, "I *was* trying to kiss you."

I let that sink in, then replied with a tinge of angered disbelief, my gaze narrowing. "And then what?" I said, shaking my head. "I'm pregnant, Todd. With my sister's children. Do you honestly think you could handle that little fact? I mean, between the dinner dates and labor pains?"

"Prue," he defended quickly. "I don't care."

"Well you should," I snapped. "Because . . . because this isn't something a guy would really want in a relationship. Not when two other people come first."

Todd's eyes narrowed, and his jaw clenched tight. "You mean *three* people," he said, and my ears were sensitive to the note of hostility. "Are you really just mad because he won't say the same thing? The very thing you want to hear from him—that you're hearing from me?" His breath was too hot and heavy against my face, and guilt swelled my chest as well as clarity.

He's right, I realized. I don't want Todd to be the one to want to be with me, to kiss me. I want Henry to be the one. I've known it from the start, the very reason I was so excited once we got home. But was Todd God's way of giving me another choice? Another option?

I wasn't sure.

Todd still held my face and tried to kiss me again, leaning forward until I pushed his hands off and swerved to the side.

"Don't ever try to kiss me again," I warned, my hand grabbing for the doorknob.

His face fell. "Prue, I'm sorry, it's just—I can't stand it!" he said. "I can't stand watching you watch him the way you do—even when he gives you nothing in return. I mean I—"

"Well get used to it," I barked, and slammed the door

behind me.

The echo reverberated off the walls, and I hoped it hadn't woke Henry. He left the downstairs light on and I crept into the kitchen to get a glass of juice, calming myself down before I headed upstairs.

A light down the hallway from my room caught my attention. It was coming from the other guest bedroom, one I had only seen briefly in my short tour of the house. Usually empty, I didn't understand why a light was on and went to it.

The sound of glass shattering against the hardwood floor crushed all attempts at silence, and I instantly heard the shuffling and deep thud from Henry's room.

But my eyes stared ahead, wide, as his ragged breathing drew closer.

"Jeez, I thought someone broke into the house." He then let out a deep, almost annoyed, groan. "I wanted to show you myself, but you stayed out later than I expected."

"Henry, wh-what is this?" I looked at him and I couldn't believe his smile.

The first I had ever seen that didn't come from a laugh. A true and genuine smile from the gloomy and brooding Ex-Officer Henry Clay. The corners were all the way up, and the crinkles around his shining eyes spoke volumes more of happiness. His beautiful straight teeth showed beneath his full lips, and I wanted to cry with shared joy.

"Go on," he prodded, and followed me as I entered the bedroom.

If first thoughts were to be pink or blue, they would be completely wrong. This was so much more.

The walls were painted to show the lake and the trees, every detail immaculate. There were two cribs, one on each side of the room, matching the color scheme with old fashion woodwork and carvings up the bars, as well a changing station and rocking chair. A small bench where two could easily fit sat beneath the opened window draped with sheer lace curtains, and I took a seat on it as my mouth hung open.

"Look up."

My neck craned and I gasped. The sky, painted so realistically, showed limitless on the plaster as stretched branches from the trees leaned forward full of green leaves. But that wasn't the only thing.

"How?" I cried at the sight of the two portraits that faced me, one above each crib. It was Hannah. And Jacob. Each smiling as I remembered on their wedding day, the very picture I took with me on my trip here.

"I found the picture in your room and thought it would be nice for the twins to see," Henry said, closing the distance between us. "Now you know why Natalie and I went to the city. I couldn't find any furniture without someone telling you about it."

"But why?" I asked, standing up, amazed.

"Chief Brandon said you could still be here a few more months until the trial. I just thought that if you had the twins here, then they would need a room." He shifted uncomfortably in his chair. "We had it done while you were in the hospital—the only time we could do it without you knowing, or seeing the designer. Think of it as an early Christmas gift."

I hugged him on impulse, my neck close against his as I squeezed tightly, not wanting to let go. "Thank you," I said.

A few seconds passed and soon his hands slid against my sides, returning my embrace, sending electric currents through my body.

When I pulled back, cold drafted into my skin where his warmth had made its home, and I shivered.

"I guess we should clean up the mess you made," he said

with a grin.

"Sorry I ruined the surprise," I said, leaning down to pick up the sharp pieces of glass. His fingers scrambled down close to mine, grabbing the last few chunks with ease.

"So . . . how was it?" he asked, and it took me a moment to realize he had meant about the date with Todd.

"Oh, eh . . . It was fine, I guess. Until he tried to kiss me."

"He what?"

"Yeah, I pulled back," I said, then threw him a line. "But when he tried again . . . ."

"Again?" Henry said, his face strangely red. "Ow!" He cried out and jammed his thumb into his mouth.

"Ew," I gagged. "Don't drink it." I pulled his hand out from his mouth and carefully inspected the skin. "You just need a bandage." A small dot of blood appeared against his thumb, and slowly grew.

"And you need to explain," he said, not giving in to my change of subject.

"There isn't much to say." I let go of his hand and led the way to his room. Soon I was searching through his medicine cabinet for alcohol and a bandage.

"Then it shouldn't take long to tell me," he concluded.

I sighed, realizing this wasn't going to end, but found the supplies I needed. I sat down on the edge of his bathtub and waited as he rolled closer to me. I began to clean his wound.

"He tried to kiss me at the door, I pulled away, told him he didn't know what he was getting into, and when his balls were busted, he tried to kiss me again."

"What do you mean?"

I looked up to his face, then quickly back to my task. "Don't worry, I slammed the door on him like a big girl."

"That's not what I meant."

"Then what did you mean, Henry?" I asked tiredly,

applying the bandage then dropping his hand, and looked him straight in the eyes.

"Nothing," he replied.

After a short moment of silence, he spoke again but with a little bit of humor there. "So, you *didn't* kiss Todd?"

"No."

"Why not?" he teased as I got up from the hard tub.

"Because I am not the type that wants the whole *'kisses-me-at-the-door'* scene. I want passion." My cheeks burned at my honesty, but Henry didn't seem to mind it. "Not just with the kissing part. I want the whole atmosphere and time to suddenly close in as we lock eyes. But Todd did get one thing right."

"What?" Henry said, and I made sure our eye contact stayed, grinning, and knowing he might not get it just yet.

"He made the first move."

CHAPTER SIXTY-SIX

I knew it was a dream. A nightmare. Everyone knows when you are having one, but for some reason, it still feels so real. And though it couldn't hurt me physically, it could hurt in many other ways.

I was back in Hannah's nursery, blood dripping down my hands, the babies inside of me gone. I cradled my stomach, not understanding where they could be, wanting to vomit, but then I saw him. The masked man as he held a bloodied knife, and came toward me. But just before he aimed the blade against my throat, he pulled off his mask, revealing a different face, and I couldn't scream awake.

"Prue! Prue, wake up!"

My eyes opened, a cold sweat across my forehead, and the back of my neck as my eyes blinked for clarity. I froze at the sight of Henry holding my arm. "W-what happened?"

"You were having a nightmare. You kept mumbling Hannah and the twins, and saying they were gone. I think you almost took my eye out." He tried to joke, but I could he tell he knew I wasn't up for that. "What happened?"

I hugged my arms close around my belly, tears in my eyes and a tremble to my chin. "They were gone," I whispered. "He took them from me."

"Who?"

"Mark Brooks."

Henry let out a deep breath, watching me, and suddenly placed a hand to my stomach, a shockwave coursing through my body. "It was just a dream, Prue. No one is going to take them. I won't let anyone hurt you, remember?"

"Not even you?" I asked, the corners of my mouth slowly rising.

"Not even me," he said. "Now go back to sleep, and you'll wake up to pancakes with peanut butter."

I nodded, saying nothing more, and tried my best to go back to sleep. But the dream took longer to shake away than times before, and the fear that something bad was going to happen coated me like a thick fog.

CHAPTER SIXTY-SEVEN

Purple flowers were left for me at the front door the next morning when Henry went to get the paper. Last night's dream was gone from my mind and my thoughts were light.

I still had yet to figure out how the paperboy made it all the way into the woods alone, but nevertheless it arrived every morning without fail.

"I guess Todd is sorry," Henry said uninterestingly as his eyes scanned the mid-section of the paper. He took a sip of coffee, a bite of toast, and another sip before lifting the pages a little higher.

I grinned, reading the small card tucked between the stem of leaves. He apologized for being so forward and hoped to see me at the Christmas party.

"So," he switched the subject easily, "what are your plans for today?"

I took a bite of my pancakes, the peanut butter causing the food to stick to the roof of my mouth as I spoke. "I don't know." I took a gulp of milk. After my nightmare, Henry said I should sleep in later, and since it was after 10:30, I could drink milk. "Any ideas?"

"We could make out."

I choked on my next bite.

"Funny," I scoffed, but couldn't deny the blush he caused. "I don't know how I could ever forget your humor."

He grinned behind his paper, and took another sip of black coffee. "Do you have an outfit for the Christmas party? You know these things are a big deal in small towns."

"Actually," my smile widened, "I bought a dress before the accident. No one's seen it yet, not even Evie, so it's going to be a surprise for everyone. At least as big of a surprise a pregnant girl can be in a dress. I just hope it stills fits." I finished the rest of my food, picked up my plate and Henry's half-eaten pancake plate, and went to the sink. He always liked to eat his toast last.

"A dress, huh?" he eyed me playfully as I sat back down.

"Don't get too excited," I laughed, "I'm still pregnant in it."

He chuckled, flipping his page, and narrowed his eyes a little more as he read with deeper thought.

"What do you read in a small town paper?" I asked, with slight mock of course. I didn't want this to be a silent day.

"And I thought you were observant," he said.

I sighed, annoyed he wouldn't play along with my joke. "Henry, I know you read a different newspaper every day." His eyes darted to me suddenly, revealing nothing, but the action alone making a statement that he was listening. "Just like how I know on Saturdays you read the comics, and Sundays the town paper."

If Henry had a toothpick in his mouth right then, he'd either been chewing or choking. "Huh." He forced out the humph.

I held my chin in my hands, watching him. "But what I don't get is you always read the smaller articles in the middle, never the front page of any paper. Why?"

"People," he said, "young and old, spend their energy writing up these articles and rarely ever make it to the front page. But they keep writing. They have no pictures, only so much space to tell their story, and when they do on the very rare occasion have a photograph, I'm sure a celebration occurs in their box of cubicles; cake is cut and praise given." Henry took another dignified sip, then continued with pleasure. "I have about five favorites in each paper. Five people I read on a regular basis.

"A girl with the pen name, *'Yellow Bundt'*, loves to discuss how weather and changing seasons represent people in daily life. Each week she picks a person she sees in the park and studies them for six days, seeing how they change from day to day as the weather changes, and even goes back to that same person when the next season comes. Plus, the names she comes up with are hilarious."

My brow rose. "Yellow Bundt?"

"Her grandmother's German, and always used to call her Yellow Bundt because of her love for cake and her gold hair," Henry replied, as if he had known this girl his whole life.

"Rudy is obsessed with basketball and constantly remarks on how much of an impact the game makes on the players, coaches, and fans. Most people want the high stories with the best scores, most damaging injuries, and juiciest scandals; but Rudy focuses on how peer-pressure influences the play of the game. He's pretty good for being a college dropout. He wanted to show people it didn't take a college diploma to work in the big leagues. *'Grandfather'* often talks about—"

"Wait," I stopped him. "How do you know so much about these people?"

"I'm friends with them," he said with a smile, but completely serious, no sarcasm at all. "I called them up years ago, told them I liked their stuff. Bundt visits me every two years or so, and Grandfather comes by for a coffee when he sees his children down south."

"But you don't have a phone."

"This was before Sylvia died, before I moved back here. I used to call them up every so often before then to have dinner and hang out. Rudy called every once in a while after Sylvia . . . and Bundt liked to keep in touch after what happened as well. But when I left Arizona and secluded myself here, I dropped all connections, until one day, after months of isolation, a paperboy rode up to the house and handed me a big wad of papers—all from them. A note inside said that just because I moved didn't give me an excuse to stop reading." He laughed again, short but true. "Another young girl I know writes poetry, and short stories. I think she must pay them to put it in their paper."

"Why do it then?"

He looked at me as if I should have known the answer. "She feels that even the greedy need to be reminded of childhood, of thoughts away from lust."

"You really like them," I said.

He shrugged. "They have something in common that amuses me. They're Christians." He waited for my response, but I didn't react, and he continued.

"I find it . . . aspiring that these people have knitted themselves in these places. I know many people would think nothing of it, or even condemn them because they feel that since they are Christians and believe in God, then they should be owning the place, right? But these people are the real thing. I've asked them, and they answered the same. They're happy. And even though they write random and out of the line stuff, they managed to keep their job in a world where not only is a picture worth a thousand words, but a lack of one and a load more of ink, is worth less."

"I like that," I agreed. Then a more obvious and plaguing question popped into my mind. "How do you get the paper?"

After explaining how all the writers send their papers on the express route the day before their story is out; a certain mysterious paper boy as deliverer; and spending the next hour telling me the different people he liked from the various pages after the front, I finally figured out what we needed to do that day.

"We need to get you an outfit for the Christmas party," I said with a smile as Henry's smile completely disappeared.

My back leaned against the tub as Henry took a bath. He thought the idea kind of girly, but Natalie said a hot bath after physical therapy was best recovery, so after a *no-discussion-face* from me, he relented. Thank goodness, he kept his boxers on.

"What?" he pretended not to hear me.

"Do I really have to be in here?" I whined back, my eyes wandering about the room trying to find something to do, and not really knowing what he was supposed to do in the bath. Didn't you just kind of sit and soak? The thought made me smirk.

"You wanted to tell me something," he reminded, flicking water against the back of my head, daring me to look his naked-chest way.

I held my urge to turn my head around. "Well, now you know." I started to rise from the floor, my hands using the tub for support when my foot slipped against a cool piece of tile.

Before I could crack my skull open against the hard rim, Henry grabbed my upper arms quickly, splashing soapy water everywhere. His fingers pressed into my skin as I tried to catch my breath.

"And I thought not taking a shower would avoid you falling, but I forgot, it's you we're talking about." He helped me steady to my feet before letting me go.

I grabbed nearby towels and began to soak up the wet floor, ignoring the tingling on my arm.

"I'll get out now," Henry said, "I don't want you leaving me in here to prune."

"Good." I smiled faintly, my hand pressing into my side, praying the throbbing pulse would cease. "That gives us plenty of time to shop for a new outfit." I took a sharp breath, a wince escaping me.

"What's wrong?"

"Nothing," I reassured. "Just a cramp."

"Get me some dry clothes," he ordered at once, authority in his voice.

"What? Why?"

"Because we're going to the hospital."

Chapter Sixty-Eight

I tapped my fingers against my protruding belly, the hospital gown the nurses forced me into stiff and cold.

So bored, I groaned for the third time in three minutes.

My gazed roved over to Henry, his own eyes guarded. "Don't look at me," he said. "It's not like I was concerned for your safety or anything. Besides, I didn't know they'd take forever."

It had been over thirty minutes since the doctor saw me, and no one came in with any news yet. Maybe this was when I should I have spoken up. We were alone, and Henry couldn't very well walk out on me.

No, I told myself, *now is not the time for confessions.*

One of my eyes narrowed, and the corner of my mouth pulled upward as an idea came. "I think you just didn't want to go shopping for a new outfit for the Christmas party."

"Prue, this is serious," he said, and I could see he meant it.

"Henry, it's nothing. I am sure of it."

But he wouldn't agree, and we waited the next ten minutes in heavy silence. Finally, the doctor who examined me after the car accident, walked in with a clipboard in his hands.

"Well," he said. "Everything looks good."

"It wasn't early labor?" Henry asked.

"No, just the twins having a little soccer match with mom's ribs." The doctor smiled warmly. "Your left side and two of your ribs are still bruised, and healing. Other than that, you are in perfect health."

"So, we're free to go?" I asked with pending joy.

"You're good to go."

I smiled, plopping down from the hospital bed and landing on my sock-covered feet. "Thank you, doc. If you don't mind, could you both give me some privacy while I put my clothes on?"

The doctor's face creased with slight confusion as my continuity broke, and his eyes said it all. *Why would a wife want her husband to leave the room while she changed?*

Henry cleared his throat, rescuing us. "She thinks she's fat, and doesn't like me to see her naked anymore." He gave a mischievous grin, and coolly rolled to my side before slapping my butt. "I keep telling her she's just as beautiful as the day we met."

My cheeks burned and I smacked his shoulder hard before I scooted toward the curtains.

"Still, sweetie," I said through clenched teeth, my head poking out of the curtain now. "I insist."

"I'll just leave you two alone." The doctor backed up slowly, and left.

I waited for the door to close and hurried to change into my jeans and sweatshirt. After I pulled off the gown, I realized I had left my pants at the foot of the bed, and only took my shirt.

My heart sank at the thought. "Will you throw me my

jeans?" *Why did Henry even have to be in here?*

"You mean these?" Henry chimed as his hand popped through the opening of the curtain, releasing a squeal out of me as he dangled the jeans like a treat.

"Henry!" I growled when I reached for them and he pulled back. I almost tripped on the smooth floor.

"Ah, ah," he toned teasingly. "What do you say?"

I gritted my teeth, the cold draft sinking in. "Would you *please* give me my pants?"

"Maybe I'll just come in instead?"

"No!" I shouted suddenly.

"Oh, come on," he continued playfully, but my burning cheeks would not cool. His free hand started to pull back the curtain and I freaked.

"Henry!" Nervous panic shook my chest. "I have never been naked, let alone in my underwear in front of a guy before, so please," I begged, "just give me my pants."

He threw over the jeans and they landed in a huff as complete silence remained on the other side of me. I stared at the curtain, barely grasping the low exhale from Henry as I quickly shuffled the pants on. I tried to recompose myself before walking out, and pulled back the curtain, expecting his slightly humored face. Instead, all I got was his back to me, shoulders hunched near the window, his head forward with forced focus.

"I'm sorry, Prue," he said, his voice low, and my ears were sensitive to the sound.

I shrugged my shoulder, not angry at his teasing, only flustered. "You were just teasing."

"It wasn't right. I shouldn't have done it, teased you like that." Henry turned and I saw grief in his eyes. "I keep forgetting . . . it's not appropriate."

"Then why did you do it?"

He opened his mouth to speak, like so many times before, but no words came. I took that as my invitation to draw closer.

Though I towered above him, I never felt so small. Never felt so vulnerable toward someone before, nor saw such of the same in his eyes, causing my heart to squeeze.

"We should probably go before it gets too late," he said.

I held the instinct to bite my lip, and only nodded in stiff response. Backing up slowly like the doctor had done, I broke eye contact as my gaze traced the floor, noticing a small smudge from a shoe, and off we went. Away from the unspoken words that so badly needed to be said—before everything between us would explode.

And I knew it would explode. It was just a matter of timing.

Timing, and gunpowder.

CHAPTER SIXTY-NINE

"I like it," I stated confidently in the clothing store, eyeing the sharply dressed man before me.

Jim turned around in a circle, and smiled. "I hope Evie likes it."

"Evie?" I inquired, my brow rising as I inspected an array of suits the shop owner brought out to us. I had pulled Jim from his own shop on the way to buy Henry a new suit, thinking Jim would most likely need one as well, and I was right.

Jim fiddled with his tie in the mirror, the ominous Henry in the background brooding like a child who didn't get his way.

"Yes. She asked me if I was going with anyone to the party and when I said no, she asked if would accompany her, and I said I would."

I beamed. "I should have seen that one coming," I chuckled to the grinning man, then looked behind me to Henry.

The night was already present through the store windows, and a few people I'd seen at church were spotted around, all the women getting their men to dress nicely for the Christmas party. I waved to a few passing by, their smiles genuine as they said hello to Henry.

"I don't know why they bother," he muttered, watching Jim and I before the mirror.

Jim laughed. "It's this girl you got, Henry—they take one look at her and know you're the lucky one. They only like you because of Prue."

I blushed, looking at Henry. "Aren't you going to try on a suit?"

His arms crossed and he looked at the garments with disdain. I didn't understand his dislike of dressing up, but figured it had something to do with the people he would be 'forced' to talk to while at the party.

"What's wrong with what I usually wear?" he asked.

"It's a party, you have to dress up."

"Conformist," he muttered, but I didn't respond.

"Prue?" Jim waved me over to his side and I quickly followed, helping him straighten his tie. "How about you take the car and go on home. Henry and I will find something for the party."

I was about to protest, but he spoke before I could.

"It will be a surprise," he said, and slowly I agreed, realizing this would be the only way Henry might wear a suit.

"It better be a suit," I warned as Henry handed me the car keys. It never occurred to me until now why he always managed to have them when it was I that drove.

"And nice. Not casual," I added.

Jim grinned, a twinkle in his eyes. "Go on, Prue. And don't worry, I will make sure it's just right."

Hours later, Henry entered the house, the rain outside subsided with barely a trace of its print on his shoulders.

"So, can I see it?" I asked peering at the black bag he held across his lap.

"Nope."

I frowned. "Why not?"

"Are you going to show me your dress?"

Not fair. I stood up from the couch. "I'm going to bed."

I heard his laugh as I reached the top step, the childish antics of my stomping feet having no effect on him. I made a point to pretend to be asleep when he came to check on me.

He only laughed harder.

CHAPTER SEVENTY

The day of the Christmas party came quickly, and I was enthralled with the spirit of Christmas as the townspeople filled the square with lights and decorated trees; the smell of holly filling every room. People with huge smiles and red noses from the cold wished Merry Christmas to everyone who passed them by.

I hadn't heard from Todd until that afternoon on my way out for Henry's physical therapy when a wrapped gift box was left at the door with his name on a small card.

I closed the door behind me and unwrapped the white paper as I walked toward the kitchen, Henry reading an article by *'Grandfather'* that had him chuckling every other second.

"What's so funny?" I asked, taking a seat next to him.

"Oh, he's just commenting on how drastic a holiday can change a person's priorities and differences. He made a comparison between the way children somehow are able to be more cunning, and parents—" Henry stopped talking at the sight of the box in my hands, and I froze under his scrutiny. "What's that?"

"Oh, it's just from Todd." My aloofness did not comply with the beating of my heart. I started to lift the lid, then shut it abruptly. "You know what, it doesn't matter." I discarded the gift at the end of the table with a good push and rose from my seat.

"Oh, come on," he said. "What did lover boy send you?"

"I'll just give it back to him at the party," I said from the living room, about to head up the stairs to start getting ready. I liked a few hours in advance to do my makeup, that way it would be easier to fix any mistakes with the added time.

Henry rolled behind me. "Why?"

"Because I don't want him thinking I like him in that way."

"What way?" he teased, but it came out like all of Henry's teasing. Completely serious with a very light edge of sarcasm. You could cut yourself with the sharpness. "I thought he made the right move."

I brushed Henry off. "I have to pee."

"Prue?"

My eyes closed at the sound of his voice, and I faced him with blatant honestly, knowing he still would not get it. I sighed. "You could have all the right moves, Henry, but that doesn't mean you fit the part. Why would I like Todd? I barely know him. He's a nice guy, but there's no connection. I don't know why you keep pursuing this topic."

I waited for his response, for his answer to my unquestioned question, but after a fifth second of nothing, I turned back on my heel, and kept going up the stairs.

Instead of taking a quick shower and readying my makeup, I stood stationary under the silky water. It helped calm me as I thought the past months over in my head. The different occurrences between the two of us—words exchanged, and others never given back. When I finally got out, the clock read four.

Natalie would be over by six with Jim and Evie; it was her idea for all of us to ride together, though Henry wasn't fond of a group. And I couldn't very well go downstairs looking like a hurried mess when Natalie got here, or else I would feel completely inferior without much effort on her part. No, I needed to prove to her that Henry and I . . . that we . . . that just because of my circumstance, it did not mean I was out of the competition.

An hour passed and I was applying my foundation when Henry rolled in, his hair disheveled, and still in his bathrobe, though I couldn't say much on that; I had on the gray robe since I got out of the shower.

"Can you hand me my razor," he said, not asked, as he shook a can of shaving cream in his hand.

I stopped my foundation sponge against my cheek, and turned toward him, a little shocked. "You're shaving?"

"You don't want me to?"

"No, it's just . . . ." I looked at his scruffy face—overly done five o'clock shadow needing attention—but I didn't want it completely gone. Or else, he would not be the Henry I knew. He would be the Henry from years ago . . . when she knew him. Clean shaven, younger, a stranger.

But I finally gave in. "Just do what you want, Henry. It will look great." I handed him his razor then looked again to the mirror.

I went back to my sponge and caressed my face roughly as I smoothed out the uneven tones. My hair was still up in curls, waiting to be let down, but I wanted Henry to leave first before revealing anything.

"I'll just use the other bathroom," he said.

"I thought it was broken?"

"I had someone come over and fix it while you were in the hospital. I guess I was running out of things to do."

"Why didn't you tell me?" I asked. "I could have been out of your way, and you could've had this bathroom to yourself. I don't want to be your way."

"No point," he replied. "Besides, the sink's lower in the other bathroom." And then he left, per his usual gusto.

I moved on to applying my eye shadow, doing a dark smoky eye and complimenting it with pale lip-gloss. The next hour passed in a breeze as I was struggling to finish my hair, all the while trying not to forget deodorant.

I had pulled out the curlers, and clipped my bangs to the sides, giving my face a clear perimeter. I could hear the others arriving downstairs, and scurried to get my dress from the other room, hidden from Henry. I pulled the purple fabric to my thighs, and a sweat threatened to break out across my forehead.

Dear God, please let it fit!

And yes! The dress shimmied over my protruded belly and clamped to my collarbone without fault. I smoothed out the bottom that flared down to my ankles and then paused, resting my hand against my stomach, feeling the life there, still amazed at how my own life turned out.

Hard to believe only months ago I was just a young woman strolling along. Hard to believe, just months ago, Hannah was alive. And now, I would soon be a mother.

I used to think I'd meet a boy in college, get married, buy a house, have kids. But I never went to college, I didn't even have a boyfriend, or my own house. Only the kids part came true so far.

Tears pricked my eyes suddenly and I dabbed them away so my mascara wouldn't run. Patting my belly once softly, I took a deep breath and faced the mirror.

The single strapped gown seemed to shine like water as it swept along my chest and stomach, the bottom fanning out to give my legs room to move.

I planned on quietly walking out, getting a first look of them, before introducing myself. If only the first step against the old stairs hadn't caused such a loud creak, then my plan would have worked.

Jim's eyes flew up toward me as he ceased his chatter with Evie, a smile across his face. He motioned to Henry, who didn't seem bothered by the sudden silence as he remained practically outside of the circle.

It all came down to this. The look in his eyes.

If only someone had prepared *me*, for his appearance.

Henry was so handsome—I thought it times before, but dressed up, it brought out the charm in his features.

He hadn't shaved. At least, not completely. A groomed shadow with bare hints of salt remained against his skin. He wore a suit, too. It made him all the more . . . I couldn't even think of a word, but my heart couldn't stop pounding loudly in my eardrums, and my hands were shaking.

I gripped the banister as I walked with care, but the entire time, Henry held my gaze. As I neared the bottom, he pushed his wheels and closed the gap between us. A sparkle lit his deep brown eyes, making my breath catch, and I wondered if this is what Jim had meant. I hoped so.

"You're beautiful, Prue," he said, and the word was clear to everyone. And even though Jim and Natalie knew Henry and I weren't really married, I could have sworn he was doing it all for Evie.

"You look pretty handsome yourself," I said, my free hand reaching out to caress his cheek, feeling the familiar scruff now sharpened. His chocolate eyes held me, and I didn't want his gaze to let me go. "I like what you did."

"Prue, you look so amazing!" Evie squealed, and Henry and I pulled away from each other, remembering who we were again. Scared. "Everyone will be in shock!"

"Thanks. I haven't had any opportunity to dress up, so I kind of went for the gold."

"You really look great, Prue," Natalie agreed, and I took in her attire. A tight pencil skirt and white blouse that matched well with her hair, down from its usual bun.

I forced a compliment out, feeling bad. "You as well." I quickly turned to Evie before she could pout at the lack of joy over her. "And I just love your dress!"

Evie beamed and gave a quick spin, her green-festive dress flowing in spite. She skipped to Jim, her black curls bouncing, and slipped her arm through his. "Are we ready to go?"

I nodded enthusiastically. The five of us turned toward the door and headed out, taking Jim's car that had the most seating. But as I went to help Henry into the passenger seat, he protested.

"I got it, Prue," he said. At the blatant look of hurt in my expression, he gave a reprieve. "I don't want you to tear your dress."

Evie patted the seat next to her, Natalie on the other side, and I tried to get in. It was a little difficult, what with me being hugely pregnant and wearing a dress I had no intention of tearing; besides, Henry's car was low enough all I had to do was slip in, with Jim's I had to climb a mountain.

Evie leaned forward and pulled my arm as I let her drag me in, and even Henry reached back his arm to make sure my legs were inside the car. I gave him a flickered glance, then turned to Evie as he let go and faced the windshield, not understanding at all his sudden change of attitude.

"I'm really glad Dr. Seymour is holding the party at his house this year," Evie chirped as Jim backed out of the drive. "He has the most room."

Oh great, I thought begrudgingly. *I shouldn't be surprised to get some looks from him—good thing they still enforce confidentially even in small places like this.*

"What are they serving?" Natalie asked politely, and I felt strange being in the same car with her, so close and us acting like nothing was strange. But I guess we had to keep up appearances for Evie, or else the whole town would know the truth.

"Oh, Christmas-type food. Ham, and all that."

Jim laughed at the wheel. "Nice description."

Evie grinned, her eyes shining even more whenever he spoke to her. I suddenly wondered how Natalie felt about the whole thing.

"Point is," Evie concluded, "Martha and I made the best pies, cakes and cookies! All shaped like gingerbread men, reindeer, ornaments, and other cute little things. Prue made something too!" She winked at me, and I nudged her arm.

"That's supposed to be a secret," I murmured.

"What did you make?" Jim asked, and I couldn't say no to him.

"Well, it's nothing spectacular. Just some homemade peanut butter cookies. I doubt they'll stand out at all against the Marthas' collection."

"No, they're really good, her secret is—" I elbowed Evie more firmly that time, eyeing her not to reveal my secret recipe.

She giggled with a mouthed *'oops'*, and changed the topic like the course of the wind. "There will be dancing too! I am so excited! You know how to dance, right James?"

The old man coughed out a laugh.

"Well, we shall see." She winked at me again. "Do you like to dance, Prue?"

"Uh," I stumbled over my words, Natalie watching me closely. "N-not really. I've never really danced before." *Or had someone to dance with,* I thought more sourly.

"Henry," she lashed out playfully, "you mean you never took her out dancing?"

Evie's careless question stilled the air in the car at once, and I knew she didn't mean anything by her words negatively. She was just excited over the coming party.

"Does it look like I can dance?" he remarked harshly, harsher than I think he realized, and I caught the sight of swelling tears in Evie's eyes.

"I only meant . . . ." She didn't finish her sentence, and it was clear she was hurt. I didn't know what was up with him tonight, he seemed fine earlier, but that was no excuse to be rude to Evie—the nicest girl in the world.

I patted her arm comfortingly. "Henry is just disappointed because he's not able to dance with me, *when in fact*, that is all he ever thinks about when we go out," I explained as my gaze travelled to the mirror of his opened visor. I got caught in his questioning stare, but continued talking, though only one person in the car wouldn't know it was pretend. "That's the second thing he wishes for, to dance with me."

"What's the first thing?" Evie's smile returned, her tears gone like yesterday. I kept contact with his eyes, another challenge coursing through me as they all waited for my answer.

My brow rose at Henry. "Only he knows that."

CHAPTER SEVENTY-ONE

Evie was right about Dr. Seymour's house having plenty of room for a party. The wide two-story estate was prim with kept flowers and fresh cut grass that managed to keep its green color in the winter month. The bare trees were strung with white lights as the house kept decorated beautifully in the spirit of Christmas.

We were greeted warmly by Dr. Seymour and his wife, the inside of the house a bustle of cheerful faces and crowded bodies, and an adjacent room full of gifts the people had brought. Longing tugged at my heart as I walked through the heated house full of friends, the homey atmosphere causing my eyes to water.

Henry kept up to my side as Natalie walked ahead, strangely out of place in a room of people she grew up with her whole life. Maybe that's what made her and Henry work so well. The idea sent a pang to my heart, but I quickly brushed off the feeling as I followed Evie to a spot on the couch, Henry pulling up to the armchair.

Others joined into the living room, filling up the various

chairs and love seats as fresh apple cider was passed around in chilled glasses.

I took a mug from Jim, who also handed one to Evie, and I wondered if this made him miss Laura more, miss Sylvia too, with everyone crowded together as a family. Natalie took a spot opposite us, Martha joining her as the nurse I vaguely remembered from Dr. Seymour's office rushed over to the middle of the room, facing us with a wide smile.

"All right now," she said loudly, and the others began to quiet, "you have to tell us the *whole* story of how you two met!" A chorus of agreements rang high.

Henry turned to me, disbelief clear in his brown eyes, then toward the nurse sitting next to Natalie and Martha. Jim watched us with detected humor, but I could tell Natalie found nothing of interest in our attention.

"Remind me again what Prue has told you so far?" Henry said, the kindness in his voice surprising me.

I jammed my elbow into his ribs as I kept a firm smile to my lips and eyes, his groan barely audible against the sudden stir of conversations between the guests.

"Well," Sarah, as I remembered her name, began, "Prue said that you two met in a hidden country, Bagheera, a little over a year ago where you saved her life, and then you got married, but it turned out the pastor wasn't legitimate, so you had to remarry in the states?"

Henry's hand clamped down on mine tightly. "I guess that sums it up."

"No way!" Evie cried out, her eyes aglow. "She never got to the part of *how* you saved her life, only that you *did*. We want the details!" The others nodded in agreement, and my shoulders shook with laughter.

"Yeah, Henry," I teased. "You tell the story best."

Another squeeze, but I didn't care.

Henry was holding my hand.

He let out a breath as his brain seemed to scramble for ideas, his eyes watching the people, then me, and back again. When he spoke, I saw why everyone loved him before.

You couldn't not listen to Henry speak, or tell a story. Though I doubted he saw it, he had eloquence, his words like honey and jasmine, and everyone wanted a taste.

"It's as Prue said. I was visiting the country because it's said they have the best medical doctors." Henry's crippled card worked brilliantly, a round of sympathetic nods occurring in response. "But you see, Prue had a little run-in with a local murderer the police could never put away because all their witnesses would end up dead before a trial could take place. She was their only hope at locking him up, but they had to catch him first, and they needed to keep her safe in the meantime."

I tensed beneath Henry's grip, the story too obvious, too blunt to not catch the details, and I wanted to jump up from the couch and run. But Henry's hand gave a softer squeeze, reassuring, and my breathing relaxed as I released my fist.

"So, they find me and at once she can't believe they expect a cripple to keep her safe!" He let out a laugh, one that carried across the room, and the others joined with ease. "You should have seen her face." He did a brief imitation of a *jaw-dropped-wide-eyed-deer*, and the crowd was rolling. "You would have thought they told her to marry me!"

I laughed too, watching him as he spoke, the center of positive attention for the first time in a long time. I was glad he held my hand.

"Was it love at first sight?" someone asked.

Henry balked. "Not for her! I mean, our first night she locks herself up in the room, and when we start to get along, she drops me down a flight of stairs!" Henry eyed me, a spark in his irises, as the others continued to laugh. "After a while we began to warm up to each other—and when the trial passed and it was time to go our separate ways—"

"But how did you save her life?"

Henry paused, grinning. "One day we went to the market and Prue just had to have a pomegranate. Well, the stand was full of at least a hundred of them, and of course, she had to grab from the bottom. The whole thing collapsed, and just before she could be pummeled, I grabbed her from the street and saved her life. Not that keeping her safe from murderers or anything was such a big enough deal." He shrugged, watching me then with a wide smile and I got a glimpse of the Henry they had known, now slightly changed.

"What did you do then?"

Henry's eyes didn't leave my face. "I thought I'd lose her, they had a plane ticket for both of us going two different ways. But she surprised me."

"How?" Evie squealed, wriggling with pure delight as the room seemed to quiet with bated breath.

"Tell them what you did, Prue," he challenged me softly. "Tell them what you said."

My smile fell.

He was going to make me say it first. So he wouldn't have to. So I would look like the foolish girl in love with her rescuer, and he would be exempt to admit anything for himself.

Well, I wasn't going to play that way.

"I have to go to the bathroom—you know, being pregnant and all," I said with a forced laugh. I rose from the couch, using both hands to help push my pregnant self up, and then Henry's hand pressed the small of my back, helping me. Tears stung my eyes, and I gave a polite smile to the crown before hurrying down the hallway in the wrong direction of the bathroom.

I hid for about ten or fifteen minutes, wondering what I should do.

I could leave now.

I banished the thought quickly, knowing that wasn't what I wanted. I knew what Henry had wanted me to say. It had to be it, what else was there? And why did he have to do that? In front of everyone? Did he truly want to embarrass me?

I splashed cold water on my face like they did in the movies during an intense scene, and regretted it at once, forgetting my mascara would run and people would think I was crying. I balled up some toilet paper and dabbed my face sporadically, soaking up the mess as my eyes continued to sting.

After one last look in the mirror, I left the bathroom and walked through the warm hallway, the sudden noise of cheerful voices jarring after the minutes of silence.

"Oh, Evie!" I called with a sigh of heavy relief, catching sight of her in the line for the food. She whipped around, cheeks flushed with heat that heightened with the close bodies and non-stop chatter. "Have you seen Henry?"

"Yeah, he and Nat went off somewhere—I think out on the back porch." She pointed to a screen door leading to the outside, my heart convulsing at her statement. I hurried on my way, my breath not able to catch up with me.

Outside the wind blew with a deep chill, the smell of coming rain evident in the air, filling my nostrils as the moon crept out after the slowing sunset.

Torchlights spread shadows over the lawn, and up ahead, beneath the veranda, stood the tall figure of Natalie next to the shortened Henry. I walked up to the white perimeter and crouched low, peering through the gaps in the wood.

"What are you saying, Natalie?" I heard Henry asked sharply as I tried to find his face.

Natalie spoke next, her back to me. "I know the others are buying into your fanatical story—but even if I didn't know the truth—I still wouldn't believe it. I would know something was up, and from the moment I met her, I knew something was up."

My calves began to burn, but I forced myself to remain still, wanting to know what the huge fuss was about.

"And?"

"And, Henry!" she snapped. "I know you are just doing your job, but don't tell me you actually have feelings for some pregnant girl."

"She is not just some pregnant girl, Natalie. She has been through a lot and I—"

"She loves you!"

My jaw dropped. *How dare she? That wasn't her right to tell him! It was mine!* My heart pounded, a ferocious lion in my chest, beat rapidly—and I almost stood, if it weren't for that dang curiosity.

"She loves you, Henry," Natalie said again more defiantly, grating my ears. "I can see it in her eyes, when you walk into the room she lights up. Not to mention—"

"What is your point, Natalie?" Henry asked. "Why does Prue bother you so much?"

Natalie crossed to the other side and I could see her profile, her trembling chin. That night I understood something more about her. That we were connected not just by loss, but by unrequited love as well. We knew how useless it was to fight things unattainable, and yet we kept kicking.

"Because I used to look at you that way. But I realize now, you're not the same Henry from high school who had every reason to leave this town. Now, you have a reason to stay."

"I told her I didn't notice her," he confessed suddenly, looking out toward the trees, his voice pure. "But that was a lie. I noticed everything. Her stubborn will to keep thoughts in, and her impulsive determination that never let her stay quiet for long. You're right when you say you saw how she looks at me, see how she feels for me. I wouldn't be surprised if it were true. Prue from the very beginning has been open. I think that's why so many people around here like her so much. She doesn't try to be something she's not. She reaches out into their world, and pulls them slowly into hers, she makes them feel important." He chuckled quietly, shaking his head, and my ears rang. "She made me feel important. I fought hard to keep her away, but she fought all the harder to break through my walls. And you know when they finally broke down?" he asked, turning his head toward her, but not waiting for an answer.

"When she came back. She said she wouldn't but she did. She could have left this place, left me when I promised nothing in return. She made me realize that not everyone wants something from you, Natalie. That sometimes people want to impart something inside of you that no one else can." He truly laughed. "That day she spilled soup all over me and then came walking in with *my* robe on—"

"Stop it!" Natalie screamed and I jumped, almost falling on my butt. "Just stop it!"

Henry looked at her, his brows sharp. "Why?"

"That's when you saw her? About the second week she was here? What about me, Henry! What about when *I* turned *my* back on the scholarship that would take me away from here? The day I found out my baby sister was dead because of you was the day my life ended too." She glared at him, a wild dog. "I stayed here. I stayed here for my father. We lost my mother, we lost my sister, and I stayed here. I hated it here, Henry! You knew that and yet you decided you didn't want to leave anymore. Until the fight with my father and you took Sylvia away from us—then you wanted to leave. And we never saw her again!"

"I'm sorry, Natalie," he said. "I was angry. You rejected me, and Sylvia stepped in. I shouldn't have left like I did, I shouldn't have made Sylvia leave without saying goodbye."

"Without coming back," Natalie spat.

"Please, hate me what for I did, but don't take it out on Prue, she doesn't deserve that." His shoulders were slumped, defeat weighing him down. After a pause, he added, "It still doesn't answer why you dislike her so much. She did nothing wrong to you."

"That's not the point," she said. "You should be miserable, Henry. You should suffer because of what you did to my sister, to this town, to my father. Besides," she quieted an octave, "it would never work between you and Prue, anyway."

"Why is that?" he challenged, making my heart soar, only for her next words to pull me back down.

"Because all you see is Sylvia."

CHAPTER SEVENTY-TWO

"Natalie, wait!" I hollered after the defiant woman storming across the lawn toward the house. I caught up to her before she could enter the party, and she turned to me, her eyes watery and red.

"Well, you heard everything. He thinks he's in love with you. Just don't expect him to admit it."

"I'm so sorry, Natalie," I said, ignoring her comment. "It was wrong of me to treat you—"

"Now you think we're connected? Now we have something to unite us? Love for a man who will never love someone back. Isn't capable of doing so." She dropped her arm that held her shoes, scoffing. "We have nothing in common." She pulled back the screen door.

"I understand what it is like to make choices you never thought you'd have to make," I said, "because of sudden circumstances. My sister couldn't have children, so I gave her my womb, and you're sister died, so you stayed behind. I mean, look at us." I half-laughed. "We try to be these people, people who are unaffected by the chaotic world around them. People that don't bleed because we made the choice not too."

"What's your point?" she said.

"We don't have to be these people anymore. Henry doesn't have to be a widower stuck in a chair for the rest of his life; you don't have to be the sister who did what she thought was right by staying here and ending up stuck in the process; and I don't have to pretend to be strong as I live the rest of my life as a single mother without her big sister around to help," I said. "We don't have to be these people, Natalie."

"You're wrong, Prue," she said, and tears fell from her eyes. "We do."

"My sister was the oldest, so all she ever did was bail me out—even when she was the one to put me there in the first place. She mediated every time it was me against my parents, or me against the world. That is what the older sibling does, they make up for the younger, protect them, step in when they can't—things that you did for Sylvia." I paused, praying my words were helping. "You picked up the pieces of her death and tried so hard to put them back together. To fix the broken vase before mom and dad got home. But she's gone, Natalie," I said, tears spilling from my own eyes. "So you don't have to do anything else. There isn't anyone to blame anymore, to do that for now. You must go on with your life and be happy, because if you are not happy, then . . . what is the point? Sylvia would want you to go after your dreams, not stay behind reliving her nightmare."

A long moment of silence played, Natalie not moving one muscle. But after that long moment, her head raised a little, and it was as if a weight had been lifted from her shoulders. "I'm not sure he loves you, Prue," she said.

I licked my lips, and spoke with confidence. "That's okay."

"You are right when you said Sylvia would want me to live. She'd want me to follow my dreams, fulfill my own plans." She choked back a sob. "But what about my father? What will he do? I have been here so long, I can't just leave."

"Jim will understand," I said. "It hurts him more to see how hard you try, when you he knows you aren't really happy here, don't you think?"

"Yeah," she said, and an icy laugh escaped her. "You're right again. So right." She stepped into the house, barefoot and exhausted, leaving me to the outside.

I watched as she quietly entered the crowd to find Evie who wanted her to dance at least one song before going. An hour later, she would be on the red-eye to New Jersey, a simple note left for Jim on his shop door found the next morning. But that was tomorrow, and the voice behind me was from tonight.

"Prue?"

I turned to Todd with ease, giving nothing away, though I hoped it was someone else. He smiled, and I took his offered hand as he led me inside the house, a warm smile on his face. "Care to dance?"

"I don't really know how to dance," I said.

He motioned toward the moving crowd. "I'll teach you."

Five minutes later, I was doing something with my arms and legs that might have resembled a dancing toddler; still, it was fun. Evie hopped to my side, Natalie next to her smiling with a red nose and enjoying herself, and I knew we would be okay. Todd spun me around twice, the third time making me want to puke with laughter. But in the corner of my eye, I caught Henry's attention as he rolled into the house from the yard, a solemn look on his face.

I stopped and told Todd I needed a breather, and he agreed to get me a drink as I made my way to Henry's side,

303

and took a seat near him on the couch.

"What are you up to?" I asked, my focus to the dancing crowd.

"I can't dance, Prue," he stated, his brown eyes roaming into mine as I turned my head to him. "If that is what you are asking. This isn't like swimming."

"I know," I said. "But we can listen to the music."

"You don't have to miss out because of me," he said. "Go have fun."

Before I could protest, Todd came over with a cup of lemonade Martha had made from lemons and berries, and handed it to me.

"Thank you," I said, sipping the iced drink.

"Ready for another dance?" he asked.

"No," I smiled, leaning comfortably against the couch as my eyes stayed with Evie and Jim dancing. Boldly, I placed my hand atop Henry's. "I'm just going to sit here and watch."

CHAPTER SEVENTY-THREE

Henry and I stayed in good spirits as we made our way to the lake house, rain patting against the windshield in a soft lullaby. It heightened everything, the chill of the air, the swirling clouds in the sky. It made me feel like being bold.

"It wasn't that bad, now was it?" I said, smiling, Jim and Evie quiet in the front seats.

"It could have been worse," he murmured, then eyed me. "And you seemed happy there, with everyone."

We reached the lake house, the moon casting enough light to see through the trees and to the porch.

"I am happy," I said, getting out the car to help him.

I swung the wheelchair to his side and he hopped into the seat with some ease and little strain. We managed up the porch steps, waving goodbye to the two others in car, and Henry unlocked the front door. My heart pounded loudly inside my chest as I followed behind him into the chilled house, my resolve waning.

"Henry," I said almost inaudibly, my throat dry, and he didn't hear me.

He dropped his keys, always seeming to end up in his hand, and hung his jacket in the downstairs closet. "I think my story was pretty good at the party—believable."

"Henry," I said more loudly, my hands balling into fists as my legs itched to run from here. He turned my way, a relaxed smile to his lips, and I almost couldn't do it, but did. "I looked in the box."

His eyes, once light, suddenly narrowed and he glared at me with a vengeance. His voice held no kindness. "What did you do?"

"I—I saw the pictures of Sylvia. She was pregnant. You gave her slippers for Mother's Day because her feet were swollen." Even now I recalled the picture of Henry, smiling, as he held Sylvia close, his hands on her growing belly. It caused a deep ache inside my chest.

I took a step closer to him as he continued to stare at me with hatred, his eyes angry with tears.

"W-was this a mistake, Henry?" I asked. "Was me coming back, wrong? Please tell me . . . was this a mistake?"

"You had no right!" he yelled, whipping around his chair toward the kitchen. But I followed.

"Natalie said you didn't love me. That all you saw was Sylvia. Is that true? Is she all you see when you look at me?"

He turned to face me, the sharp line of his mouth meant to scare me off. But my body moved with what my heart wanted and not what my mind fought against as my palms planted firmly on the arms of his chair, and I leaned down so that our eyes were level.

We were so very close as his dark gaze looked into mine, our noses but an inch apart. I tried not to think about how insane I was being.

"Tell me that you see me, through all the gloom of your world, tell me that I am the clearest." His mouth twitched, causing my heart to stop mid-race, and I dared to ask such a risky request. "Be the boy who kisses me first."

He stared at me, his brown eyes hard and unyielding. But I knew his heart had to be thinking something—this couldn't be for nothing—could it?

"What you heard between me and Natalie wasn't what you think," he said, his eyes moving back forth against mine, his voice low. "I don't want this Prue."

Ouch.

That hurt more then I let myself believe. It knocked the tears out of me and they slipped down my cheeks as I released my grip from his chair. *How foolish I had been to think . . . to even hope.*

I closed my eyes, taking a step back as my heart slowly crushed inside my chest with nowhere for the fragments to fall. Breathing was difficult. I didn't know heartbreak caused your lungs to collapse.

"Think about it, Prue," Henry protested, getting louder. "Look at our circumstance. I'm twice your age, the children inside of you aren't even mine. Aren't even yours."

I was in a daze. *How could I have been so wrong? No, I had to be right.* I knew it. I knew it like some people knew the weather, ever changing.

"You're not twice my age," I said, opening my eyes, and wished he would just be honest.

"And you're not going to win this one, Prue."

"There is something about us. I feel it, deep inside my heart. Don't you?"

"I feel nothing."

Heat burned in my chest then, and I grabbed his hand and pulled it to my belly.

"Do you feel that?" I said. "Do you feel them kicking inside of me? It happens whenever you laugh, when you touch me.

When you make me feel like I've never felt before. They know you, Henry. *They know you.*"

The brown eyes so easily lost, fled to my hold with amazement. I felt pressure applied from his palm as he felt the miracles thudding inside me. But all too quickly, he dropped his hand, and the vacancy was like a knife in my chest.

"I'm sorry, Prue."

I took his face in my hands boldly, feeling the warmth of his cheeks. "Don't make me say it first, Henry," I said, my eyes filling with more water. "Don't."

"Say what?" he replied, taking hold of my wrists and we were locked together, neither one of us daring to give in or give up. "Don't be so vague."

But I was first to let go.

My hands slid from his rough cheeks, and I knew my eyes flickered defeat. If only he hadn't held my wrists seconds after my withdrawal, hadn't stared moments longer into my eyes. Because he did it again. If he would have just dropped my hands like the very nothing he said was between us, then I would have no longer been stuck. Because now when I stepped away, my heart stayed with him.

I ran up the stairs and into my room. I pulled off my dress, undid my hair, pulled it into a ponytail, grabbed jeans from the drawer, pulling them on, and dragged a shirt over my head before taking my jacket and heading back downstairs. I slipped into my sneakers, ignoring Henry who remained in his spot in the kitchen, and hurried to the front door.

"Where are you going?" he asked as my foot hit the front porch, water rushing from the roof in a flood as the rain grew heavier by the second. A cold wind blew, chilling my skin, and I zipped the jacket higher.

"I can't stay here," I cried as I gasped for breath. "I need to be alone."

"It's pouring outside."

"Any other reason?" I said, then turned toward him when he didn't respond. I let out a deep breath before speaking, "Let me just say this, so that I am not too vague. I love you Henry. I don't care how old you are, or that the children inside me aren't yours. I don't care that you're crippled. I just want to spend the rest of my life with you. And I don't care if you feel the same way, because that's what love does, Henry. It forces us to be selfless. It forces us to give up everything and face the truth. True love doesn't know how to be any other way."

I turned back to the pouring rain, my hand gripping the doorframe for support, the other on my stomach.

"When I came here I was broken, and so were you." I glanced back a final time, not strong enough to completely let go just yet. "But as you can see . . . *something* put us back together. Because I'm not broken anymore."

"If you knew the truth," he murmured like a shadow in the wings. "You would take it all back."

Every fiber within me called to know what he meant, but another part, somewhere in align with the back of my thoughts and the shudder of my heart, did not . . . was afraid to know. So I ran.

CHAPTER SEVENTY-FOUR

I was drenched by the time I stumbled onto the shore of the lake, my jacket clinging to me as my hair stuck to the sides of my face. The moon lit up the woods around me as I laid against the ebony rock near the crashed waves. I curled onto the slick surface as I let myself cry, my heart beating with pain, and my face heated with rejection.

Could I have been so foolish? I asked myself again through the drumming rain, the small drops of icy liquid a smooth caress to my wounded soul. *Did I imagine everything? Did his words to Natalie mean nothing? And the box—why did I have to look? Why did I have to know? Could all of this been avoided, could he have still fallen in love—no, no.* No.

My face kept pressed against the cold surface of the rock as I took deep breaths, trying to still my gasps.

"You would be so mad at me, Hannah," I chuckled pitifully. "You would say I shouldn't be out in the rain like this, let alone pregnant with your children. How reckless of me. But you aren't here, Hannah. You aren't here to pick me up and tell me that it will be okay. You're not here." I cried, my shoulders shaking with sobs.

I closed my eyes and bit my lip. I knew I would have to go back, that I was acting like a child, and this was no good example to anyone. But I didn't care—who said I was good? Who said I was perfect? Not me.

Someone called my name from miles away.

Again.

And.

Again.

I tried to ignore the puncturing sound, but such a thing would not relent.

"Prue!"

I had to open my eyes to believe it to be true. I lifted myself from the rock and planted my feet firmly against the uneven ground as icy waves broke against my heels.

"Come back!" Henry said. There was about ten feet between us and I wasn't about to step forward.

"Why?" I countered.

Rain poured down his face, his clothes soaked. "I lost Sylvia to a fight. I can't lose you too."

"That is all you see when you look at me, isn't it?" I said, trying to figure out the best way of accepting such a hard fact.

"No," he said, shaking his head and his eyes stared hard into mine as he came closer, the brown irises vibrant with plea. "It isn't like that."

"Then what is it like, Henry?" I snapped, and when he had no reply, I turned away.

"You are the clearest thing I see, Prue!"

I stopped cold as warmth forced itself into my chest with his words. "Through all the gloom, you gave me light. It was my fault Sylvia died. Five months into her pregnancy, she miscarried. I was so angry at God and at her. She got counseling from our pastor and improved while I sank deeper. We fought constantly, and one night she left. She was coming back here to live with Jim and Natalie. But she must have changed her mind; she was on her way back when the driver hit her." His voice broke, competing with the rain, and I strained to hear his next words. "When *I* hit her."

The blood drained from my body as I faced him again, seeing the truth. Seeing why he had been so broken, so hard, dripping with self-hatred. Finally, I understood—understood where all the true grief came from, why the people in the town—and Natalie—said he was the one who killed her.

He was.

"I killed her, Prue," he sobbed, looking down. "I said it was a drunk driver, but I lied. I wasn't drunk. I went speeding after Sylvia when I found out she left. I was so mad. I wasn't paying attention and the bridge was full of traffic." Henry paused, breathing hard. "I couldn't believe I hit someone and when I got out of the car, I realized who it was . . . I jumped in the canal after her, the vehicle was filled with water—but she was too far under, I was too late. And then cops pulled me out when the pipe struck me."

His sobs subsided, hardness taking place. "The judge didn't even convict me—Sylvia was the only casualty. And I was a cop, we had history. They wouldn't put me in jail even though I deserved it! I told them I was reckless but they didn't listen!" His fists balled up in anger. "I deserved death, and they let me go free!"

"Henry," I cried, closing the gap between us. My hands cupped his face as his eyes shied from mine. "I am so sorry."

"You say you love me Prue, but how can you now knowing I killed my wife? Knowing it was my fault she died?"

"Because I love you, Henry," I said, pulling him to face me. "And God loves you too. He wants to free you of this pain. He knows it was an accident, He knows you are sorry for what happened. He forgives you, Henry. You just have to accept that."

"The hardest part," he said weakly, "Trusting someone other than yourself. Trusting God when you don't see Him. Trusting God when you don't deserve it."

"None of us deserve it," I said.

The pattering rain filled the following silence, and I began to wonder if maybe the only reason God brought me into Henry's life was to help reconnect him to Him. Maybe not so I could fall in love, perhaps that was my human mistake. Maybe I was just to show Henry that there is hope in chaos, there is light in darkness—you've just got to open up your eyes and look for it. You have to seek to find.

"You trust me, don't you?" I asked. "And I trust God. You can trust me, and you can trust Him. I may make mistakes but He doesn't."

His jaw moved in my grip as he spoke. "That's the problem, Prue. I started to trust you, and the more I trusted you, the more I forgave myself, and I couldn't—I just couldn't let myself get off so easy. I deserve to be unhappy, but with you . . . it's impossible."

I pushed aside all theories of us not falling in love and being together. I knew deep inside of me that I was made for this man, and he was made for me.

"Then why did you come after me, Henry?" I said. Another challenge, and the last one.

His eyes stared into mine, and for a moment, I thought I was imagining his hand touching my face.

"Do you love me, Henry?" I asked, searching his face for a sign. The pressure of his hand against my cheek pulled me closer, confirming this was reality.

"I love you," he said, and without second hesitation, his mouth touched mine as he made the first move.

Heat blasted through my skin, exiting my pores with a hot flush. Rain continued to pour, soaking my clothes, and I started slipping in the soft sand. Henry pulled me closer, and I couldn't breathe.

I didn't know what the heck I was doing. I always looked away in the movie theatres when the couple kissed, and was starting to regret that. *Would if I was making a complete fool of myself again?*

"Stop thinking," Henry murmured during a brief breath as I pulled away, embarrassed. He tugged me close again, the world around me dark as I kept my eyes closed. Somehow he got me sitting on his lap, and I smiled at his enthusiasm though my cheeks burned even brighter, but Henry didn't seem hindered by my inexperience.

He pulled back and his hand caressed my cheek, his eyes holding my gaze. I couldn't believe this was happening, and yet, here we were. Two people once connected by tragedy now connected by . . . love.

Love? He loved me. Henry loved me?

Henry chuckled, pulling my face close to his again. "What is going on in that head of yours? I've never seen you this quiet—it's a new record."

My mouth rose in a smile, my heart beating fast. No words could come, my thoughts unable to travel from my mind to my mouth. I think shock had momentarily stopped the nerves from connecting. You're not supposed to shock a person whose heart is still beating. But I didn't care. I would risk electricity for Henry to kiss me again.

When his lips touched mine once more, I realized Henry felt the same.

CHAPTER SEVENTY-FIVE

I made it all the way down the stairs and into the kitchen the next morning without a problem. Pancakes with peanut butter and fresh cold milk with a glass of water waited for me and I sat down without a word as Henry read his newspaper with diligence. Only when I grabbed the glass of water to drink, did I lose control, and giggled.

Henry peeked from the side of his paper, and a deep blush burned my cheeks as another, louder, giggle escaped. His face seemed to redden as well and he chuckled.

"What?" I asked.

He coughed. "The comics are good today."

"Mhmmm." A grin burst through my lips, and I was having trouble controlling myself again. Henry slid his paper to the side, revealing his contemplative face, and I bit my lower lip as a snort let out ridiculously.

"Well, last night was embarrassing," I said.

His brows flickered to an almost furrow, but I could tell the difference in his features. Happiness was there. "Why?"

"*Well*," I said again with a shorter pause. "First, you kiss me, which was an embarrassment of its own on my part, and then, you sleep on the couch before I even head upstairs."

"I thought it best."

"Really?" I laughed, my chin now in my hand.

"You know, you losing control and all." He smiled, and a spark kept to his eyes as he sipped his coffee.

"Yeah, right."

He shrugged as he tried to return to his paper. If only that had worked. His eyes darted to mine soon enough.

"You're staring," he said, and yet there was still that edge of happiness again.

"No, I'm not," I lied uselessly, and tried to focus on Sheridan dozing against my leg. Her stomach was getting so huge.

Henry set the paper down for good. "Come here," he said, rolling out from beneath the table.

I took a deep breath, not sure if he was about to tell me how stupid I was for believing all of last night—that the kiss was a mistake, or just sucked.

That would be really embarrassing. My face was already burning before he could say anything else.

"You're not just grinning because you are happy," he said. "You are really embarrassed by this."

"Not because of you," I said quickly, "But because of me."

"What? Prue—"

"Look," I said. "I have never done this before. Had a—" I stopped before the word *boyfriend* could escape and make me feel even worse at any sign of rejection. "Kiss."

Then again, hadn't we said we loved each other? Ugh.

Henry's brown eyes studied me, and then he said in complete seriousness. "Kiss me."

"What?" I freaked. "No!"

He waited, relaxed with a hidden smirk beneath his

316

serious façade, making his lips all the more appealing as my own mouth tingled with memory. My mind and my heart were at war again.

I didn't make a move and he sighed, leaning forward, only inches between us. "Is this better for you?" A smile then bloomed on his face. "Or did you like the challenge?"

I rolled my eyes, trying not to notice the grin that forced its way up to my lips. I couldn't deny the leap in my chest, or the adrenaline pumping through my veins, shortening my breath.

"Why are you doing this?" I asked.

He grinned. "Practice makes perfect."

"Is that you saying I did it wrong?" I felt the color burning on my face, and I wanted to run and hide in my room.

"No," he groaned, his brows pulled together in sincerity. "It was a joke. Now, come on, kiss me. I'm waiting."

"Are you going to keep your eyes open the entire time?" I asked, my voice higher than usual.

His eyes suddenly closed as a smirk played his features. It didn't help my nerves any.

My palms were sweaty against my thighs as I leaned in close, my butt rising from the chair, and I tried not to breathe, my mouth parallel to his.

Could he hear the pounding of my heart? I wondered. *Did he see how terrified I was of making a fool of myself again?*

"Don't do that," he said, his eyes opening as I inched further away. "Don't be self-conscious." He started to draw me close again, when I went for it.

I felt his surprised reaction against my lips. I wasn't sure if I was breathing yet, and his response made me even more panicked. *Henry was kissing me back!*

What was I supposed to do now? Last night I was swept up in euphoria, but now reality had its day, no smoke, no mirrors—just us, vulnerable in daylight.

Fear rose in my thoughts as I struggled to stop worrying as well as make sure I was doing it right. It was a wonder I didn't go into anaphylactic shock. His hands slid to my sides, my protruding stomach a barrier he didn't mind.

"Remember," Henry teased, his brown eyes glancing into mine. "Don't think."

And for the first time in months, I listened.

CHAPTER SEVENTY-SIX

The bell on Jim's shop door announced our arrival. Henry and I kept close as we followed Sheridan's wagging tail toward the counter where three iced cokes awaited, unopened.

"Good afternoon." Jim smiled to us, popping open one bottle after the other. He handed me the first, then one to Henry, and we drank obligingly, an odd and awkward silence taking place.

Jim eyed us, but then said, "Natalie left a note for me last night."

Did she take what I said to heart? I wondered. I prayed Jim wouldn't hate me for it.

The older man sighed, seemingly too tired for this world. "She said she was sorry for the sudden departure, but that she knew the both of us needed it. She said she only wanted to fix what had happened and finally realized it was impossible, and now she needed to live her life instead of Sylvia's death."

Henry winced next to me. "I'm sorry, James."

"I still have you two to keep me breathing." He grinned, then faltered, "at least until you have to leave."

Suddenly all went silent, and I took a hesitant sip of fizzy coke, my eyes darting quickly to Henry who seemed to want to keep a low profile.

"What is with you two?" Jim's eyes narrowed. "Huh?"

My cheeks burned, and I bit my lip as I smiled in spite of Henry's shifting gaze. Somewhere, Sheridan was sniffing the floor.

"Henry?"

A smile edged the corners of his mouth, but other than that, he gave nothing away, though everything to me felt so very clear. "James?" he said.

Jim's eyes zeroed in on me and my giggle sealed the deal.

"Hmmm?" I hummed, shaking with laughter.

"Well," Henry feigned a sigh. "We have to take Sheridan to the vet." He turned his wheels toward the door, but Jim wasn't about to give up without an honest answer.

"Henry—"

"We'll talk tomorrow, James." Henry waved as he reached for the door, holding it open as he waited for me.

I thanked Jim for the cokes, giving a soft smile, then whistled for Sheridan to follow. I could hear Jim's laughter even after the shop door shut, and the response caused Henry and I to lose all restrain.

The wind was cold and refreshing as I walked, and Henry strolled, across the pavement, our breaths coming out in white puffs. Sheridan wagged her tail merrily beside us.

"We're just going to the vet, right? No other errands?" he asked, and his calm, languid exterior did not match his voice one bit.

"Yeah, why?" I asked, wondering what was up his sleeve.

"Just tired."

"Oh, well it shouldn't take long. He just wants to check her progress."

We reached the small building and I pulled open the door for all three of us. After a ten minute wait, we were led into a room where Sheridan's vet arrived.

"Congratulations, folks," he said after the examination. "Sheridan should be due within just a few days."

Henry's face fell at once and he turned pale. "Few days?"

"Yes, and I would guess at least three pups."

"Three?" Henry seemed ready to pass out, but I squeezed his hand, grinning inside.

"Now, to be on the safe side, I would recommend keeping Sheridan here for observation for about a week, just in case she gives birth earlier than expected. But, if you would rather have her with you, then that's fine too. Just bring her by when she starts acting funny."

I looked Henry, waited for his eyes to meet mine, and whispered, "Do you think we should keep her here?"

Slowly, color returned to his cheeks, and he blinked for the first time in the passing seconds. "I—"

"It is probably best, Mr. and Mrs. Clay, if Sheridan stays here. She could have them today for all we know. Plus, given her earlier health situation, I would feel better about it."

That settled it with Henry. He told the vet to make a room for her, paying up front even, and I was given only a few minutes to say goodbye.

I rubbed her jaw, scratched inside her ears just like she liked with my knuckles, and kissed her scalp a thousand times before she nuzzled away, but not before licking my cheek for comfort. However, it wasn't my goodbye she truly wanted.

"Henry," I grinned as he tried to sneak into the waiting room. "She wants you."

He came to a stop and sighed, my cue to let her free. Sheridan, with complete restrain, walked up to Henry and with a sudden jump, rested her white paws on his motionless legs, her nose reaching for his.

Unbelievably, Henry gave her what she wanted. His hands cupped her face, massaging her cheeks roughly like she loved, and rubbed his nose against her wet snout, whispering his goodbye. I remembered the way he held her when she was sick, and my heart melted even more.

It was hard leaving. Hard, saying *'see you later'*. Especially when you knew how it felt to have to truly say goodbye.

"Ready to go home?" Henry asked once outside the vet building.

I nodded my head with light surrender, but was cut off by an interloper.

"Prue!" Todd called, jogging toward us until stopping at my side, his breathing rattled. "Hey," he said.

"Hey," Henry toned, not quite sure what the deal was, obviously. I only smiled.

"I'm glad I caught up with you," Todd continued, taking deeper breaths. "I didn't get a chance to really talk after the party. I wanted to know if you opened my present yet." His eyes found mine easily.

"No, not yet. Actually I—"

"She wanted to tell you that she couldn't accept it," Henry blurted, and I glared in his direction, but his features were controlled, and arms crossed.

"I think she can make that decision on her own, Chief," Todd retorted.

"Todd, can I talk to you for a moment?" I said. He nodded and we stepped toward the car before Henry could protest.

"Look, Todd I—"

"Don't let him control you, Prue."

"Can I just say something without being interrupted, please?" I groaned, and Henry's chuckle in the background was evident to all. "Todd, I want you to know that I appreciate what you have done for me, and the time we did spend together, but—"

"But Henry finally gave you what you wanted?" he said, and the bitter edge made my stomach ache.

"No," I said, crossing my arms, completely offended. "I just don't like you in that way, and I don't want to hurt you, but you need to know the truth."

Todd's jaw clenched as hot air blew from his nostrils, but it seemed to help calm him down. "I'm sorry," he said, looking to the concrete. "From now on, I'll just come by for doctor visits, and that's it."

"Thank you," I agreed, giving a small smile, but his face kept its hard surface and I knew that it was my time to leave. But when my back turned on him, a chill ran up my spine and I had to shake the feeling off before Henry noted anything.

"Prue," Todd said, and I froze, listening. "Keep the gift."

I gave one more nod, and went my way, feeling his eyes on me the entire time, and hoping I had not just caused a permanent rift between the two waging men, though I doubted there ever was peace to begin with.

CHAPTER SEVENTY-SEVEN

"Why are you so ready to get home?" I asked Henry once inside the car and on our way to the house.

"Three's a crowd," he said and I wondered how much longer his mood would go on. *Didn't he realize by now that I liked—loved him?* My heart leaped at the thought.

I smiled. "I did not think you could get jealous, Officer Clay. After all, you did say when it came to *me*, I had nothing to worry about you being jealous." I waited for his smart reply with open ears, but I was deeply surprised.

"I was wrong," he said, and my eyes flickered toward him for the briefest of moments, catching the raw stare in his gaze.

I coughed, not knowing of any other way to respond; his words were so matter-of-fact. Thankfully, we both kept quiet until reaching the house.

But once we got onto the porch, Henry slid me onto his lap and I started laughing. "What are you doing?"

He smiled and wrapped my arms around his neck before kissing me on the lips, and I had to hold back my squeal of excitement as he rolled us into the house.

"What is wrong with you?" I asked playfully as we entered the kitchen, the open windows letting in rain-filled air.

When he continued to remain silent, I pressed a different issue. "Why did you wait until after we left town to kiss me? Hmmm? Are you ever going to kiss me in public?"

His eyes wouldn't meet mine and he said, "Remember when I told you, you owed me for getting chocolate all over my pants?"

"Yeah?" I chuckled.

"Well, I finally thought of something good."

A knock came at the door and he let out a loud sigh that was more of a growl. "You know, ever since you came here, I have gotten more visitors than I care to count."

My smile widened and I boldly kissed his cheek before getting up to answer the door. More knocks continued as I reached for the knob, and I was quickly faced with a very flustered Evie.

"Evie? What are you doing here? Is something wrong?"

A huge smile lifted her face. "I know it's an odd time, but Martha and I have something to show you that cannot wait!"

I glanced to Henry, asking. He muffled an annoyed groan, then came into Evie's view.

"Oh, hey Henry," she said.

He only nodded at her gesture, then looked back up to me. "I need to make a phone call anyway," he said with no enthusiasm, and reminded me more of a deflated balloon.

With that note, Evie whipped around and headed for her car. It took me only a second to see the shaded figure in the passenger seat, and my skin prickled.

"Is that Todd?" I whispered as Evie hurried to her car, starting up the engine.

"Something is up with him," Henry said, causing my heart

to go into panic mode. I moved in front of him so that my back would block both of our faces and moving lips. Henry looked at me intently. "I am going to call Brandon and make him do a full background check on his whole family."

"You don't think . . . ." I couldn't even finish my thought, I turned so cold.

"I don't know, Prue," Henry shook his head. "He could be perfectly innocent—he is your doctor after all—who just so happens to be in love with you." I couldn't tell if he was trying to make me feel better or worse. "But I'm still going to check it out."

"Maybe we shouldn't go," I mumbled, anxious to even turn back around.

Would if Henry was right about Todd acting weird? What could it mean?

"No, that would be too suspicious. We need to act normal."

I chewed my lip, a shiver coming with the wind, and took a deep breath for courage. Henry reached up and grabbed the sides of my face, drawing me down to his lips to plant a light kiss on my mouth. But I wasn't about to count that as a real kiss in public. After all, my pregnant self was covering the whole show.

My worries lightened a little as I hopped into the car, helping Henry along the way.

"Hey, Prue, Henry," Todd said, all smiles. "Guess what?"

"What?" Henry and I asked at the same time.

"You're going to be parents!"

CHAPTER SEVENTY-EIGHT

Henry and I rushed into the appointed room with held breaths, our hearts pounding in heavy rhythm as I led the way and he chased after. Evie called after me down the hallway as she tried to catch up—but I wasn't missing this for the world.

Almost an hour later, and squeals of joy from both Evie and me, Sheridan gave birth.

Three beautiful and sleepy puppies cradled against Sheridan as they drank her milk with the idea of never eating again. The two females were the exact image of their mother; pure black with scarves of white; and the small male was what the vet called a Merle Blue Border Collie with black, blue and gray colors patched together on his face and back. He said he must have gotten if from the father, and I grinned at Henry.

"Sheridan and I have something in common, then." I laughed, staring down at the beautiful pups, Evie to my right and Henry to my left.

"What?" Henry said.

I giggled. "We like our men rugged."

Evie laughed and even Henry's frown lines twisted up into a grin with a shine to his brown eyes.

The vet told us we could take them home in a few days, and Henry wanted to get a dog bed and other supplies the vet recommended. I scratched behind Sheridan's ear, missing her even more, and she looked up at me with her soft eyes, a new wisdom in her irises I hoped one day I would retain. I cradled my belly as we left our little family of four.

"What are you thinking about?" Henry asked.

"Seeing Sheridan give birth, and seeing her pups, makes me think of our future." I spoke without thinking, and caught myself on the last two words. "The babies and me," I whispered just low enough for only Henry to hear.

We said we loved each other, I thought to myself, *but what did that mean when reality came and I had to go back to Arizona? Did I have to go? What did Henry think? When could I find the opportunity to ask?*

"Did you want to get the supplies today?" Todd asked as we walked to the parking lot.

"Actually," Henry said, "I'm going to go make a call first."

He headed straight for the payphone, leaving me to lead the two confused participants.

"Is something wrong?" Todd asked, watching the back of Henry get further and further away. I picked up my speed to follow.

"He's just tired," I excused. As the four of us neared the payphone, Jim stepped outside, but no iced cokes were in his hands. I said a brief hello and followed Henry, Evie stopping next to Jim, with Todd trampling behind.

I came up to the booth and watched as Henry pounded the number keys, inserting nothing into the coin slot, and soon the phone began to pick up a ring.

He was angry. Nostrils flaring, arms tensed, and all I could do was stand by, playing patient, when all along I wanted to be doctor.

"What's wrong?" I nudged, breaking my resolve to wait for him to speak first.

He didn't even look my way, but soon he said in a loud voice. "Yes, can I speak to Chief Brandon, please." I was surprised he even added the last sentiment. "Scott, I want everything you can find on the kid."

I chewed my lip, anxiously awaiting some form of news. In the background, I saw Evie close to Jim as she explained the situation with Sheridan, and Todd oddly distant, and ever attentive of Henry and I.

"There is something not right, Scott," Henry said lowly into the mouthpiece, clearly restraining the full extent of his anger. "I don't care who you have to call, but call them. I mean it, or else you'll have a dead body on your hands."

My brows rose at his last words. I took a step back as my hand reached forward, my heart and mind torn as to what to do, per usual.

"Look Brandon," he continued. "If you haven't dug something up by tomorrow morning, I'm putting him in handcuffs." He slammed the phone back on its hook, and didn't move his gaze from mine.

"I want to call Juliet," I said, trying to keep my voice even. "The trial is just around the corner, and I don't care if someone is desperate enough to tap her phone. Please?"

After a brief moment of hesitation, he reached into his pocket and pulled out a quarter, and I took it with care. I kept my eyes on the faded black numbers, steadying my breathing as best as I could. A woman's voice came clearly.

"Dr. Hayward."

"Juliet," I gasped, emotion rising up my throat. "It's Prue."

"Oh, Prue! It is so good to hear from you! The police at the station won't tell me anything! What's been going on? How are the twins? How are you?"

"Good, good," I assured. "The twins are healthy and kicking—and my dog just had puppies of her own a few minutes ago."

"That's good to hear," she said, and I was a little surprised to hear a sniffle from her side escape.

I leaned my back against the plastic wall, watching Henry roll over to Jim by the car. "Actually, things have been a little different with our new addition."

"You mean the puppies?"

My head shook even though she wasn't there to see the action. "No," I said, my heart pounding loudly in my chest. "The intern you sent, Todd. He has added some drama to my plate, but all the same, I guess it's good to have a doctor around, just in case.

Juliet said nothing. Dead silence on the other end but I couldn't stop.

"He gave me a present. I told him I hadn't looked at it yet, but I lied. I looked. I saw."

"Prue, I never—"

"It was the necklace Hannah had bought for the baby before she died." I continued to stare straight ahead, my nails digging into my palm to keep my steady. "I figured at first he only got it from the police, and thought it a kind gesture. I didn't want to be right."

"Prue!" Juliet screamed in my ear, but I wasn't listening anymore. "I never sent anyone!"

"I prayed to God I wasn't."

"Prue! You have to tell the police!" Juliet's voice was trembling. "I will call them, just stay away from Todd—and tell Henry the first chance you get!"

My mouth began to bleed, I had bitten too hard into the skin, and I tasted metal.

"It's too late," I said.

I hung up the phone as Juliet's shouts broke through the plastic device. The police wouldn't get here in time, not before something happened. I knew what to do, whether it worked or not, wasn't a concern.

With frozen fingers, I took a step away from the payphone. Evie's laugh rang out in a daze, not clearly registering with my senses, but I managed to reach the small group.

"I see congratulations are in order," Jim said with a smile, and with all the energy I could muster, I faked my own. "Todd was saying you were going to buy things for Sheridan and the pups?"

I nodded.

"Shall we go?" Todd asked.

I eyed him for a split second, and forced another smile.

"Yeah, Henry," I said, "Are you ready?"

The only place that had things for pets was the standard grocery store next to the courthouse. The five of us were an odd bunch if you looked close enough, but we passed by fellow shoppers with ease and conversation that I had a hard time hearing clearly, my focus elsewhere.

I was the first to grab a cart and pushed forward, every hair on my body wired to the sudden movements of Todd. Even though Sheridan slept on Henry's bed at night and on the green couch during the day, Henry thought it best to get her a bed where she could feed the pups and keep them warm. I let him choose which one, and moved along down the aisle of leashes and toys. I made sure not to go near the food, and diverted the four's attention by suddenly remembering Evie wanting to show me something important.

"Oh, yes!" she squealed, slapping her forehead in bewilderment. "How did I forget? I guess with all the excitement!" She hurried to the checkout. "You have to come to the bakery at once!"

Henry trailed in the back as Evie led the way out the store doors—*after we charged everything on Henry's tab of course*—and as the others followed in her excitement, I dropped my pace to meet with Henry's.

"I love you, Henry," I said quietly to the ground and he took my hand in his. "You don't have to say it back. I know you feel the same, I just wanted to say it again."

Henry looked at me, his brows hovering above those deep brown eyes as his mouth kept closed. He was trying to figure me out, and I wasn't going to let him.

"Come, on." I motioned forward, the bakery only feet away now, and the chill started to get to me then. I didn't wait for his response.

Evie jumped from behind me seconds later, and her hands enclosed my eyes, telling me not to peek.

"Okay, ready—look!" Her fingers plied away and I was already smiling. My first glimpse though was of Todd, and I quickly looked up before I could glare.

I gasped, my stomach filled with butterflies and kicks of life. Thuds, really. This was theirs, as much as it was now mine.

The sign on the bakery with its pink lettering was now gone and replaced with fancy gold script across covered glass. *Marthas' and Prue's Bakery and Café*

I choked on my own emotion. "Evie, how—?"

Evie squirmed in her skin, bubbling with smiles. "Well, you *have* added a large selection of new desserts, and our new coffee! Me and Martha just thought it right to have your name, too!"

I gave her tight hug, breathing in her hair that smelled of flour and chocolate, wishing with all my heart that we could be friends forever. I needed a friend forever.

"Thank you," I whispered.

She pulled back after a moment, her nose red with winter, and looked back toward the building. "Now that we have the sign right, me and Martha need your advice on the reconstruction. We want to remodel the whole bakery, inside and out! It doesn't say bakery *and* café for nothing!"

"I would love that," I replied, choking again. A warm hand slipped into mine. Henry smiled at me and it knocked the wind from my chest. If I didn't let go, he would hold me here forever.

"Come on." Evie pulled me forward. "We need to start our plans."

But I kept my footing, and she looked at me, confused. I was quick to soothe her hurt. "How about I come tomorrow morning? I'm getting tired—and that way the three of us will have the whole day to plan everything out."

The idea struck well with her and she nodded happily. "I'll tell Martha to make a notice to the customers that we're closed for remodeling."

"And now you can help me and Henry set up for the puppies—they need a warm welcoming too!"

"Of course!" she cheered, jogging back to the car.

"I will come too," Todd said. "I need to give Prue a checkup anyway."

I eyed him, no smile to my lips, repeating Evie's habitual phrase. "Of course."

CHAPTER SEVENTY-NINE

The shaking started before I realized—before I could even take note of it. Henry was the one to see, and comment.

"What?" I asked Henry as we sat quietly in the backseat.

"Are you cold?" he said more firmly. "You're shaking."

"I'm fine." I swallowed for the third time in the last passing minute. But I wasn't fine. My fingers were trembling and my heart would not stop with its anxiety shots. The time was coming, and I only had so much of it left.

We reached the lake house too quickly, and I tried not to notice how close Henry's hand was to mine. I rushed out of the car as fast as I could, pelting rain soaking into my clothes. I knew I had to be quick. Todd was already at the door holding the groceries.

"You know what?" I said before anyone else could get out of the car. "We forgot the dog food."

"We can get some more tomorrow when you help the girls at the bakery," Henry replied, reaching for his chair.

I clucked my tongue, my head shaking in disagreement. "Yeah, but I don't want her coming home to a house that isn't ready for her. I want everything prepared in advance."

"We can go to town tomorrow."

"You should go now while you are still dressed," I prodded. "Evie can take you to the store, you know the right brand to buy."

"Prue," Henry argued, "I will go tomorrow."

"Henry," I said, hating how condescending my tone was. I didn't want to hurt Henry, to give him a reason to think the last twenty-fours meant nothing. But I had to face Todd alone. "I know how you feel about Todd, but you don't have to be *jealous* of him." I looked to the surprised intern on the porch. "Right?"

After moment of hesitation, he nodded.

"See? Nothing to worry about. Evie will take you to the store while Todd gives me my check up, and when she gets back we can set up the place for the pups."

The plan sounded good—smooth as room temperature butter—and with nothing, no margarine, out of the ordinary. By Henry's reaction to the jealousy bit, I knew I hit the right target.

"Fine," he said, obviously trying to prove me wrong by sounding careless when it came to Todd.

I gave him a gentle wave from the front door as they backed out of the driveway. I entered the house, the door closing behind me, and the true challenge began.

CHAPTER EIGHTY

A loud pounding took place between my eardrums, muffling out all sound, including Todd's blurred words he spoke so carelessly.

Didn't he know I knew? Hadn't he gotten the hint yet? I guessed I needed to give the extra push.

"Prue?"

I blinked, clearing all distraction. We were in the kitchen. I backed up until my butt hit the stove, and my hand crept secretively in search for something. "Huh?"

A half smile crossed his evil lips. "I said, are you going back home once the twins are born? You're due soon. Only one month left, really."

My mouth twitched as my fingers encircled the handle of a knife. "Would that make it harder for you?" I asked.

His eyes narrowed for a split second, his brain thinking my words over, trying to taste if there was something between the lines. "Make it harder for me to *what*?"

"To kill me."

A flicker, or phantom, crossed Todd's features in a quick

shadow, as if the mask he wore was suddenly falling apart, and soon, his true face surfaced. I almost dropped the knife at the sight of his sly, cold and psychotic grin. I suddenly knew why he looked so familiar before.

"About time you figured it out," he sneered. "I wondered how long it would take. Henry was easier to give alert—though I only gave one clue away." Todd circled the island counter, not quite coming to me yet, not quite ready. "The car crash," he explained. "I drugged your food and made sure it wouldn't kick in until after you were on your way home."

Todd laughed, chilling my blood. "That man you are trying to put in jail, the one your brother-in-law started his company with? My uncle."

I knew it. The murderer was Todd's father. Why didn't I see it before? And what was my plan now? I had only thought to get everyone out of harm's way, leaving me to face the monster of my dreams.

"How did you find me?" I asked.

He shrugged. "Simple. We had been tracking your sister, seeing if she was expecting, and after so many visits to the fertility clinic, we had our suspicions. It was only after you came back to Arizona and identified my dad that we realized our mistake: we killed the wrong girl. Such a shame."

He clucked his tongue but I remained immobile.

"Getting here undetected though, was a bit tricky. Still, my aunt was pretty convincing as Juliet, and it always helps to have a man on the inside."

I cringed, unable to take my eyes off his. I tried to kick his ego. "Why did you wait so long? You had plenty of chances."

His head cocked to the side as his eyes took me in, and he spoke with strange enjoyment, ignoring my question. "Now all I need to do is figure out the best way to kill you without causing much of a stir. I'm not cruel, you know."

He reached into the small space between us, and I pulled out the butcher knife, swinging at his face. He howled in pain, grabbing his cheek where blood began to spill, and I ran out of the kitchen to the staircase.

"Prue!" Todd roared and I looked back just in time to see the flash of his gun. When I stepped toward the front door, he shot the knob.

I dashed to the stairs, fear trying to freeze me, and I wasn't fast enough. His hand grabbed my ankle and my body slammed against the steps, my mouth pooling with blood. My hands reached for my stomach, fear paralyzing me.

"Don't even think about running," he snarled, gaining way up my calf as my nails dug into the wooden step, struggling to gain freedom.

The front door opened, slamming against the wall, and my eyes stared at Henry in the doorway.

"Prue," Henry shouted familiar words. "Run!"

The moment of distraction worked for Todd as it did for me, and I kicked him in the face, knocking him back as I made my escape. In the corner of my eye, Henry lunged from his chair and attacked Todd. Remembering what he said, I ran.

I reached the attic door and pulled it open only to slam it shut again, and then quietly as I could, hurried into the bathroom next to the nursery, hiding inside the tub.

I pulled the curtain as a shield and tried not to cry. I could still hear the footfalls, groans, and thuds of Henry and Todd, until all at once and without warning, a shot rang out, echoing off every wall.

Dear God, I cried, but could think no further.

Heavy footsteps reverberated off the walls, my heart hammering at the sound, and something in me fell away.

CHAPTER EIGHTY-ONE

I kept my breathing shallow, listening for the right sounds. Todd must have taken the bait and started his search in the attic. Slowly, I got out from the tub.

I tiptoed across the hallway and to the banister as I tried to prepare for the worst.

The silent scream ripped out of my throat as I looked down to see Henry on the floor, legs bent inward, and a growing red stain at his shoulder. The image of Jacob quickly came back to mind and I ran down the stairs.

"Henry," I cried, kneeling down to his face, tears filling my eyes. My fingers swept his brow, praying for him to be alive.

"Prue?"

I gasped. "I'm here, Henry, I'm here," I said, leaning closer. His eyes blinked a few times before focusing, and soon his brows furrowed as he pointed at me.

"Prue? You're—"

The attic door shut and I jumped.

"Come on," I said, "We have to go." I pulled at his arms but he pushed me away.

"No, go into the woods, to the lake—has he been there before?"

I shook my head as I tried to fight down hysteria, memories flooding to my mind. "No, no—I never took him there." I almost sobbed aloud. Even in pain, Henry had to know where he stood—where my heart was—when he was never able to see that it was always with him.

"Good, good," he said, pushing me again toward the door. "Run, Prue, run!"

"Prue!" My head whipped to the staircase where Todd stood in full vigor, the shining gun pointed at my head.

"Go!" Henry said, and it was the final break I needed. I dodged for the outside world, almost landing on my ankle after jumping from the porch.

I looked behind me, an instinctive habit, and watched Todd shoot Henry again, then kick him in the face. I couldn't catch my breath as I part of me wanted to go back.

Thunder clapped the sky as a bullet whizzed past my head and hit a tree. I took a right into the woods, running with all I had in me, my sneakers crushing into the earth with each step as one hand held my stomach and the other tried to gain momentum.

Another clap of thunder rang, and I took another right when appointed. I had a distance before me, and pain within me, but I would not—*could not*—falter as branch upon branch scratched against my limbs. I only let a short cry escape as tears fell from my eyes.

Dear God, I prayed, *please save him!*

And a voice whispered back through the coming storm, *Have faith.*

CHAPTER EIGHTY-TWO

Henry

It was as if a truck had hit him, that's how bad he felt. As if his very body had been plowed through a field raid, and the truck came back to make sure he was really dead, not just pretending.

Henry's eyes flicked open, his shoulder and lower side soaked in dark blood, as he began the struggle to rise into sitting position. Clutching his jeans, he pulled himself up. A groan screamed in his body from the effort, his wounds unrelenting, but only one thing occupied his thoughts.

Prue. Prue. Prue.

Her name sang through his mind, demanding him to do something, to save her. She was in danger, the truth reminded him, and she was . . . hurt?

His eyes squinted, trying to think, to remember. The kick to his head made him dizzy and out of sorts.

Come on, Henry! He yelled at himself, forcing his body to

gain stability. His arm reached for his chair, but it was no use, it was too far away. After a frustrated sigh, he cupped one knee, and lifted it up with shaking hands—then lifted the other as both feet planted firmly on the floor.

Both fell within seconds of each other and he felt nothing as the dead weights gave in. His fists slammed against the floor, a deep pounding beginning in his chest, a thundering as awareness lit the room.

Henry didn't want to do it. He didn't want to feel the forcing tug within the cage that surrounded his heart—but it was no use to deny it any longer.

God was watching.

He had always been watching. Even in the darkest moments.

"No!" he growled.

Again, he lifted both legs, and again they fell. His fists pounded into his shins and he felt nothing. Only his palms crushing against something that had died long ago.

All those years of exercising these lifeless limbs—and for nothing! No wonder I didn't tell anyone—there was no progress to show for it!

The rising tide increased its course through his body, the adrenaline surge flowing within his skin. His teeth clenched as he fought against the voice, his mind trying to find another way but the voice came all the same.

What do you do when you're on an airplane and the oxygen masks come down?

His brow furrowed in response.

You adjust the mask on yourself first, then help the person beside you.

Water pricked his eyes as a loud breath escaped him. He understood what God was telling him. He understood that in order to help someone else, you must be helped first—or else you give oxygen to the other and suffocate yourself.

But Henry wanted to suffocate. He wanted to die. At least he thought did, until . . . until he fell in love with Prue.

I don't deserve her, he thought. *I deserve misery, pain. Not life, not happiness, not love. Not healing.*

"None of us deserve it." He recalled Prue's words.

His shoulder began to burn with heat—the one without the wound—as if a large hand were holding it tight.

"Forgive yourself."

"What?" Henry gasped, eyes wild as he looked behind him, having clearly heard someone speaking aloud. But no one was there.

You adjust the mask on yourself first. . . .

Henry closed his eyes. Even before the accident, he had lost Sylvia to anger and bitterness, and he wasn't going to lose Prue over the same.

So, for the second time, Henry made the first move.

"God!" Henry yelled, and his voice echoed off the walls. A thick silence resounded, and fear tried to keep him quiet. But love was so much stronger.

"God, I'm sorry! I blamed You for Sylvia's death . . . for my child's death . . . Please, forgive me. Please, I ask You, God . . . to help me forgive myself!"

The anger inside of him vanished like mist in the morning, and the warmth surging at his shoulder shifted and moved into his heart, lighting it on fire. The hardness burned away, and soon peace instilled.

But if someone were watching and expected fireworks, thunder, or even a shaft of light, they would be sadly disappointed. Because the things for show are not always real, but the things inside are what matter the most.

"God," Henry said, "I need to walk—I need to go after Prue—she's in danger. You brought her here for a purpose. I love her, God. Please, help me walk again."

Henry let out a shout as an electric current charged through his legs, and he fell onto his back. Every fiber, every nerve, every muscle to the deepest marrow came alive at once. He let out another shout, his legs writhing to relinquish the raw fire that swam through him, twisting and pulling, squeezing tighter and tighter—he could feel it all—until finally, it released.

Henry gasped, amazed and shocked. His entire body pulsed—he never felt more alive— and a bubble of joyful laughter escaped. "Thank You."

He slowly sat up and surveyed his position, then reached for the railing of the stairs. Holding his breath, he pulled himself up and onto his feet, using the stairs for balance. His legs wobbled like a newborn foal, but he took a step forward, again, and again, getting stronger.

He smiled. The world wasn't so dark anymore, his eyes holding a new light as revelation came, and Henry could see so clearly.

Prue hadn't been hurt like he had thought.

Her water had broke.

CHAPTER EIGHTY-THREE

By the time I reached the black rocks, I was hunched over my knees in pain. I took deep breaths, and prayed the fall on the stairs had not harmed the twins, but at the same moment, all I could worry about was keeping the three of us alive.

Hidden behind the largest rock, I poked my head out to see if anyone was coming. My eyes then roamed to the lake.

Should I try to swim away? I could hide in the water—I would at least be farther from Todd than I was right now.

The water would be freezing, I knew, but for twins . . . .

I looked behind me and paled at the sight of Todd running through the trees and onto the shore.

"Ah!" I growled through clenched teeth, pain shooting at my hips and back as my fists curled against the ground. The first time I felt it was back at the house and figured it was from the fall, now I wasn't so sure.

In the bathroom, I remembered, then looked down to my jeans and reached my hand against fabric. My fingers came back wet, and my stomach coiled as I thought of giving birth right here and right now, with Todd ready to kill us all.

I pushed myself up from the ground and stumbled toward the crashing waves, the white foam resembling snow. My sneakers filled with water and I stopped, gasping for breath as my feet burned with immediate cold. The water sloshed back and forth against my ankles and it felt like needles plunging into my flesh.

I can't go in there. The water would kill us in a matter of minutes . . . . Facing Todd wasn't a better option, though. *What could I do?* I couldn't do anything.

"I knew I'd find you."

Todd's voice made me jump, my back toward trees, and I turned around. His face was pale and he was sweating, his eyes wild and bright.

God help me!

The pain shifted down toward my thighs, and the pain was so intense, I had to hunch over again, gasping for breath. My knees sunk into the thick, wet sand as freezing water splashed over my body.

Todd's eyes registered everything at once and his gaze scanned me whole. His tortuous grin widened.

"Just in time, I see." He cocked the gun. "Are you ready?"

"No," I said, stretching out a hand toward him as the other shielded my stomach. "Don't—"

A loud shot broke out, and I screamed.

Todd stared at me, confusion in his light eyes, and he clutched his chest before hitting to his knees. The gun had fallen out of his grasp and when he reached for it, he was hit again. He choked, then fell on his face.

I scrambled to my feet, sand sticking to my hands as pain screamed throughout my lower body. At the sound of my name, my gaze looked ahead, and I stared in shock.

There was Henry—*walking toward me.*

He held something in his hand, a gun, and step by step, he

came to me, a smile on his face. I ran to close the gap, his arms opening to me, and I slammed into his embrace.

"Thank God," he spoke into my ear as he held me close.

He's alive! I cried. *Thank You, God!* I squeezed Henry tighter and felt his lips kiss my cheek, then my mouth.

"You're freezing," he said, his arms wrapped around my shoulders, and I couldn't explain the burst of joy in my heart.

"I'm okay," I said, smiling, then asked, "but how are you—"

He locked me in his gaze with those shining brown eyes, the curve of his mouth held up in a grin. Somewhere in the atmosphere sirens wailed, trying to force their way into my current world of Henry and me, the both of us very alive and together.

He kissed me again, and his arms pulled me closer. My fingers touched where his arm had been shot, the area around the hole in his shirt soaked in blood—but when I touched his skin, there was no wound.

My jaw dropped as I stared. I quickly pulled his shirt up from his waist, and though his stomach was smeared with blood, the wound there was gone as well. Tears stung my eyes, and I gave a soft cry as I collapsed against his chest.

Henry kissed my temple. "I'll tell you all about it once we get to the hospital." He slid one arm around my waist, leading me away from the shore. "But let's just say, you got another miracle."

"We both did," I said, taking in all that had occurred, amazed.

We left Todd's barely moving body and headed toward familiar figures in the woods next to an ambulance.

Evie and Jim were leading the way for the paramedics, running at the first sight of us. I had to laugh, my split lip hating me for it, and I squeezed onto Henry, joy filling me to the brim as well as exhilaration.

"Prue!" Evie cried, rushing up to me. "I was so worried! Henry told me to turn the car around when we were on our way to the store, and he said I had to get Jim and tell him to call some Chief Brandon in Arizona! Prue, what is going on?" She began to sob, black mascara running down her cheeks in the most beautiful way.

I could only smile. "I'm having twins!"

Her eyes widened. "Jim! Jim!" she screamed, though the relieved man was standing right beside her in full earshot. "We have to get Prue to the hospital!"

The four of us trekked toward the awaiting ambulance as men in blue went after the waking Todd. Evie continued to fret and cheer over the passing events that took place, and she even asked if Todd was okay.

If the hospital was not fully aware of my pregnancy and labor, they were the moment we arrived. Evie scrambled inside the hospital when truck stopped at the entrance, and like a cheerleader, gathered every available nurse and doctor to my side. Jim took the offered paperwork at once and only stopped to ask for a pen. A nurse came up to me with a wheelchair, which Henry gladly took and plopped me on his lap as he ordered the nurse to take us to the room. Evie said she would call Martha to bring a camera since the nurses forced her to remain in the waiting room, and I couldn't stop smiling.

As I was being prepped, a surgeon came in to look at Henry's shoulder, befuddled to find not even a scratch remained. Another doctor masked in scrubs scurried in and pulled up a stool to my show. If I hadn't been so happy, I would have been completely embarrassed.

More people flooded in, saying different things, naming names, and the shooting pains increased as an IV stuck my hand, a cool liquid running through my veins. The doctor checked my status, and it was time.

I watched the world through a daze, hearing two distinct gurgling screams that filled my heart with a happiness I never knew existed. Nurses took the two bundles to be cleaned and examined as the doctor finished with me. Henry held my hand the entire time, smiling with warm tears in his eyes, watching me with awe and with love, and I knew Hannah was watching too.

Thank You, God, thank You, God, thank You, thank You, I repeated the words in my heart, soul and mind over and over.

My eyes started to droop and I barely recalled the surgeon returning with a needle and telling me to rest. Henry said he wouldn't leave me. So I let myself sleep, knowing that when I did wake, Henry would be there to tell me it wasn't all a dream.

CHAPTER EIGHTY-FOUR

When I woke, he was there, just like he had said. Except now, he had someone else with him.

"She compliments you," I said quietly, my eyes clearing of sticky residue as my throat craved a glass of cool water that I really didn't care about getting.

Henry looked up from the pink-wrapped baby girl cradled close in his arms, and smiled at me.

"Your turn," he said, his eyes motioning to the waiting nurse to my left. I reached up with both hands as she leaned forward to hand me my own pink bundle.

The smile that erupted from my lips could not be contained as I looked to the beautiful face of Hannah's daughter. Her small eyes kept closed as her lips moved in repeated motions as if she were speaking.

"Girls," I said, not losing my smile through the blurring tears.

"Three of the most beautiful girls I have ever seen."

I loved the way he held her in his arms, the way he already loved them both without question or thought; the way I loved them so much.

"Would you like me to take a picture?" the same nurse asked kindly, a throw away camera in her hands.

The hospital room door swung open suddenly, and Evie dashed inside, all smiles.

"Me first!" She whined, grabbing the camera Martha held in her hands, and rushed to the nurse's place. Henry and I both laughed as she held it up, waiting for us to pose. Henry rose with the babe in his arms, and leaned close to me, smiling ear to ear.

The camera flashed, he sat back down, I cried, and our friends, *our family*, swept in like a gush of wind.

Evie took pictures of everyone and everything. Ones with me holding the girls, then Henry holding them, then Jim and Martha, and of course, Evie herself. She even managed to get my doctor in one of them, much to the chagrin of Jim. And a few other surprise guests appeared, much to the astonishment of me.

Mom and Dad rushed to my side, tears running down their faces as my arms flew open to wrap around them. Words of what happened in the passing months weren't exchanged, nor of what the future would be. Only love was to be shared right now.

Evie got them together in a picture, then them holding the twins, smiles on their faces. And even ones of me introducing Henry, and I could tell by their twinkling eyes they sensed something between us. I was glad I didn't have to explain everything right away. Though, the next picture of Henry giving me a full kiss to the lips just because I joked he still hadn't really kissed me public, seemed to be explanation enough. Then finally, a nurse managed to gather us around the bed just before visiting hours were over, and took a final picture for the day.

Henry and I sat in the hospital bed together, each holding one of the girls, with Jim on his right side and Martha next to him, and my parents to my left with Evie squeezing in front. It wasn't a fake picture or pose. Martha was crying with a tissue against her nose, Jim told Henry something funny because both of them looked at each other, laughing, Evie was explaining the new bakery to my parents with whimsical detail, and I was in the exact middle, smiling at it all, smiling to the camera, to the world, and all who would see this wonderful picture.

I had the perfect spot for it too. Just above the fireplace where there was no TV; in Jim's shop on the wall behind the counter; in the bakery where the cakes were displayed; in Martha's home next to where her own family portrait of three boys one day would be; and in my parents' house back in Arizona, right next to one of Hannah and Jacob.

The time came for everyone to leave and Evie was already planning a welcoming party for the twins, which got spirits up again. I said goodbye to my parents who would be staying at the inn for a while, and to Jim who gave me a kiss to the cheek before going. The nurses took the girls to sleep, and soon it was just Henry and I once more.

"Thank you for saving me," I said as he continued to sit next to me in the hospital bed. My eyes then narrowed playfully. "Now explain."

The corner of his mouth rose, his eyes shining.

Yes, I could see a change by the way the lines of his face were softened and not so daunting; and his shoulders didn't carry a heavy weight like before.

"The truth is," he said, "I repented to God for the way I had been living in bitterness toward Him. It was my foolishness that lost Sylvia long before the accident, and I realized I couldn't forgive myself for it. But God helped me. He healed my heart." Henry smiled again, his hand close to mine but not touching. He explained the part about his legs coming alive, and tears shined in my eyes.

"I'm so happy for you, Henry, and so thankful you're alive." Something caught in my throat then. "But . . . what do we do now?" I focused my gaze on our hands, unable to look him in the eye. "I mean, because Todd admitted everything, the trial shouldn't be difficult, and Brooks will be arrested. Now what? You and me . . . ."

Henry let out a deep sigh, and I glanced up just in time to see his eyes roll. "You always have to rush things, don't you?"

"What?" My heart skipped a beat, I was sure the monitor picked up on it, and Henry let go of my hand and reached into his pocket.

"Remember when I said, you owed me for getting chocolate all over my pants?"

"Yeah . . ."

"I had planned on doing this back at the house earlier but then—"

A black velvet box spilled out from his hand and onto the white hospital bed, startling me into silent shock and internal hysteria. Henry quickly picked it up, still talking.

"I deserve to at least ask for your hand properly," he said. "Prue, when you first came here I had no idea how drastically you would affect my life, and I wouldn't trade a single day with you for anything. You made me do things and face things, and even say things no else dared to. You smacked me when I needed it, and didn't let me sink inside of myself. You gave me a reason to be happy. You showed me that even though something bad happens it doesn't mean you give up. You may hurt for a while, but God will bring joy again, and laughter. That is what you bring me—hope, joy, happiness, and laughter—and I love you." He flipped the box open. "Prue Collins, will you marry me?"

I stared at the gold band with three intertwined diamonds, and a swell of happiness filled my chest, but I couldn't speak.

Henry then cleared his throat, a look of worry in his eyes. "If you hate the name Prue Clay so much, we can change it."

"I love it," I said, biting my lip that couldn't contain my laugh. "I love you."

His head cocked to the side, the corner of his mouth waiting. "Don't be so vague," he said.

I rolled my eyes before rushing to kiss his lips. "Yes, Henry Clay, I will marry you." I pulled him close, and he slipped the ring on my finger.

EPILOGUE

Seven years later

The sun was high in the sky and covered with beautiful snow-white clouds by the time we made it to the lake. The water glinted with hues of evergreen and dark aqua, the pebbles of the shore shinning with each new wave, like most Sundays when we came after church.

A flair of dark gold curls bounced in sight as feisty Charlotte ran down the beach, the purple ribbon in her hair flying behind her, until finally she stopped at the sight of Jim who sat yards away on a blanket Evie had laid out minutes before.

"Uncle Jim! Uncle Jim! Look what I found!" she squealed, holding up something in her fist.

"What did you find?" he called back, giving her full attention with a smile. Charlotte never liked to be ignored, especially when she had something to show.

"Wait for me! Wait for me!" Elizabeth cried out from feet away, her new dress completely soaked with lake water, her light brown hair clinging to her face.

"What is it, Elizabeth?" Evie asked, as she set a picnic basket down.

From this distance, I could barely make out the pebbles the two girls held out before their Uncle and Aunt, but I smiled all the same. Soon, Mom and Dad strolled out of the woods and joined the small group, bringing with them more containers full of lunch. When the trial ended, the judge gave Jacob's company to them until the girls came of age. They decided to divide part of the year in Arizona, and the other in Oregon, not wanting to miss any milestones from their growing family.

"Papa! Grandma!" the girls squealed at the same time. "Look at what we found on the beach!"

The locket Hannah had bought that turned into two necklaces, shined at both their throats, a picture of their parents inside. Henry and I told them the truth, never hiding anything, and they still loved us as parents. We kept Hannah and Jacob's memory alive, knowing one day they would meet again for the first time.

I stood on a small hill, inhaling the wonderful feeling the sight of them brought, remembering the struggle it took to get here. The memory of pain was a dull ache in my chest, and on days when it sharpened, seeing their faces, seeing Hannah in Charlotte's eyes, and Jacob in Elizabeth's smile, gave comfort to know that not all had been lost.

Tears stung my eyes as a wet nose nuzzled my thigh.

I scratched behind Sheridan's ears just where she liked, her light pant proof of her contentment. Two younger collies ran out, both resembling their mother in color and size, and the twins welcomed them with giggles of delight. They still didn't understand why they couldn't bring dogs to church, and often argued that dogs liked to sing praises too.

"Gemma!" Charlotte purred, rubbing her dog's face with love as Elizabeth did the same to Lady. I smiled as I recalled the day Evie helped me pick out the puppies' names.

It was amazing how different the girls were, and yet I was thankful for it too. When I was first pregnant with them, I had wanted a boy and a girl for Hannah, that way she had one of each. Now, seeing Charlotte and Elizabeth, I thanked God for giving me this gift. The very thing I had lost when Hannah died, God gave back to me through her children. *Sisters.*

A warm hand touched my arm and I turned, knowing full well the person. I wasn't surprised when I found that Henry only stood a few inches taller than me. He greeted me with a long kiss; something he never shunned of doing in public ever since that day in the hospital. I slid my free hand against his cheek, feeling the scruff, and my own cheeks began to burn, as they always did when I thought of Henry kissing me.

"You okay?" he asked, his arms circling my waist.

I smiled. "Fantastic." And I meant it.

Henry grinned, kissing me again.

At the sound of a small bark, my eyes opened and I watched as a third dog ran out, looking nothing like his siblings with his blue-gray mixed colors. A young voice hollered after him.

The little boy, almost three years old now, came up to us with his blue eyes like mine, and brown, almost black hair like his Henry's, giggling.

Henry bent down and picked up our son easily in his arms, keeping him close between us.

"Ready to eat, James?" he asked, tickling his belly.

James laughed. "Ah huh! I'm starving!"

"All right," he said, stepping forward as I took his offered hand. "And I'll tell you and your sisters' your favorite story of how mommy dropped daddy down the stairs!"

"Yeah!" James agreed, and I laughed, Sheridan at my side as we joined our family.

Once we sat down, we each joined hands and Henry said a prayer over the food, thanking God for all He had done, and was doing. Everyone said 'Amen' and to little James' delight, it was time to eat.

Evie passed out the plates as Martha waved from the hill, her share of boys and husband with her, carrying dessert. Jim inspected the pebbles the girls had found, Mom and Dad watching with smiles. Henry and I kept catching glances at each other, smiling randomly because of it.

The girls laughed, and I heard Hannah. I sucked in a deep breath, a sharp pain in my chest.

Seven years, and sometimes it seemed just like yesterday.

Henry's eyes missed nothing, though. He took my hand in his again, reminding me it was okay to be happy. It was okay to live. It was okay to heal, and it was okay to love.

Love is what made all this possible.

Have faith, God had told me that day I feared for all our lives. *Have faith.* I now saw the fruit of it. I saw the people around me, my family, safe and happy, and my heart sang with joy. *Thank You, God!*

"Daddy," James called, chocolate smeared all over his lips as he had eaten dessert first. "Remember what you were going to tell us!"

"Oh right," Henry said playfully. Then, eyeing me, added, "Remind me again?"

I rolled my eyes, gently slapping his leg with my free hand, and laughed. "You tell it best," I said.

He grinned, rubbing my wrist with his thumb, his gaze not leaving mine. "Maybe we should start with that first day?"

"Yeah!" the girls agreed, their pups (as they called them) panting heavily beside them as they wagged their tails.

"All right," he said. "It was raining. I had just reached the top of the stairs to go to bed when I heard this loud banging on the front door."

His face became more animated as he spoke, holding everyone's attention. The wind blew gently through his hair, his brown eyes bright with passion. Bright with life.

And I listened closely, as Henry told the story of us.

[Acknowledgements]

I want to thank God for giving me the ideas for my writing and helping me get them onto paper. Through doubts, triumphs, highs and lows, ripped up pieces of paper, and multifaceted tears, You never leave me, and thank You Jesus Christ for all You have done for me!

I want to thank my family for their support in my creativity, for loving me and being there no matter what. Thanks for home-cooked meals, driving me to school, late night talks, and much laughter. I'm thankful to have a sister who is my best friend (*and Henry's #1 fan from the start!*). Most of all, they have helped instill in me that in the end, there's only God, and He can change any situation for the good.

I have always loved reading since a young age and spent hours living and learning through characters I seemed to connect with better than people. Though I did some short stories, writing really began for me in the fourth grade when I learned poetry. I loved, and still do, how words could rhyme and mix so beautifully—how easily I could express things I could not normally speak aloud. I want to one day publish a poetry book.

People I want to thank: Melanie O'Hara, the first person to read this book other than family! Mary Holden, for your encouragement, and answering my many questions! JP Jones (Collipsis Web Solutions), for the awesome book cover!

To you readers, thank you for taking the chance and picking this story. I hope you have enjoyed the journey of Henry and Prue, and if you don't mind, I would like to offer this advice:

Go after your dream. Go after that thing that lifts your heart from the ground and makes you soar to the heavens—pulls at you every night and every day—that fire that keeps you burning through the mediocre.

Don't ignore it, don't let it go unanswered. Run to it. Charge ahead though others may brace against you. Charge ahead though flaming arrows come your way. Charge ahead, even in storms, even when lost at sea. No matter what, hold that hope, and do not give up.

You were made for so much more.

- Sydney

[ABOUT THE AUTHOR]

Sydney Paige McCutcheon lives in Arizona.

She loves coffee and rain, and when she isn't writing, she loves spending time with her family.

One of her favorite places to be is Maui, Hawaii where she learned to surf, realized zip-lining isn't a leisure activity, and that shave ice is best served with ice cream and condensed milk.

Rarely one to be competitive (except when it comes to board games), she enjoys playing tennis, and is a collector of random facts.

Though growing up she had wanted to become a lawyer, at age fourteen she chose to answer a different call.

Eight years later, *Henry* is her debut novel.

14867757R00221

Made in the USA
San Bernardino, CA
07 September 2014